Baubles to Die For

A SHELL ISLE MYSTERY

TONYA PENROSE

This is a work of fiction. Names, characters, places, and incidents are products of the author's imagination or are used fictitiously and are not to be construed as real. Any resemblance to actual events, locations, organizations, or persons, living or dead, is entirely coincidental.

World Castle Publishing, LLC
Pensacola, Florida
Copyright © 2025 Tonya Penrose
Hardback ISBN: 9798891263857
Paperback ISBN: 9798891263864
eBook ISBN: 9798891263871
Second Edition World Castle Publishing, LLC, June 23, 2025
http://www.worldcastlepublishing.com
Cover: Cover Designs by Karen

For those who love their baubles

CHAPTER 1

"How utterly curious." Page's sapphire eyes narrowed to focus on the cryptic exchange happening between a couple seated a few feet away. Their words traveled across the café's table on a yellow paper napkin rather than in conversation.

"What'd you say?" her cousin, Betsy, asked, distracted by the three remaining French fries on her plate.

"Oh, nothing, just a personal observation about that man and woman seated to your left."

Betsy's head swiveled.

"No, no. Don't look." Page grinned at Betsy's evident inner battle to resist temptation by jockeying around in her seat.

Both women had savored an early Saturday lunch at the trendy Beach Bistro's outside terrace. Betsy had appeared at Page's door only hours before, declaring she needed a vacation with Page on Shell Isle. Another relationship malfunction had sent her usually extroverted cousin scurrying into hiding, more from herself than her last guy. The family's summer haven had always filled unrequited needs for them both.

"So, can I look now?" begged Betsy, starting to shift again in the metal chair.

Page's attention snapped back. "Sorry. They just left."

Betsy glanced over her shoulder at the empty table, seeing the waiter now busy clearing. "So, exactly what did I miss? And why must it always be you that attracts the strangest doings?"

An abundance of wavy auburn hair framed the flushed face of Betsy. Her tall frame, once called willowy, testified now to her passion for food. Betsy embraced flamboyance in the way she lived and dressed. She fixed her gaze on Page's delicate features. Style clung to her cousin like ketchup in the bottle that Betsy held suspended over her plate. Page's blond hair shimmered in the sun, and a sprinkling of freckles across her cheeks presented the image of someone much younger than fifty. Betsy often confessed to her cousin that she envied the put-together package Page seemed to create effortlessly, and the grounded way Page lived her life. Celebrating the same birthday and age, along with their moms being twins, helped the cousins forge an early bond, almost as if they were twins themselves, albeit not identical.

Page broke the silence, dropping her napkin next to her half-eaten colossal shrimp salad. "I'll enlighten you in a bit. Are you finished?" Page left money on the table to cover lunch.

"My plate's cleaned, so guess I'm done." Betsy licked the ketchup off her finger. "How about an ice cream cone, my treat? I spied a dairy bar a block from where we parked."

"Ice cream? Okay, I'm considering." Page sighed, thinking about her favorite flavor and an expanding waistline if she allowed the food aficionado Betsy to lead her to daily confections. Still, one itty bitty cone couldn't cause too much harm.

"Well? Oh, come on. You can tell me what fired your curiosity gene while we walk toward our cones." Betsy waved and winked at their waiter as they left.

Shell Isle was an atypical beach town tucked away on the southern coast of North Carolina. Absent were the tourist traps; present were an eclectic group of shops that beckoned one to explore their inner selves, eat healthily, wear hip, natural fibers, and be a full-time islander. It was a town in support of both a happy and fulfilling life for those having ties to the place. However, there existed a peculiar essence clinging to the island, which seemed to shun discovery by newcomers.

The cousins plopped down on the marina's park bench and gazed out at the bay. Two tugs chugged toward the dock, sending plumes of charcoal smoke skyward, signaling their captains' yearning for home. The azure water glistened from the sun's rays as if fairy dust was sprinkled over the surface. Vintage homes, moss draping their trees, were designed with southern charm testifying to Shell Isle's historical pedigree. The beach side of the island presented a face of quaint bungalows and cottages tucked behind the façade of majestic live oak trees.

Betsy licked the drips from the sides of the cone. "Tell me what you saw back at the Bistro."

Page handed her cousin a napkin. "Well, it was probably nothing. I mean, a good explanation for what I saw could be—"

"Stop waltzing me. You know how much I detest slow dancing." Betsy unfastened the top snap of her white pants and tugged her navy striped nautical shirt back down. She gave a little shrug.

"Okay, well, first, I noticed this seedy-looking guy and society-type woman writing notes to each other on a napkin. I'm telling you, these two characters were total contrasts. You know, it just didn't square they'd be together, but get this, just before they left, he slides a small silver pistol under the table to her." Page turned her attention back to her cone.

Betsy studied her cousin's face. "No. No. No. Not again. You've been in town for a short time. What, a week, tops? And I've only just arrived at Shell Isle to have a glorious laid-back summer thanks to our Aunt Tilly's gift to you." Bothered, Betsy did the unthinkable. She tossed the remains of her treat into the trash receptacle.

"Oh, just forget what I saw. I want a relaxed summer, too. I came here to do exactly that and, well, of course, to see about putting Hibiscus Cottage up for sale in the fall."

"What? Sell Hibiscus? You mustn't! Aunt Tilly left it to you. She wanted you to have a getaway to call your own at Shell Isle. This place means so much to you…to us, the memories and all. Hibiscus Cottage has always been our place to ground. Aunt Tilly understood…" Betsy's voice trailed off.

Page released a weighty sigh and dug in her handbag for a lipstick. "I know, Betsy, but what I don't know is if I want the responsibility of two homes. We do need this sojourn, but you forget I have my bookstore to run."

"Of course, I haven't forgotten. Nor, that you've lived in that reclusive mountain village for what, three years now? It's past time if you ask me, and you should ask me, for considering a new adventure because—"

"Curious, so very curious."

Page's words alerted Betsy, who swiveled in the direction that had captured her cousin's interest. "What? What'd I miss now?"

"That woman from the Bistro just sashayed into Garrett's Insurance office." Page motioned left with her head.

"Geez, why did you have to go and see that? Forget her. You aren't listening to me."

Page grabbed her handbag and stood. Indecision played across her face.

"Don't do it. Whatever it is you're planning, don't do it. I'm telling you right now I refuse to budge from this bench and get snookered into another mystery-solving expedition with you."

Ignoring her cousin, Page watched the mysterious woman's exit from the insurance office. The stiletto heels didn't slow her pace, nor did the dove gray pencil skirt with the high side split meant to show off a shapely leg. Page noted the manila envelope the woman clasped to her chest. Her signature wide-framed sunglasses were still in place. *Funny how glasses hid so much*, Page thought. "Something's up with this one. I sense it. We've got to follow her. You know your role, Betsy."

"Yeah, and I'm not playing it. I've got a new role, and it's staying as far away as I can from anyone acting remotely strange. Seriously? You're leaving me?" Betsy hollered to Page's back.

CHAPTER 2

Betsy caught up with Page, bringing plenty more words with her. Short of breath, she managed to release a few of them. "Need I remind you of the promise?"

"Nope." Page stepped behind a palm tree, pulling Betsy alongside.

Ignoring the nope, Betsy pressed on, whispering, "You promised your buddy, Detective Larsen, that if he ran your bookstore for the summer, you'd stay out of mischief and not even say hello to a cop at Shell Isle. That was your solemn promise, kiddo. And this I know because he told me when I called to confirm you were at Hibiscus. And right now, this feels like mischief to me."

"Shh. I know. I know, but you forget Larsen just retired and was bored out of his gourd. I rescued him. My bookstore needed him, and he needed the bookstore to break his addiction to trout fishing. The guy kept showing up at my place with his catch of the day and a DVD Who-Done-It flick. I couldn't fry another mess of that man's fish. I'm not even sure I can eat fish again. Besides, I haven't broken my promise."

"Still." Betsy couldn't resist peeking around to see the woman who'd caught her cousin's eye.

"See her? Tight skirt, Jackie O sunglasses, and gold bangles dripping down one arm?"

"Yeah, yeah. La-di-da's somethin' all right. Wonder what she's rummaging for in that Italian designer handbag? Forget it. I don't care. Come on. Let's go to the market." Betsy started to turn away.

"Wait. Not yet." Page saw the woman shove a smaller envelope in a drop box outside the Brakem Law Firm. "Did you see that?"

"Sure. La-di-da is leaving something at that attorney's office. Big deal. Hey, I just remembered I'm the one driving, and I'm leaving you. Go ahead and have an affair with this coconut palm tree if you want." Betsy started walking in the opposite direction.

Page trotted after her cousin. "Oh, okay, you're probably right, but this isn't the first time I've seen La-di-da acting odd."

"So what. Get in." Betsy laughed and opened the car door.

Page liberated a frustrated sigh. "You're the most uncooperative sleuth I could ever have gotten paired with in this lifetime."

"Listen up, Sherlocka; we've been retired as sleuths. We agreed, after that spa murder escapade you got us involved in, that we'd hang up our spy glasses. Listen to my grand idea. I'd planned to pitch this later, but now feels right. Why don't we spend our summer exploring some fun joint business venture? I'm ready for a fresh beginning, and you need one, too. And maybe Shell Isle is just the place for us. We've always adored the beach life. Come on, at least ponder my suggestion."

Page offered a smile. "Okay, okay, I promise to consider your latest wild idea." She didn't bother reminding Betsy that cases tended to find them regardless of where they roamed.

CHAPTER 3

"Well, I'm off to look for shells. I want to fill a snifter with them to dress my abode." Betsy held up her neon green bucket, which any six-year-old would proudly claim.

"Ah, you're going to make your bedroom feel even more beachy, if that's possible, with Tilly's decor." Page covered her grin with her hand and laid the *Coastal Points of Interest* magazine on the nearby table.

"Why don't you come along? You can park that fanny in the deck chair any old…"

"What's wrong?" Page craned her neck to see over the deck's railing, wondering what had grabbed Betsy's notice.

"Wrong…it's wrong for any man our age to look that good. Over there." Betsy tipped her head in the guy's direction.

"Oh, him? He's got the bungalow next door." Page picked up the magazine. "And you need to hold to your oath of this being a man-free beach vacation."

Betsy tucked already damp curls under her bonnet. "Know something? I liked you better quiet. I withdraw my invitation." Betsy scrunched her nose at Page and ventured down the steps, humming.

"Just trying to keep you on the straight and narrow," Page yelled back too late. Betsy had chartered a course right toward the aloof neighbor.

Page watched Betsy extend a hand while the guy ignored her outgoing cousin's attempt at conversation. He'd chatted a big five minutes with Page yesterday, introducing and apologizing for his spaniel's overly friendly greeting. She was curious why he'd given his dog's name but omitted his. What did she know about the guy? He called his dog Barnacle because he had a penchant for chewing crustaceans off his boat. And he'd recently purchased the bungalow next door. Page usually experienced little problem in getting a reclusive type talking, but Barnacle's companion bested her.

From her chaise, Page turned back to reading, releasing her mind's chatter. A shadow descended on her magazine. She glanced up, expecting Betsy's form to be towering over her.

"Hi again. I uh wanted...sit Barnacle."

"What's up?" Page reached down to pat the spaniel's back, offering her best nonchalant expression to his owner. Blast the man for being so attractive in cut-offs and a blue tee shirt. She bet he spent his life at a gym since easy conversing wasn't top on his list.

"Listen. I need to ask a big favor here." His eyes caught sight of Betsy circling back.

Page read her neighbor's mind. It wasn't hard. She'd witnessed the same reaction with other guys around Betsy. He wanted to get his say in before the man-eater arrived.

Page grinned to torment him a bit.

He cleared his throat. "A favor —"

"Yeah, I think we covered that part. What kind of favor?" Page had crossed over to being intrigued. He seemed like the kind of man who didn't like to ask favors but preferred to keep to himself. So far, he'd done an excellent job of the latter.

"It's Barnacle here. He's developed a keen desire to jump ship and come over to your place."

"Really? I've not seen any evidence —"

"You've been gone the three times that I've found him camped out on that...lounger."

Page glanced down to see the dog hair clinging to her white top. Yep, there was the proof.

He watched her try to brush off the hair. "Look, I'm sorry."

"And this favor, mister—?"

"Umm, Steve." He managed to put out his hand to grasp Page's.

"Nice to know at least half of your name." Page tendered a weak smile and placed the tortoise-framed sunglasses atop her head.

They both witnessed Betsy closing in.

"So, look, if you'd just walk Barnacle back over to my place and give him a talking to, I think we can break him of his—"

"Friendliness?"

"Who's friendly?" Betsy asked breathless, climbing the steps and depositing her near-empty shell bucket on the railing. She dabbed her flushed face with a nearby towel.

"Oh, just Barnacle. Steve's dog has come calling, and I've just agreed to help teach him the importance of waiting for an invitation." Page raised a perfectly arched brow toward the man standing next to her. She noticed his shirt said, 'Live to Surf.' His yellow-striped surfboard waited a few yards away. A surfer. Never her type, well, except for that one time. "Sure. I'll bring Barnacle back home next time he appears at our place."

"Great. Listen, I need to get out there before the sun drops." Steve moved toward the steps and a waiting Betsy.

"Why before the sun drops?" Betsy cocked a sideways grin.

"Because the sun blinds me when I'm riding a wave in." His tone came across almost patronizing. Steve moved to escape the two women, especially the one called Betsy.

"Makes sense, I guess." Betsy glanced at Page, who appeared engrossed in her magazine.

"Be seeing you." Steve walked around a dune with Barnacle following.

Betsy looked toward the beach. "He's plenty handsome

all right with those dark looks, trim physique, and all, but the man sure got shortchanged on personality. I bet his dog is more interesting than... Page, are you even listening?" Betsy parked both hands on her generous hips that the bright floral colors of her beach shift had done an excellent job of concealing.

"Of course, I'm listening. Why would I want to read this article about the disappearance of honey bees and the effect it's going to have on our civilization when I can discuss the guy next door's lack of social graces."

"Ha! Funny you. I've got a feelin' about that one. Something's just not adding up. Oh, forget it. I need a shower, and then tonight, I prepare our dinner. Yep, you're in luck; I'm in one of my creative cooking moods."

"Sounds good," Page answered absently and then registered too late Betsy's pronouncement to cook.

The door slammed. Page resigned herself to eating one of her cousin's eclectic meals.

And she thanked her lucky Feng Shui star that she'd enjoyed a filling lunch and ice cream. Secretly, she agreed with her cousin. Steve's behavior was more than just aloof.

CHAPTER 4

After chewing two antacids following Betsy's single course of cayenne kale and quinoa tossed with cantaloupe balls, Page's tummy felt settled enough to go in search of her cousin.

"There you are," said Page.

"Yeah, I love being out on the screened porch in the evenings. Gosh, how old is this hammock?" Betsy attempted to sit upright while balancing her computer tablet.

"Old. Want to go for a stroll on the beach? Tides out and the evening sky is awash with the most amazing colors of indigo with swirls of apricot. Besides, it's the perfect time to find sea treasures deposited on the beach."

The cousins enjoyed a quiet walk, stopping to shine the torch on anything of interest that'd washed ashore. A few expired jellies were all the evening yielded.

"Guess we'd better turn back. Judging by the few people on the beach, it must be late." Page slowed her pace, waiting for Betsy to agree.

"This little meander has done me good." Betsy made the turn.

"Really? How so?" Page stepped around an abandoned beach chair.

"I've made peace...finally made peace that I don't need to be on a man's arm to be happy. Big epiphany at fifty, huh? A little late, but still..." A wave caught Betsy's ankles, causing her orange flip-flops to make a squishing sound with every step.

"But still a significant shift toward wholeness." Page hoped the revelation would bring Betsy a more centered way of living. And should another man present, maybe her cousin's new awareness might provide for a healthier relationship. Two failed marriages and numerous relationship malfunctions were a testament to a needed shift.

"So, what about you having male companionship? Had any epiphanies?" Betsy's tone punctuated their serious mood.

"Me? Nah. One husband satisfied me in that department. I'm content with my life as a merry widow, and I don't want to look for the impossible." Page released a sigh, feeling the sadness of Jeff's passing wash over her like the last few waves toppling the afternoon's abandoned sandcastles.

"Ah, Page. I know Jeff's not replaceable. He was one of the finest men I've ever known, but surely, you're open to—"

"Look, I'm not closed exactly, just not seeking. I'm good." Page leaned in, hugging Betsy, slowing their walk. She wanted her cousin to understand and more, accept that truth.

"Okay, I'll shut my yap, but know if I come across a man that I think is perfect, I will be trotting him over to introduce."

"Yeah, and good luck with that perfect part. Come on. We need to pick up speed. I don't see anyone out here."

"We're almost home. I can see our yellow porch light up ahead," answered a winded Betsy, trying to keep pace.

"Stop," Page whispered.

"What now? Another jellyfish? I can't see. Turn on that flashlight, will ya?" Betsy begged, glancing down at the sand in search of a lurking jelly.

"Look over there. See that ginormous window? The inside is lit up like a stadium event. See who that is? Come on. We've got to get closer." Page walked toward the showy beach house two doors from Hibiscus Cottage.

"Not again. It can't be. I don't want it to be," Betsy pleaded, following on Page's heels.

"It's her all right with all that tall, willowy manufactured elegance. Shh, they're coming outside. Duck down." Page pulled Betsy to her knees behind the sea oats.

"My body's too old for these fast movements." Betsy rubbed her knee and whispered, "Geez, we're stuck hiding here now until they go back inside. Why couldn't you have just kept walking?"

"Hush. Can you hear what she's saying?" Page watched the woman from the bistro in a heated discussion with two men and an older woman. Each stood on the deck holding cocktails. The breeze carried La-di-da's words to Page and Betsy.

"Hear me on this, Garrett. You will put that insurance binder on my newest bauble from Evan, or I'll be inclined to let it slip about your latest dalliance." La-di-da put some distance between herself and the other three by moving to the railing and taking a sip of her drink.

"Ah, Garrett Insurance. La-di-da got a manila folder from him this afternoon." Paige whispered.

"Catherine, please. I reviewed the paper you dropped off. You have to understand that the value of the canary diamond necklace isn't anywhere near the five hundred thousand you want me to insure it for." The man she called Garrett wiped his brow with a handkerchief. The tight-fitting gray dinner jacket didn't improve his stocky shape.

The other man piped up, "He's right, Catherine. And no way can I change Evan's will about the jewelry's ownership without his express—"

"Bet that's Brakem, the attorney. Remember she dropped a file in his box earlier?" Page elbowed Betsy. "Listen."

"Enough. All of you are here to serve me in Evan's absence. And I'm not feeling well served at this moment. Should we call Evan in New York and interrupt his important meeting?" Catherine's fingers swept blond hair over one shoulder as she stared down the three others.

"No, that's not necessary, dear Catherine." The other woman moved with a regal air to Catherine's side. The deck lighting showed her age to be well into her sixties. Impeccably dressed in a pastel yellow suit, her height matched Catherine's, but not the strength of voice.

The cousins remained quiet and crouched, taking in the unfolding scene.

The older woman continued, "Evan's my only brother, and we all want what he wants. Don't we, gentlemen?" Her tone tried to make the words a command.

"Of course we do, Gwen." Garrett raised his glass.

"The law states — " Brakem made another attempt to plead his case.

"The law is subject to interpretation, Mr. Brakem," Gwen quickly intervened, evidently still trying to appease the now simmering Catherine.

Betsy gave a huff. "Are you believing these people? Honestly, I…"

Page reached over and covered Betsy's mouth. "Shush. Our voices carry out here. Great, we just missed what Catherine said."

Both women turned their gazes back to the four people a few yards away in time to catch the next exchange.

"I've heard enough from you three leeches. Leave me. Leave now." Catherine turned, taking a few steps toward the glass door.

"Catherine, come on. Be reasonable. We each need time to think about what you're asking." Garrett released the button on his jacket, allowing his full paunch exposure.

Catherine moved within inches of the man. "Asking, Garrett? I'm not asking. I'm telling."

Garrett recoiled, taking a few steps backward.

"Not one of us dares to execute what you say are Evan's

wishes without his verbal go-ahead," Brakem's voice broke.

Catherine turned to face the trio. The iciness in her voice was colder than her cocktail. "You've heard why I brought you here. This is the last time I will ask you cordially to leave."

No one moved. Confusion registered on the three faces.

"Ty?" Catherine called out.

A burly man appeared at the open door. "Yes, Mrs. Lange?"

"Please show my guests out. They each have urgent matters to attend." Catherine walked through the open French doors, not looking back.

"This way, please," Ty stood aside, motioning the three toward the door. His muscular build sent the message he'd not hesitate in carrying out his employer's wishes.

"What do we do?" Garrett found his voice first as his eyes darted toward Ty.

"Leave for starters." Brakem stepped aside to allow Gwen to pass.

"I couldn't hate her more than if she just stabbed my brother." Gwen moved past, ignoring Ty.

The other men followed, disappearing inside the pretentious oceanfront home.

"Wow. Did you get all of that?" Page stood, pulling Betsy upright.

"You bet I did. That's one mean, conniving, spoiled, evil, uppity La-di-da." Betsy relished her adjectives.

"Isn't she, though. I knew those envelopes Catherine was prancing around with earlier carried troubles. And don't forget she's packing a silver pistol, too. Why are you limping?" Page slowed her pace.

"Cause I'm stiff from that long crouch, sista. I've got more girth to manage, and you're a pretzel. Wait a minute, will you? I need to flex a few things." Betsy stood on tiptoe and flapped both arms in the air.

"What are you doing? Preparing to levitate?" Page waited for the sideshow to end.

"If only…I need a hot shower and some smelly pain ointment." Betsy pointed them south.

Page couldn't let go of the scene they'd just witnessed, and why did that unpleasant woman keep intruding in her quiet little world? She'd invite Betsy to join her in pondering. "So, what else do you think this Catherine wants them to do besides pump up the insurance on a canary diamond necklace and—oh—make some changes in her husband's will?"

"Beats me, and I wonder what she's demanding of the woman? What was the dowager's name again?" Betsy asked, pausing to stretch her knee.

"Dowager? You said dowager. What book are you reading? Betsy Ross?" Page couldn't contain her laughter. "Her name's Gwen."

"Yeah, dowager already. That's what she is, too. Never mind what I'm reading. A girl's gotta find romance where she can, don't ya know?" Betsy's lilting voice mirrored her style of humor. She paused, taking in Page's expression. "I'm not liking that arched eyebrow of yours. It bodes badly for my serenity. You're way too curious about La-di-da."

"And you, Betsy Ross, are way too perceptive."

CHAPTER 5

Page awoke to an unusual sound coming from the living room. She padded down the hall to locate its source. Barnacle stood outside the screen door, banging the Sunday newspaper against the metal frame. Amusement danced in her eyes as she opened the door a foot.

Barnacle read that as an invite. His muzzle held the newspaper for Page.

She'd have to walk him back home and deposit the paper at Steve's front entrance. Barnacle's sweet face didn't mesh with a scolding. Page smiled at her canine buddy. "Let's go, boy. Your owner can do the disciplining."

Page had just dropped the paper at Steve's front door when his black SUV turned onto the gravel driveway.

"Morning. What's up?" Steve approached Page, seeing Barnacle round the corner.

The dog dropped his head and tail, sensing a rebuke.

Page nodded. "Hello." She tightened her flowered robe's belt, noting Steve's eyes running an assessment of her attire. "I uh had an early visitor. Not exactly the traditional paperboy, as you see." She snatched up the newspaper and handed it to Steve, adding a bright smile, showing off her success at teeth whitening.

"I see." He turned his focus toward his dog. "Barnacle, I thought we had covered this subject pretty well about your staying in our backyard." Steve projected a stern look.

Barnacle offered a whine before high-tailing it down the side of the bungalow.

"Sorry about this. I swear he's a canine Houdini. He finds

escapes that don't exist."

"I believe you. Barnacle's a good spaniel at heart." Page noted Steve's attire. The black jeans and pullover had no trouble finding well-developed muscles to showcase, but the expensive leather loafers, diver's watch, and a backpack hanging from his arm left her baffled. "So, are you just getting home?"

"I am." Steve's voice chilled the air.

"Were you like…working? I mean, do you work?" Page stammered, sensing her inquisitive nature had overstepped. She needed to work on that highly evolved character defect.

"Helllooo. Page? Where are you?" Betsy's voice interrupted Steve giving a reply.

"Coming, Betsy!" Page hollered back. Resigned that her neighbor wasn't going to answer her question, Page tossed him some triteness. "Well, be seeing you."

"Yeah, thanks for bringing Barnacle home and my paper."

Betsy stood at the cottage's front door. "So? What ya been doin'?" She drew the words out for effect.

"Returning a dog and morning paper, Miss Nosey." Page frowned.

Betsy chose to let the nosey remark slide. "What's the frown about?"

Page walked past her. "The frown is about Steve arriving home at seven in the morning."

"Maybe he had a hot date last night." Betsy fanned herself for added effect.

"I don't think so. Our neighbor was dressed all mysterious in black and toting a backpack. A real enigma and I'm thinking we ought to find out who this guy is." Page disappeared down the hall to her bedroom.

"And if I have a say, I say let sleeping dogs lie," Betsy called back, heading for the shower with the most fantastic menu idea for their breakfast.

"Ah, but that's just it, cousin, that dog ain't sleeping," Page answered as she passed the closed bathroom door, laptop in hand. She dashed to her closet and grabbed a pair of jeans and her lilac tie-dyed tee. She'd hurry and dress and seize the opportunity to get lost in the screen while Betsy did her hour-long morning ablutions. Still, plenty of time to fix them a light breakfast.

Page parked herself on the porch's glider, the laptop poised to investigate a few of this peculiar group, starting with Steve. With any luck, she'd have a good sixty cherished minutes of solitude before Betsy appeared with her constant hunger.

~*~

"Come and get it," Betsy shouted from inside.

Page peeked at her watch. How had an hour slipped past her? Ah, it hadn't. Betsy's primping time had suffered a dramatic cut to twenty minutes. "Coming!" She feared the breakfast awaiting her still unrecovered digestive system.

"Have a chair. I've got just the thing to wake up those sluggish taste buds of yours." Wearing a proud face, Betsy placed the crimson polka-dot napkin in Page's lap and took her seat.

"Wow, what do I have here? Such a generous serving, too." Page felt her stomach roll and prayed the bottle of antacids held at least two remaining chews. She'd need to stop by the pharmacy later and grab a colossal bottle to carry her through summer.

"It's my newest recipe. It came to me this morning—red chili pepper French toast with either cinnamon maple syrup or honey goat cheese. You've always loved any honey bees' offering. Go ahead. Dig in." Betsy took the first bite, rolling her eyes heavenward.

"Sounds…zesty." Page slipped the tiniest morsel into her mouth, nodding. The hot exploded in her throat. She downed her glass of water.

"Good, huh?"

Betsy's constitution trumped hers. "If you wouldn't mind, I'm going to need that bottle of syrup and a refill on my ice water, please."

"Of course." Betsy's floral shift shimmied toward the kitchen.

Barnacle's face appeared at the screen door.

Page thought quickly. She grabbed the French toast and raced to throw the slices out the door to the waiting dog. Mission accomplished. She sat back down and pretended to be chewing when Betsy returned with the water pitcher and more syrup.

"Here you go. Goodness, you've positively devoured your toast. I'm sorry not to have any more to offer." Betsy's attention shifted to the sound coming from outside. She rose to investigate.

Fearful, Page followed.

"Well, if it isn't Steve's dog having some coughing fit. Whatever is wrong with him?" Betsy cracked the screen door, and Barnacle zipped past, heading straight for their table.

"He's in a bit of distress. The poor dog." Page knew she was the cause, too.

Both women watched in surprise as the dog knocked the plastic water pitcher over with his paw. Barnacle commenced lapping the spilled liquid from the floor.

"How strange for him to be so…thirsty." Betsy stared, perplexed.

Page stooped down to check Barnacle. His eyes were tearing from the hot peppers. He did manage to give her face a lick. "I'm so sorry, fellow," she whispered, relieved his hacking had subsided.

"He seems fine now." Betsy had sat back down, eyeing her plate.

"Listen, since I've finished breakfast, and you haven't, I'm just going to walk Barney back home."

"Good idea. My toast is getting cold."

"Doubtful," Page muttered under her breath. That toast would never be anything but insanely hot. "Come on, Barnacle. Back you go. And I promise I'll make this up to you somehow."

CHAPTER 6

"Sir, this lady is up to something...a big something. And I happen to be ideally positioned to watch and observe her movements."

Page stood at Steve's screen door, hearing his rich baritone voice declare his certainty about who she didn't know. She paused with her curious nature to listen. Barnacle waited by her side, swallowing big gulps of air while his tail wagged against her leg.

"For starters, I can tell you there was a meeting last night at her home with some guests you might find noteworthy."

Page surmised the Sir, whoever he was, must be talking.

"Not now. In person. I'll be there before you fly out."

Page gathered her composure. She'd have time later to ponder who Steve might really be and if he was sinister or safe.

Barnacle whined.

"Who's there?" Steve appeared within seconds, cracking open the screen door.

"Me again with your dog." Page held Barnacle's collar and passed him back to his owner.

"Are you kidding me, Barn? Go to your crate. Now."

Barnacle suffered another minor coughing spell, causing Steve to drop to his knees and check out his dog. The love shone in the man's eyes. "Barn, what's the matter? Did you eat another crab, because the vet —"

Page knelt and hugged Barnacle's face. "Forgive me, boy."

"Forgive you?" Steve's steel gray eyes fixed on her.

"Yeah, you see, Betsy made some spicy French toast. And I shared my lot with Barnacle here. I never dreamed he'd react like...he has. I thought dogs had strong constitutions, and I mean yours eats crustaceans and such."

"Do go on."

"Well, Betsy's not a great cook. Actually, she's a horrible cook." A giggle escaped that she dared voice her feelings out loud.

"I'm inclined to agree." Steve watched his dog move toward the water bowl.

"Is there anything I can do? I swear he's doing much better than a few moments ago. I'd offer some antacids, but I'm probably all out." Sensing Barnacle was over the worst of the encounter, Page suppressed the grin, trying to escape.

"I think he'll be okay once I get some food into him to cut any remaining fire. Maybe this escapade will keep him home. Right, my man?" Steve grinned.

Barnacle managed a tail wag but kept drinking.

"Anything else? I'm in the middle of something."

Page registered the dismissal. "Nope. Just one more I'm sorry. Bye, Barnacle." She let herself out but planned to keep Steve on top of her investigating list.

~*~

"What took so long this time? Honestly, if you hadn't given me that dissertation of you being a one-man kind of gal, I'd swear you were hanging your beach bonnet on our hunk next door." Betsy shut the dishwasher door and pushed the start button.

"Nope, but I'm on a mission to learn what type of work our neighbor is doing. I sense he's not your average nine-to-fiver."

Betsy grabbed a pen and notepad.

"No, Betsy. I don't need you to take notes just yet, but soon," chuckled Page.

"I was getting ready to write my grocery list. I need to grab a few things at the market for my next culinary extraordinaire."

Page panicked. She felt the adrenaline pump kick open. "Totally unnecessary. I'm relieving you from cooking another meal today. You're on vacation." She grabbed the notepad and pen, tossing them in the drawer.

"But really, I love—"

"I won't hear another word. I'm treating us to a meal at..." Page's mind scrambled to come up with a place. "At...the Crab Shak."

"The Crab Shak? Where the bikers go?" Betsy's mouth hung open.

"Yep. There will be plenty of local color. You love color. Let's add a different kind of spice to our day. We can have an early dinner." What in the world had her make that restaurant choice, never mind the reference to spice?

"Guess I'm game. Okay then, the Crab Shak it shall be. Hey, are we getting tats too?" Betsy pointed to her forearm and laughed.

Page envisioned them inked with a seagull image. Her next words came as a tease. "Hmm, let me think about it. For now, let's run some errands and then enjoy a swim this afternoon. Give me about an hour to make some calls, and I'll be ready. You?"

"Oh, I'll sit on the porch with my historical romance novel. Big doings because Laura's ready to tell the Dowager Gertrude..."

Betsy turned to find Page had disappeared into the study.

CHAPTER 7

Page's index finger flew solo, punching a series of numbers into her cell phone. "Hey, Larsen. How's the bookshop?"

"Hey, yourself. Shop's good," Larsen quipped. "You'll like this. I just took a thirty-piece book order for the third graders. It seems the homeroom mothers have banded to have their spawn read some manners book called, "Say Thank You." Larsen's words came tinged with amusement.

"Sounds like a good idea to me. Good for those moms bringing back the forgotten rules of etiquette. What else you got to share?" Page twirled her pen. She'd have to dance carefully with the retired savvy detective.

Larsen's crisp voice came back through her phone. "Well, I've been familiarizing myself with where certain fiction genres are in the shop. It's kinda embarrassing when the customers must lead me to the right section. Know what I mean?"

"I do, but everyone understands you're new to running a bookstore, so don't stress. Just promise me you won't close early to go fishing." Page clipped her hair back. "That's what I care about, Mister." She delighted in goading her one male friend, who always took her bossy words good-naturedly.

"Define early." Larsen cleared his throat.

"Early would be two o'clock." The rascal had plans with his fishing buddy, Harry. She felt it. Page glanced out the window in time to see Steve hop into his SUV and tear off toward town. *What's his big hurry?* Larsen's voice beckoned for her attention.

"Then no worries here," Larsen assured Page. His waders wouldn't be on him until three p.m. "What's new with you?"

"Me? Oh, just trying to survive Betsy's cooking one meal at a time. Getting a few walks each day. And for entertainment, I'm encouraging a male neighbor to develop manners like the third graders' moms." Steve's face flashed in her mind.

"Hmm…want me to send you some books on the subject? Wait, this one's perfect—*Manly Manners in a Fortnight*. You know I hear the Brits are very proper and good at this sort of thing," Larsen added, with his best attempt at a Cockney accent.

I doubt a book would help this guy," Page responded, believing her words.

"Hey. Got another one especially for you, *The Art of Ordering Take Out*. That should help with the Betsy problem." Larsen laughed loud enough to wake one of the mountain village's hibernating brown bears.

"Listen. I appreciate your showing off learning my inventory and all, but I need something else from you. And when you hear my next words, don't lecture." Page sucked in a breath.

"Lecture you? I only lecture when you start that sleuthing business up, and, gal, you'd better not tell me you're—"

"Only a tiny bit. Tiny, Larsen. And before you start in, I swear I just happened to be at The Bistro…wait a minute. I'm calling you about my neighbor." Geez. Whatever made her start blabbing?

"Page Wright, if it wasn't my lunchtime, I'd be giving you a long talking to about whatever you've gone and put that cute nose into." Larsen peered into his lunch sack.

"You should enjoy your meal. I'll make this quick. I need you to run a check on a guy named Steve Tanner. Page felt proud she'd hit upon his last name when Barnacle brought her Steve's newspaper with the monthly bill attached.

"And just why do I want to bother the guys at the station with this?" Larsen prodded.

"Because I've got this inkling, and it so happens he lives

right next door. And you want me safe...don't you?" Page's
spirits buoyed with her pitch. Larson's caring about her would
trump his usual sermon on minding her own business. "So? Are
you going to help me?"

Page knew that Larsen probably had his favorite ham and
smoked gouda sandwich spread out, waiting for his first taste.
"Okay. Okay. Your blasted inklings again, though I hate to admit
this, they're always on the mark. I'll see what I can dig up, but in
the meantime, you steer clear of this guy. Agreed?"

The bell jingled on the shop's door. Page could hear
Larsen's pal Harry in the background. "See here? Guaranteed to
snag ol' granddaddy trout."

"Listen, I heard the bell. You've got a customer," she lied.
"Talk to you later and big thanks." Page rang off, appreciating
Harry's timely interruption. She'd scratch checking out one
mysterious-acting but oh-so-fine-looking neighbor. Where had
that last thought originated? She must be hormonal or something.

"Page? You busy?" Betsy's voice sounded bored.

"Come on in." Her call to the real estate agent could wait.

"Can we please, and thank you, go eat lots earlier than we
planned? I can't stop thinking about a Crab Po' Boy sandwich,
and the dowager is off to summer at her country estate at Dorset.
I can leave her to settle in." Betsy's electric blue striped handbag
dangled from her arm, punctuating her earnestness about the
meal.

Page chuckled. "Well, I'm sure the dowager's escape from
her London home is a huge relief for you. Come on. Guess I'm
a smidge hungry, too." Page flicked off her laptop, but not her
mind. She knew Steve was hard at work reporting on someone,
but who and why?

CHAPTER 8

Page maneuvered her vintage European four-wheel drive past the Crab Shak's overflowing parking lot of vehicles. The restaurant knew how to draw the business. The building looked like it had suffered additions more than once, judging by the different colors adorning the metal roof. And the lack of architectural detail only enhanced the Crab Shak's unique appearance.

"Isn't it a glorious day?" Betsy gestured her arm out the SUV's window, inviting a look. She'd tucked her untamable auburn hair under the broad-brimmed straw hat. The marigold flower attached to the front testified to Betsy's showy side.

Page slowed, taking a second to observe what had amplified Betsy's lightheartedness. "Yeah, if you can see past the glare of chrome." A dozen or so Harleys were lined up with helmets dangling from the handlebars, affirming their owners were nearby.

"Ah, come on, Page. You're just cranky from hunger. Park us somewhere, will ya?"

Page cut a grin. "Okay, okay. Guess I'll head over to that sandy spot next to the dumpster."

"Sand?" Betsy screeched. "Don't go there. We'll get stuck."

Page pulled in the spot. "These beloved vintage vehicles don't get stuck, silly. They live for all terrain. Hop out." Page headed for the Shak's entrance.

~*~

Orders placed, Betsy turned her attention to the Crab Shak's patrons. "Get a load of that group to your right. Must be the bikers."

"Ya think?" Page teased, taking in the Shak's décor. Roughhewn floors dotted with peanut shells announced everyone's movement around the place. The walls displayed every possible biker memorabilia, and the tables suffered distress by patrons who excelled at imbibing with gusto into their tankards of brew. The two cousins presented an anomaly to any patrons still able to focus. Page wondered why she'd blurted out the name of this joint for them to have a meal. Geez, she needed to get her mind and mouth in sync, but there were too many distractions finding her at Shell Isle. Steve's face flashed again. Page released a pent-up breath and felt an inkling. She'd better stay alert.

Betsy broke the silence. "You know, I never went out with a biker type. I bet I missed —"

"Can't you just forget about men for a full five minutes?" Page teased, allowing her attention to stray. "No way. You've got to be kidding me." Page stared at two familiar faces sitting in a corner booth.

"What ya see? Tell me." Betsy grew serious, reading her cousin's expression.

"Two men…" answered Page, her attention trailing off. The inkling had rewarded her.

Betsy took a cooling sip of the water placed on the table by their retreating waitress. "Men? Oh sure, you can talk about men, but me, I'm supposed to act like a holy sister or something and ignore my inner yearnings," huffed Betsy.

"Forget your yearnings. That guy, Ty, and the seedy-looking one from the Bistro are drinking a beer." Page turned back to Betsy, her eyes as bright as the silver hubcaps hanging from the ceiling.

"Don't you dare tell me not to look." Betsy stole a glance. "Wow! It's that Ty fellow, all right. That dude is one intimidating-looking specimen."

"Yep, and I wonder what they're discussing, and if our Catherine knows about this little meeting?" Page saw the waitress bringing their Po Boy baskets. Fast service took on a new meaning.

"Here you go, gals. One Crab Boy with an extra-large order of fries for the big eater." She placed the food in front of Betsy. "And for you, the Oyster Boy." She set the last basket in front of Page.

Betsy sent a glare the waitress's way but wasted no time grabbing the tartar sauce cup off the serving tray.

The demeanor of their waitress brooked no idle chit-chat. "Need anything else?" Her red shirt's message stretched across her overly endowed chest flashed the words, 'Order Up,' summing up the Crab Shak's failed attempt at humor.

"We're good, but thanks," Page answered, noting Betsy's cheeks pooched like a chipmunk who'd just gorged on another stash of acorns. She shielded her grin with the napkin.

They watched the waitress sway toward the bikers' table. Her chest arrived before the rest of her. Page bet one of the guys would score a date before he left the Shak.

Betsy spoke first. "Golly, we're getting a real show here between our dastardly villains in the far booth and the bikers' Ol' Lady who's busy hustling — or serving if you like." Betsy cocked her eyebrow for effect and took another bite of the sandwich. "So, what are our two bad boys doing now?"

"One is on his cell phone. The other is fiddling with his wallet." Page looked down and gulped her iced tea, wishing to avoid any eye contact with the men.

Betsy stole another glance. "Good. They're leaving. Pass the ketchup and eat up."

"Not good. Not good at all," Page whispered.

"Will you please ignore whatever is not good and eat what is good in front of you?" Betsy grabbed a handful of napkins to dab at whatever dripped into her lap.

Page leaned forward. "Listen. They're both packing heat, and Ty just grabbed Seedy's arm. That's when I saw their guns in their shoulder holsters." Page swallowed. "I'm telling you that these two are majorly up to—"

Betsy jumped in. "See, that's why we need to stay at Hibiscus, and let me cook for us. We're incapable of eating a meal out without some high drama latching on to you." Betsy's knuckles rapped on the table to get her cousin's attention.

Page ignored her. "They're leaving. Come on. We're going, too. Let's see what they're about."

"I'm not leaving a perfectly good basket of crispy fries to chase after you like Dr. Watson on some eavesdropping escapade. Nope. Not budging," Betsy declared, waving a French fry in Page's direction.

Accepting her cousin's resolute tone, Page nodded and released a heavy sigh. Maybe her nudge to follow the two men came from her mischievous mind. She heard Betsy's chattering and turned her attention to the outer world.

"There's a good girl. Get things worked out in that head of yours. We don't need to concern ourselves with these menacing people." Pleased to have won a round, Betsy sprinkled some of her coveted fries into Page's basket.

"I guess." Page witnessed the Shak's screen door close on her opportunity to find out.

Betsy brightened. "Wait a minute. You still need to tell me about what happened at Steve's this morning. Out with it, sista."

Page noted the cheerful tone in her cousin's voice. Probably because Steve's looks appealed to Betsy's forever roving, now sans astigmatism corrected, left eye.

"Hello?" Betsy snapped her fingers in front of Page's face. "Where'd you go now?"

"I'm here. Oh, all right, here's the scoop. I take Barnacle

back home, and Steve's on the phone talking to someone he calls Sir."

"Sir, huh?"

"Yeah, Sir. And get this, he tells Sir that he's watching some lady, and he's well positioned to do so. Next, he talks about a strange meeting that happened last night at a house." Page felt the familiar flush wash over her body. Something was brewing nearby besides the Shak's craft beer. She forced herself to focus on Betsy's chatter. The flushing ceased, but not her thoughts.

"Well, what do you make of all that? I mean, who's the Sir? Our Steve is undoubtedly involved in tailing, but hey, wait, we don't care. Do we?" Betsy flagged the waitress.

"We might care just a touch," Page answered, taking a sip of the cooling beverage.

The waitress swung by their table. She cast her eyes on Betsy's breadth. "What ya need, honey? Dessert?"

"As a matter of fact, yes. I saw a piece of chocolate layer cake whiz by a minute ago. Box me up a slice." Betsy squinted at the woman's name tag. "Will you, Velma?"

"Sure thing, Toots." Velma totaled the check and handed it to Betsy. "Your box will be at the cashier's." Not waiting for a reply, she headed to the kitchen.

"There's another one missing a personality." Betsy shook her head. "Okay. Back to your saying, we care a touch about Steve and some Sir person."

"Yes?" Page's hopes flared.

"I've decided that I don't care. Nope, I can't care a whit. Last I looked, he's a man, and I'm not allowed to be any kind of interested in the opposite sex." Betsy sniffed, testing Page's resolve.

"This is different," Page interjected.

"Nope. A man's a man. None for me." Betsy snagged her hat from the seat. "Let's get out of this dive. I want my cake."

"Well, I guess you aren't interested that I've got Larsen running a check on our neighbor?" Page followed her cousin to pay their bill.

Betsy turned and faced Page while the cashier made the change. "Please tell me that you didn't call Larsen over some un-neighborly guy who had a private conversation with someone —"

Page waited until they were outside to reply. "I did. I want to know who he is. And you know why, cousin?" Page replied, as they walked toward her SUV.

"Let's see." Betsy halted. She cast her brown eyes upward, pretending to think.

Page didn't wait. "Because I've had another one of my inklings. That's why."

"No. This I don't want to hear; besides, I've got my own kind of inkling." Betsy chided. "And it goes like this: I sense we're stuck. Your tires have sunk down into that soft sand. Take a gander." Betsy stood next to the SUV, squinting and assessing the situation.

"Isn't this swell? I should have known those tires sold to me weren't any good," Page mumbled.

"And I repeat, this jalopy ain't all that," retorted Betsy. She frowned at her cake box. The confection would never survive the heat.

"Jabs I don't need; however, a push would be appreciated. Let me start 'er up and see if I can roll out. Betsy, you get behind the vehicle, and then I'll holler when —"

"I'm not pushing anything except my chocolate cake around a plate later...if it survives out here." Betsy held up the box to drive her point.

Paged ignored her cousin and got behind the wheel, and put the SUV in reverse. Gently touching the accelerator, the tires spun, sending sand flying toward a surprised Betsy.

Page cut the engine. The rearview mirror showed Betsy

covered in a fine dusting. They were stuck and in need.

CHAPTER 9

"I've had it with these two snoops," Steve spewed under his breath, taking in the scene fifty yards from his vehicle. "Why do these blasted women haunt my every waking moment?" He slammed the driver's door and started walking.

While Betsy was busy spitting out sand and choice words, Page saw her neighbor's approach. He wasn't smiling, but that wasn't new. Page plastered a helpless expression on her reddened face and offered a shrug. Her makeup was seconds from a total meltdown. She jettisoned her pride, "The angels must have sent you. We're sort of…"

"We're stuck," Betsy chimed in, seeing Steve, "and mind you, we're stuck in this ancient four by four that I'm told never gets stuck, even on dunes in the Sahara."

"Not now, Betsy, please. It's faulty tires." Page waited expectantly for Steve to offer something.

Ignoring the women's volley, Steve's cold as a polar ice cap voice replied, "I can see the situation here. Bad sand for any vehicle. Listen, I'll pull you out with my winch. Let's get this done. I don't have time for your—"

"Great! Just tell me what to do." Page tried to exude appreciation with her eyes.

"Betsy, you stand over there. I'll give you instructions for Page once she's behind the wheel. Got that, ladies?" His exasperation followed him back to his vehicle.

To the man's credit, he had them rolling down the road in less than ten minutes, carrying his suggestion that Page keeps her inferior tires on pavement.

With the ordeal behind them, Page added another concerning observation to her growing list. Why was Steve hanging out at the Crab Shak's parking lot? Had he spotted what she'd witnessed happening nearby?

~*~

The cottage's paddle fans welcomed the two exasperated women inside.

Fork suspended over the chocolate cake, Betsy posed the first question, "So, why do you suppose Steve parked behind the trees at the Shak?"

"Maybe he'd come to eat." Page drug her finger across the cake's frosting. "Hmm, that place may be rough and tumble, but icing, they do smooth."

"I don't think so." Betsy took another bite and stared at the ceiling.

"You don't like that yummy frosting?" Page asked, puzzled, never knowing her cousin to criticize any dessert.

"No, you ninny. I don't think Steve was there to eat. Didn't you notice that he left with us?" Betsy's face showed a frown. "Forget I asked. I don't care, and don't you either."

"Oh, he was there observing." Page snagged her cousin's fork and stole an impressive bite.

"Observing who?" Betsy asked, unable to resist a taste of intrigue.

"He was parked incognito so that he could watch Seedy and Ty, of course."

"What? I didn't see those two still around." Betsy grabbed back her fork, realizing the slice of cake had morphed into a sliver.

"I know you didn't because you were too busy busting my so-called jalopy to notice." Page went to the refrigerator for a bottle of sparkling water. "Aren't you curious just a little about what I saw?"

"You're such a taunter, Page Wright. That's my new word.

What did I miss this time?"

"Well, they had a long navy duffle bag parked on the hood of one of their vehicles." Page fluffed the seat cushion and sat down.

"Like maybe holding some guns to pull a job?" Betsy offered, tossing her empty cake box into the trash.

"Who knows, but your idea sounds plausible." Page always relished the shift when a hooked Betsy became a cooperative sleuth. She'd fold with the objections soon enough.

"And you're sure Steve was surveilling Seedy and Ty? Who is this guy?"

"I'm as sure of Steve's watching them as I am of us getting more chocolate cake from Velma. It's insanely decadent. Anyway, good that I've got Larsen trying to sniff out something on our neighbor.

Page heard the cell phone chime from the porch table. She abandoned Betsy to ponder the dump of information and for her cousin's curious nature to settle in.

CHAPTER 10

"Oh, hi, Gail. Funny, you should call. I had planned to ring you in a bit. Yes, well, word does travel up and down the beach." Page knew Betsy was in earshot. "How about tomorrow morning around eleven?" Page rang off.

Betsy struck a pose next to the open sliding door. "Gail, the real estate agent, is stopping by tomorrow at eleven?"

"Yep." Page waited.

"I don't like it." Betsy's lips puffed up like a blowfish.

"Just a quick talk about getting some market information," assured Page.

"I don't like even the quick talk of selling Hibiscus. I want to talk about us settling here and doing some little somethin'. We need to have fun." Betsy moved to stretch out on the hammock with her pout fully established.

"I like fun. How about a game of Scrabble? You can express yourself differently," suggested Page, and feeling a game was a healthy way to discharge some of their emotional angst.

"Okay, but I'm on to what you're doing here." Betsy attempted to extricate herself from the hammock. "I swear this thing acts like a Venus flytrap. I'm starting to loathe it. Go fetch the game while I try and get free."

~*~

Page closed the game's box lid and smiled at Betsy. "Know what? We need to celebrate your win. Get your sandals while I grab my handbag," Page instructed.

"Yeah, I never beat you at Scrabble, and I'm suspicious this was a pity win. Wait, where are we going? I don't like surprises, especially yours." Betsy hurried to slip her feet into her favorite orange flip-flops. "Give me a hint or something."

"You'll see soon enough," Page answered cryptically.

CHAPTER 11

Page settled behind the wheel, waiting for Betsy and clueless about where to take them. She knew the time was approaching for Betsy to begin rustling pots and pans. Her hunger pains made the Shak lunch seem like last week. What she spied sitting on the kitchen counter called for quick action. A can of tuna, spinach linguine noodles, and strawberry jam couldn't possibly produce something she'd want her fork to touch. Never mind the ever-present bottle of ketchup Betsy treated like a vegetable serving.

Dressed beach casual in petal pushers and a yellow bumble bee printed shirt, the blond sleuth forced her mind to return to the present quandary. Page tapped the steering wheel and twisted her lips to the side. Where to celebrate Betsy's win? While running a mental list of possibilities, she glimpsed Catherine's red Italian sports car pull out of the garage. The nudge to act hit Page's solar plexus.

"Here I am," Betsy announced, settling in with her jumbo-size woven tote and closing the vehicle's door.

"Quick, look to your left," Page urged. Freshly applied coral lip gloss went back into her purse.

"Nope. It's gonna be something I don't need to see." Betsy's willpower collapsed, and she stole a glance.

"Change of plans. Buckle up." Page put the vehicle in drive and joined the parade. A familiar black SUV pulled out ahead of Page.

"Who is this guy? I ask again." Betsy craned her neck, looking ahead.

"He's someone I suspect is following La-di-da, and for a

reason we need to know." Page noted both vehicles were turning right. She dropped her speed to fall further back.

"Why do we need to know?" Betsy gripped the armrest. "Slow down, will ya? Steve's vehicle has stopped."

"Just great." Page braked.

"Not good. He's walking our way." Betsy slumped down in her seat.

Page lowered her window, but her curiosity stayed up as she noticed his nightly attire of all black closing the distance. He moved stealthily, with an air of confidence cloaking him.

Steve bent down, peering inside. His tone left little doubt he was irritated. "You two yet again."

"I could say the same thing about you, but I won't. I have manners." Page's smile never found her eyes. He'd let Catherine go to stop them. Why?

"Hear this, you two busybodies. I haven't figured out exactly what you're about, but consider this a warning. Stop your snooping...now."

"Snooping? We're not exactly..." Betsy's voice petered out.

"Page?" Steve's eyebrow raised, ignoring Betsy.

"Well, we felt a smidge curious about..." Page faltered.

A high-tech-looking phone clipped to Steve's belt started talking. "Steve, are you positioned?" a man's terse voice asked.

Steve unsnapped the phone off his hip and jogged a few yards away to answer. He returned seconds later, eyes stormy and boring into Page. "Get out of here...now." He hurried back to his SUV and, within seconds, disappeared around a corner.

"Well, wasn't that a pleasant exchange?" Betsy huffed. Her back now ramrod straight, meant to show she felt empowered and bothered. She hugged her straw tote to her chest, staring out the windshield.

Amused, Page replied, "Clearly, we interrupted something

important. And my question…why is our next-door neighbor following our other neighbor?" Page sat perplexed.

Betsy pointed her chipped, nail-polished finger out the window. "Can someone please tell me who this tall, dark rogue who has an affection for anything colored black is? And when is Larsen supposed to call you? I agree there's unsettling doings, cousin, and I fear we've stumbled upon something unsavory. Page, we've got to be super careful, better yet—"

Page didn't let her cousin finish. "I don't know who he is for sure, but he's tied to surveillance. And as for Larsen, maybe he'll have something tomorrow."

Betsy pulled a frown. "And the doings? What do you think about—"

"Drat. He's back."

The dark SUV pulled up beside Page's. "What part of 'get out of here' has you confused?"

The heavy dose of sarcasm in Steve's gruff voice left both women temporarily speechless.

"You've got exactly ten seconds to get this classic moving."

Page gave him back one of his saucy salutes and stomped the gas pedal. The engine responded, pressing both women into their seats. "Still a fine piece of kit." Page smiled, using a British turn of phrase.

"What the heck are you doing?" Betsy managed to ask while grabbing the door handle for steadiness.

"Showing the jerk that ten seconds is too long to wait to be rid of his bossiness." Page circled the block to see if she could catch sight of Steve. Instead, the rearview mirror rewarded her with the blue lights of a police vehicle. "Seems we're due for more attention. This time, keep quiet. I'll do the talking."

"What now? This night isn't any fun at all." Betsy blew out a breath, glimpsing the approaching silhouette on Page's side.

"Evening, ladies." The man flashed a badge their way

while his words failed at sounding friendly. His head appeared in the open driver's window. "I got a call about two suspicious types driving a white SUV in this area. Could that possibly be you?"

"Well, honestly, I hardly think we fit the description of suspicious types," Betsy blustered, unable to resist the taunt.

Page pinched her cousin's arm and offered up her best innocent smile. This guy's demeanor booked little patience. His worn leather belt was on the first notch and not because he was overweight, but more likely he didn't waste money on appearances. Page saw his brown eyes awash in smile lines that thrived on finding humor, including the current situation. These observations came before her reply. "Officer, we only stopped here to discuss whether to take in a movie or bingo at the Lions Club this evening."

"It's detective," he drawled the words out. "And the decision is?"

Page cut her eyes to Betsy. "Which did you decide?"

"Movie's good." Betsy fidgeted, staring ahead to avoid the detective's gaze.

Page nodded to the detective, hoping Betsy's reply would encourage him on his way. He didn't budge. No doubt, options were playing around in his head.

"So, can I count on seeing this vehicle in the theatre parking lot when I swing by in, say, fifteen minutes?"

The crooked grin proved Page's take on him. "You absolutely can, Detective Koch," Page answered, reading the badge pinned to his belt. "May we go now?"

Back in character and with a curt nod, Koch pointed them toward the main road.

"Boy, what a night. And about the only thing I'm celebrating is not being arrested." Betsy took a tissue from her bag and blotted the perspiration prickling her forehead.

"Don't worry." Page turned on the blinker, and as she rounded the corner, she passed Steve's black SUV parked on the side. She caught his ridiculous grin and aggravating salute as she drove past. Thankfully, Betsy missed the exchange. Page's mind considered the possibility that Steve might be the reason Detective Koch pulled them.

CHAPTER 12

Closing the cottage's front door, Betsy tossed her handbag on a nearby chair. "I can't believe I just sat through a movie titled *Vampire's Revenge.*"

"I'm truly sorry, Betsy, but it was the next movie playing. At least it was a short flick. What say we go bicycling since it's not too awfully late. It will get our minds off bloodletting, and you always call bicycling fun," offered Page.

"Yeah, biking is supposed to be fun, but with you...." Betsy's mind considered the offer. "If that's all we'll be doing on the beach, count me in, but if you've got any ideas—"

"A bike ride, Betsy. Only a simple late-night bike ride. Fun." Page hoped she could honor those words despite their growing magnetism toward troubling interactions with others. And wasn't this pattern exactly how they ended up in the middle of other murder investigations? The inklings always came calling when trouble brewed.

Betsy followed her cousin toward the waiting bikes. "Hold up. I'm concerned that we're getting ourselves entangled in something we best try to avoid. It all feels sinister. I mean it, Page. You heard Steve warn us to stop snooping."

The battle waged inside Page. She couldn't walk away from whatever was playing out. She sensed too much depended on Betsy and her abilities. Free will was highly overrated. She looked at her cousin. "We've just got to be more careful, more alert, from now on."

Betsy reacted, throwing her arms in the air. "What? Careful, as in careful not to do another thing involving meddling? Then yes, I completely agree, but if you mean careful, as in not getting caught again, then count...me...out." Betsy's eyes showed enough intensity to rival a bullfighter staring down an animal ready to charge him.

Page acted to deflect the emotion. "Oh, you! Listen. We've got a neighbor spying on our other neighbor, and we—"

"No, you listen, kiddo." Betsy's index finger came to life and began pointing Page's way. "We've got our neighbor, La-di-da, who's intimidating others and has acquired a pistol, no doubt illegally. And, a guy named Steve, who comes and goes at odd hours, tails her and reports to someone called Sir. Sir, of what? Gosh only knows. That's what we got, and I might add we are steering clear of starting now. I'm no longer allowing my curious genes out. I'm zipped." Betsy settled on her bicycle's seat.

"But, Betsy, don't you see the similarities? When we were enjoying our vacation at Serendipity Spa, things started happening around us, just like now.

Betsy jumped in. "And your intuition told you something was afoot. Yep, those inklings of yours have sure landed us into some prickly predicaments over the years, but not this time. I want a vacation. I want to see how the Dowager Gertrude will handle her family's total disregard for propriety. I want to consume large amounts of seafood. I may even want to contemplate the ocean being a sentient being."

Page opened her mouth to speak. She needed to explain that the intuiting had returned.

"Stifle yourself while I enjoy my overdue hissy fit." Betsy released a loud exhale.

Page held back her laugh. "Look, let's go ride and forget this detecting. You're probably right. Nothing to worry about with our neighbors. Just some harmless PI making sure Catherine isn't having some tawdry affair."

Betsy took a moment before nodding. Her wrinkled

forehead relaxed. "Yep, I bet that's all it is, and the gun is protection that she couldn't bother getting the proper way." Betsy took a sip from the water bottle Page placed in the bike's cup holder. She toasted Page mid-air. "We've got us a supremely fine explanation."

"Supremely fine." Page sat astride her bike, happy they'd moved past the hissy. She tossed her windbreaker and cell phone into the bike's basket and wished she could release the feeling that she and Betsy's involvement would soon prove pivotal.

CHAPTER 13

The cousins allowed their troubling thoughts to ride with them into the night. Their silence hung as dense as the humid coastal air shrouding them. The portended gray fog would undoubtedly usher in a melancholy mood for beachgoers come morning. The ever-changing sea landscape defied boredom. And the mysteries held within the depths had beckoned questioning seekers for eons. The pull to visit the beach—any beach—felt primal, like spirit healing. Both cousins answered the call of Shell Isle, acknowledging their yearning each year.

Page trusted in her unique gift and the ways it chose to manifest. An 'inkling' might appear like a willowy breeze against her physical body, alerting her. A 'nudge' often felt in her solar plexus was a call for action. Page learned the intensity presented in direct proportion to the speed she needed to react. When the more powerful and insightful 'intuition' came calling, her path was illuminated toward the person, place, or thing. She'd already been experiencing the signs. Signs to serve she couldn't ignore. More troubling, she discerned something ominous was gathering force around them this night.

The last days of witnessing Catherine's doings, beginning with the first sighting of her at the travel agency had put Page on notice. She hadn't yet shared that story with Betsy.

Her cousin's lighthearted, live-in-the-moment nature was merely the outer shell worn by someone having suffered repeated hurts and disappointments. The absence of lasting male relationships had proved to be Betsy's Achilles heel in this lifetime.

Over their many years, Betsy had remained steadfast whenever Page had needed her cousin's sleuthing assistance. Though Betsy could be counted on to question and even beg Page to ignore the sensations when they intruded on her fun, Betsy's loyalty reigned, and she always did her part with a willing spirit.

Page's next words punctuated the heavy silence. "You thinking?"

Betsy answered with a sigh laced with weariness. "Yeah, I am. I've tried convincing myself that you're not getting any of those blasted impressions, but you are. Right?"

"Probably, yes. Okay, yes, I am. A strong nudge came tonight."

"Figured. Know what I wish right now?" Betsy slowed her pedaling.

"What?" Page's heart beat with empathy.

"That you could somehow go back to the way you were at sixteen when you first started sensing things. No complicated cases to solve. Everything was all pretty innocent and even hilarious at times."

"For you, sure. For me, I felt strange, different than everyone else we hung out with back then. Thank goodness our grandmother had "the touch," as she liked to call it, or I'd have begged for a straitjacket," answered Page in jest, wanting to lighten the mood.

"Yeah, but your special knack worked dandy for me. You could tell me when a pop quiz was coming in Mr. Ellison's geometry class. Back then, your intuition warned us about simple teenager concerns. Like the day at summer camp that you advised me not to hike that trail." Betsy's melancholy weighted her words.

"And as I recall, you hiked that trail anyway to be with that jock jerk Joey and brought back to camp the ugliest case of poison ivy I've ever seen. It was all over your lips. How does anyone get it there and so quickly? You ended up spending three days in the infirmary, begging me to bring food that wasn't liquified."

"Don't remind me. I still hate straws. And was Joey ever lousy at both kissing and choosing the location to do it. That's all you're getting out of me on that subject. Except, those anti-itch shots hurt like the dickens, whatever that means, but hey, I did lose a few pounds." Betsy let the memories slip away and grew more reflective. "Still, you know I'm with you here...not thrilled...but with you, Page. Maybe this time, nothing dreadful will happen. You know, things get sorted out by the powers, and we won't be needed?"

"I don't think so, Bets. Listen, we'd better turn back. The stars have disappeared." Page lifted her gaze. "Rain must be coming."

"Nah, it's just the light from the full moon hiding the stars, but my thighs do feel like jelly from all of this pedaling." Betsy stopped and put her feet on the hard sand, and pounded her thighs. "Can't feel a thing."

Page laughed. "Poor thing has awakened muscles that have been sleeping."

Two teenagers ran past them. The boy chased a squealing girl who had slapped his back with a towel. They'd both just braved the dark ocean for a night swim.

Betsy and Page watched them do a slow fall onto the beach, never breaking their kiss.

"Come on. I can't bear to watch young love," Betsy groaned and settled on the bike's seat.

Page's mind drifted to the blessing of personal freedom gained once children reached maturity and nested elsewhere. She reflected on Betsy's two sons, both in their early twenties and living abroad. They preferred that lifestyle over settling down and sporting rings on their left fingers. Page knew their parents' divorce had jaded the boys' views on marriage. Hopefully, time and the right girls would prove to them that love could be trusted.

For Page's daughter, the fear played differently. Hannah knew her parents had enjoyed an exceptional marriage, which only made Jeff's death even more crippling. Hannah, while in another tepid relationship, shied away from allowing herself to love freely. She'd made a success of that pledge by taking vows to the corporate world and the jets that whisked her away from serious commitment. As an understanding mother, Page always supported her daughter's happiness wherever it took her.

Page admitted Betsy's and her lives were in flux and that Shell Isle always called them back whenever reflection was needed. The beach provided neutral territory for inner work. Both stared at a crossroads with change plotted on the map. Betsy's voice pierced Page's meanderings.

"Would you look over there? Just up ahead." Taking one hand off the handlebars, Betsy pointed. "Some dummy is stretched out, letting the water wash over—" Betsy hopped off her bike and let it fall to the ground, seeing Page already running toward the water.

Betsy caught up. She grabbed Page's hand as they looked down at a lifeless woman's face resting sideways in the sand.

CHAPTER 14

"Is she…?" Betsy croaked.

"Dead? Yes, I'm afraid so." Page had checked for a pulse. She covered the face with her windbreaker and stepped back to join Betsy. "So sad." The body lying in the sand now validated the nudge. They had their next case. Page sniffed and reached for her cousin's hand.

Betsy managed a nod, turning away. She shivered, wrapping her arms around herself as if that could offer comfort from such a tragedy.

They took a few moments and failed at collecting themselves as the reality of what this meant swept over them.

Betsy dipped deep inside to find her trusty humor gene. "Well, I guess it's time I abandon my happy sojourn of denial that your intuiting gift won't ruin yet another vacation." She wiped a tear, straightened her shoulders, and pulled a coin from her pocket. "Heads or tails?"

"Tails," replied Page, sympathetic to Betsy's coping strategy.

"Heads. You lose. Make the call." Betsy waited, watching Page punch 911 on her cell phone.

"Yes, my name's Page Wright, and I'd like to report a body on Shell Isle Beach." She tapped the phone's speaker button, wanting her cousin to hear the full exchange.

The dispatcher's voice responded. "Can you be specific about where you are on the beach? Give us a lifeguard chair number or anything to better pinpoint your spot?"

Page focused on her surroundings and walked toward the

nearby lifeguard's chair. "It's number eleven." She returned to Betsy.

"Great. That's precisely the info we need. I'm sending an investigator to you now. Are you alone?" The woman's voice showed concern and compassion.

"My cousin is here with me." Page hugged Betsy.

"Hold, please."

The two women stood in silence as minutes ticked up their anxiety. The beach appeared empty of walkers. The moon vanished behind a cloud, wrapping them in blackness.

"Forgive my silence. I was communicating with Detective Koch. He'll be there at any moment. Hold tight." The dispatcher spoke in a muffled voice to someone else.

Betsy mouthed, "Detective Koch. Just swell."

Both women watched the shadow of a man approaching. "That's him. Our favorite cop of the night," Betsy whispered.

The moon reappeared just in time to illuminate Steve's masculine presence. He stooped down and removed the parka to see the face. Steve scanned the women. "You two and standing over a dead body, no less. Why am I not surprised?"

"And just maybe I'm wondering what you're doing here?" Page planted her hands on her hips. Whatever made her act confrontational to this man she knew zip about?

His eyes sparked. Hers fired back. Page saw his fists clench and unclench.

"Law enforcement is here." Steve stepped back.

Betsy nodded, squeezing Page's hand, signaling her to behave.

Detective Koch approached the body first and then spoke to the dispatcher and, after a cursory look, joined the three waiting. He reached over and disconnected Page's phone, turning his gaze on the women.

"Well, look who we have here—my two movie mavens

finding a dead body. You've had quite a night for yourselves, ladies. Now, I'd like some answers, truthful answers, if you know how to give them." Detective Koch clipped his phone on a black belt.

"Of course, we know how to answer truthfully," Betsy replied indignantly.

Page wondered why Steve was being ignored but turned her attention to the detective.

Koch focused on Page. "Let's start with you. Am I correct that you are Page Wright and the one who called this in?"

"Yes, that's me. We're summering at Hibiscus Cottage two doors down. It belonged to my Aunt Tilly, but she's passed and bequeathed it—"

Koch's expression held a scoff. "How nice for you. Can we get back to what you're doing on the beach next to a dead body?" The sarcasm dripped from his voice like honey onto biscuits.

Betsy jumped in. "We went for an evening bike ride." Her arm motioned toward their bikes.

"You..." Koch pointed his finger at Betsy. "Be quiet. You'll get your turn next."

Betsy managed a loud "Humph."

Page's voice took over. "Like she just said, we were riding our bikes before calling it a night. We felt unnerved after the vampire movie you made us see," Page retorted, immediately regretting her hasty words.

"I made you see?" the detective leaned in closer to Page's face.

She caught Steve's smirk from the corner of her eye. Blast the man. Wait until Koch took on his smug self. "Well, maybe 'made' is the wrong word...sir." Page's frosty tone canceled the attempt to show respect.

Betsy chirped up, "Page didn't mean 'made.' She meant... she meant that your pulling us over and all made us late for the movie we'd planned to see. No big deal because I've got a thing for vampires."

"Enough. Both of you stick to the facts about your being here. Please, Ms. Wright, continue if you wouldn't mind?" Koch's patience was fraying.

"Fine. We were riding our bikes home and glimpsed a person stretched out here." Page pointed and gulped. "We went to check. When we got closer, it was obvious the woman wasn't alive, being in that awkward position and all. And the water was washing…" Page felt the first twinge of a migraine hit and rubbed her forehead.

The gesture struck Koch's only caring nerve. "Now there. You did right reporting this upsetting occurrence." He gingerly touched Page's arm. "Treat yourself to some relaxing breaths." He turned to Betsy. "Is that your story, too? You agree?"

Betsy eyed Koch straight on. "Yes, of course, I agree. It's what happened. And add to your fancy-lit clipboard computer thingy that Page called 911 immediately after she showed respect by covering the body. And my name is Betsy Ross. We are law-abiding cousins. And keep the jokes about our names to yourself. Our mothers suffered from an outlandish sense of humor, and we don't."

Page caught the detective's glance at the silent Tanner. Surely, it was Steve's turn to be grilled.

Koch shifted his attention to Betsy. "All duly noted." The detective studied the cousins while crafting his next words. "I'm inclined to believe you and doubt you're involved in anything but a severe case of nosiness. This may be my last question before I let you go on home. Do you know this woman's identity?"

Steve watched Page and Betsy, waiting to see who had the most gumption to answer. His money was on Page, and she rewarded his astuteness.

"Her name is…Catherine Lange."

CHAPTER 15

Page caught the surprised looks of the two men. "Yes, she's Catherine Lange," Page repeated. "And she's our neighbor."

"She lives two doors down. Of course, we don't really know her," Betsy supplied.

"No?" Detective Koch continued making notes of further questions.

"No. We just know her name." Page glanced at Steve. "Like we know, our neighbor standing here is Steve, but not much else." Page felt pleased with the comparison.

"Well, we do know that Steve here has a super friendly dog…"

Page frowned at Betsy.

"A spaniel named Barnacle that visits…" Betsy's voice trailed off. She gave a sheepish shrug.

"All right, ladies, did you notice anyone around the body as you approached? Or possibly pass someone riding your bikes who seemed suspicious acting? Anything unusual?" Koch prodded.

"Nothing at all. It's been a quiet night on the beach for us until now. Oh, we did see two teenagers making out, but they don't fit the model you described," answered Page.

Koch glanced at Steve and back at the women. "If that's the extent of your knowledge of this Catherine Lange, I'm inclined to let you return home. However, if anything comes to you, I want to hear it. I may have more questions for you later, so please remain at Shell Isle until I excuse you from the investigation of this apparent suicide or drowning."

"Suicide?" Page blurted out, regretting her words yet again. She watched Koch weigh his response.

"Yes, full moons make for crazy behavior. Maybe this Catherine took a night swim and drowned. Accident or intentional. We may never know," he replied dismissively. "You two pedal those bikes home and try to put this unfortunate experience behind you. Thanks for your cooperation." Koch waited.

Page sneaked a peek at Steve as she mounted the bike. She caught Steve's dismissive nod and meaning. "Thanks, Detective Koch. Let's go, Betsy."

Whatever muscle stiffness had plagued Betsy earlier evaporated into the ethers. Page witnessed her cousin's pedaling spirit, which was worthy of competing at the Tour de France. She didn't catch up with Betsy until Hibiscus Cottage.

"Impressive speed," said a winded Page.

Betsy paused for her breathing to allow words to flow. "Remind me to never, never I say again, beat you at Scrabble. Your idea of celebrating is way too adventurous for me. Geez, this has been some ghastly night. Ghastly."

"Full moon," Page mumbled, recalling Koch's words.

Betsy ignored the planetary talk. "All I've got to say is that I'm claiming the tub. There isn't a muscle, a tendon, a joint, that isn't screaming at me."

Page allowed the hilarity of watching Betsy gingerly touch various body parts to provide the emotional release. "Maybe an aspirin will help the screaming? I'll put the bikes away. Go claim your tub." Page pushed her bike toward the shed.

A flash of lightning lit up the beach. The women saw other officers arriving on the scene, along with EMT's. Page guessed Koch had alerted them not to rush. Catherine Lange wouldn't benefit from their capable hands.

Betsy hadn't moved. "This is all beyond awful. I'm going inside to have a big cry." She sniffled and climbed the few steps to the screened porch.

The door banged in unison with the next thunderclap. Drops of rain emptied from the inky sky, hurrying the police to get a tent erected around the scene. The hush that surrounded the area seemed to palpitate with a heavy beat. Page sensed a frightening presence nearby, watching the scene.

She shivered, trying to release the feeling. She'd make cups of spirit-soothing hot chocolate for herself and Betsy later. Then she'd inform Betsy that Catherine's life ended by another's hand. And suspects? Well, she saw no shortage of them.

CHAPTER 16

Page tapped on Betsy's door. "I'm ready to talk about tonight if you are? Made you a cup of hot cocoa."

The cousins positioned themselves on the sofa. The hour was late, but neither could sleep. The image of Catherine on the beach haunted them and would for a long time.

"I'm listening." Betsy claimed the sofa.

The cuckoo clock informed them it was one in the morning, and all was far from well.

Page gathered her thoughts. Her eyes linked with Betsy's. "Catherine was murdered."

"Murdered? Are you sure? How are you sure? Cause inklings aren't—"

"Betsy, I'm sure. I saw the bullet hole behind her head. The water had washed away the blood. You weren't standing where I was to see."

"Holy smokes. Murdered." Betsy chewed on her lower lip.

"A person committing suicide wouldn't put the gun to the back of the head or bother wearing strappy heeled sandals on the beach." Page paused, giving her cousin time to process this information.

Betsy stretched out on the sofa, clasping a pelican print pillow to her chest. "No, I suppose not." She closed her eyes. "So, do you have any ideas who did this terrible thing to Catherine?"

"Well, we witnessed some people who weren't members of her fan club." Page set her empty cup on the wicker end table and folded her legs under her. Thankfully, the aspirin had calmed her migraine, and the chocolate helped tamp her weariness.

"Hold on. I gotta ask you this before you continue my debriefing." Betsy's eyes opened, turning dark as onyx. "How come you didn't enlighten Detective Koch that we'd seen Steve tailing Catherine earlier? Or that you saw the bullet hole in her head?"

"Because what if Steve was the one who shot her? I didn't want to put us in any more danger than we could be in right now."

"Good thinking. Wait. Us in danger? Hells bells, Page, I hadn't gotten to that place yet." Betsy hopped up and moved to close the blinds and dim the lights.

Page didn't blame her cousin for playing it cautious. The way she viewed their situation cautiously was precisely the way they needed to move forward. They'd seen things that Page wished they hadn't.

Betsy plopped back on the sofa. "Do you think Steve is capable of killing? I mean, a lack of personality doesn't make for a murderer. Does it?"

Page managed a chuckle. Bless Betsy's dosing of humor. "No, but talking to someone he calls Sir about being positioned to watch is troubling. Let's not forget he was observing Ty and Seedy. Add to that, he followed Catherine and then showed up on the beach tonight."

"You're right. That's plenty of times Mr. Personality appeared around the action. And I'm sure you noticed Koch not questioning him earlier. That was way weird, too." Betsy looked longingly at the candy bar, waiting on the kitchen island.

"Maybe Koch didn't want us to hear him grill Steve." Page didn't buy that option but allowed it to remain a possibility.

"I guess." Betsy grew pensive. "Let's hope that Larsen comes through with the scoop about this guy soon. I'm feeling unsettled with him next door."

"Yep, I admit it's taking him longer than usual to run a

check." Page's brow furrowed.

"Why don't you call Larsen later this morning when he's at the bookshop and confess we've gotten entangled in another murder case." Betsy saw her cousin's head shaking no. "What?"

"I can't do that. No way. I promised him not to...." Page's voice cracked.

"Sure, you can. Now isn't the time to worry about that stupid promise you made to Larsen about steering clear of mischief and cops. We've got troubles. Big girl troubles. The kind that could get us lying flat out on the beach like Catherine. And you're not listening."

Page contemplated the current predicament. "I heard, but if we find out Steve's not Catherine's killer, we're safe enough. Remember, no one knows what else we've seen and overheard. That leaves two unfortunate women who happened upon a dead body and called the police." A plan began formulating in Page's mind.

"I don't know." Betsy's escalating fears circled her like a whirling dervish. "Everything feels dangerous and dark like the ocean out there."

"Look, for now, can we suspend our worry until Larsen gets me the low down on Steve. Agreed?" Page put out her hand.

Betsy returned a weak shake. "I can't think about this anymore. I'm beyond exhausted." She rubbed her eyes and stood. "I'm going to bed, and if I'm lucky, I'll awake to this being a dream...albeit a horrible dream."

~*~

Page gazed at the clock on her nightstand. Three in the morning, and still, her eyes refused to close out this nightmare of a day. Larsen's report was vital before the next logical step manifested. That awareness finally brought her freeing sleep.

CHAPTER 17

The morning sun burned off the fog and brightened the spirits of beachgoers. High tide brought out the surfers to claim their share of barrel-shaped waves. Judging by the plethora of swimmers already bobbing in the ocean, the lifeguard's whistle would enjoy a busy day of cajoling and scolding. Sailboats scattered amongst the fishing boats tried to tack and come about in a purist way. To the unknowing eyes, the beach looked untainted.

"He's back," Betsy announced from the porch.

"Who?" Page sauntered out, encouraging her sips of espresso to restore her wits. "Ah, I see."

"Yep. A real regular, that one." Betsy smiled, pushing her reading glasses atop her humidity-curling hair. Her newly polished lavender nails flew across her laptop's keyboard, placing orders for three paperback romance novels and various summer shades of nail polish.

Page glanced at the computer screen as she passed by. "Busy ordering, I see. Pretty nail shades." Page cracked the screen door. "So, Barnacle, what have you brought us this beautiful morning?"

The dog's jaw held a chew bone freshly dug with clumps of sand clinging to it. He released the treasure on Page's silver-sandaled foot. "Yuck." She promptly tossed it into the yard and closed the screen door.

"He'll be right back," said Betsy, stating the obvious. Satisfied with her shopping, she closed the laptop. "Is that your phone?"

Page scurried toward her room. "Hi, Larsen. Am I ever

glad to hear your voice." Page turned on the phone's speaker as Betsy entered.

"How's it going? Got your tan well established?" asked Larsen with a teasing inflection in his voice.

"It's on my list. Listen, I don't mean to cut you short, but did you find out anything about my neighbor?" Page grabbed a pen and notepad, putting her index finger to her lips for Betsy to remain mute.

"Matter of fact, I do have a little something on this, Steve Tanner. And, if you're doing more than a casual wave his way, you've broken your promise to me," Larsen's words baited Page.

"I told you he's not exactly known for his sparkling charm and friendliness," Page attempted to direct focus from her.

Betsy rolled her eyes.

Page grinned and thumped her cousin's arm. "So, who is this guy?"

"I'll start by saying he's what I'd label an impressive and versatile kind of fellow. Yep, a Navy Seal until he decided to let the Feds sign his paycheck. He's versatile, all right. Larsen's voice couldn't hide the respect he'd garnered for Steve Tanner.

"Feds? What exactly do you mean—?"

"He's associated with the FBI, Page. Sort of independent type work is the way it got explained to me. Anyway, don't worry your noggin about your neighbor. You've got protection in spades, I'd say."

"Wow," Page and Betsy said aloud.

"Who's there with you, Page?"

"It's only Betsy." Page made a fist at her cousin.

"Sorry," Betsy mouthed, dropping her head in mock shame.

"Blast it all, woman! If Betsy's around, you're into something. I feel it in my left arthritic fly-fishing elbow. You two together always cause me to lose sleep—"

"No, we're good. You can sleep easy tonight. Just whiling away our days with eating and walking, walking, and eating. No particular order," explained Page. She needed to end the call before Larsen showed off his interrogating skills. "In fact, Betsy's waiting on me now to go…" Page poked her cousin.

"Why, yes, I sure am. Come on, Page! Time for our walk," Betsy hollered loud enough to wake her last ex-husband sleeping in Sydney.

"Well, go already. Don't give a thought to the shop, and for Pete's sake, leave poor Steve Tanner alone. He's not the type to suffer the likes of you two the way I do." Larsen laughed.

Page puffed up. "Suffer us? We are two of the—"

"Sweetest gals I've ever had the misfortune to meet. I nearly got fired the way you involved me in that spa murder." Larsen chuckled.

"And we're still ever so sorry. Betsy, stop pulling on me."

A confused Betsy sat with her hands tucked in her lap.

"Okay. Bye, Page. Bye, Betsy. You two behave. No sleuthing."

"Thanks, Larsen," They both chorused.

The women returned to the porch, relieved Barnacle had moseyed back home. Betsy settled herself into the hammock, ignoring her novel and the Dowager Gertrude's latest ball. Page went for the glider and her glass of warm orange juice. Her croissant had deflated like a flat tire from the humid air. She sipped the juice while pondering the man she'd felt an unsettling attraction from the first meeting and his notable reputation and standing among law enforcement.

"How about that Steve being involved with the FBI?" Betsy had the hammock swinging at an impressive rate.

Page chuckled. "Yeah, he's a pretty big deal. Don't you bust through that screen."

Betsy ignored the warning. "And a Seal. I knew that body

of his was extra fine for a reason."

"Well, at least we know now that we've got extra protection nearby."

"Only if you do what Larsen told you...keep us out of mischief." Betsy offered in a warning.

"But, Betsy, we know stuff...stuff we need to tell Steve. He's investigating this Catherine or was, and Detective Koch must know who he is, too. That explains why Koch stopped us and why he didn't even question Steve's presence on the beach last night. See?"

"You finished?" Betsy struggled to pull herself to a seated position. She waved her arms in Page's direction, signaling a bossing was coming.

"For the moment."

"Good. Hear me roar. I'm not about to tell Steve or a flea on his dog any 'stuff' we've seen, heard, or surmised. What I am going to do is pack my beach bag, grab a chair, and spend the entire day with Dowager Gertrude. And let me suggest you be smart and join us." Betsy heaved herself out of the hammock, not waiting for a response.

Page didn't have an answer yet; instead, she had a brilliant notion that she could take down to the beach and give more time to brew in the sun's warmth. She'd hide her plotting behind sunglasses. Her spirits buoyed, and she moved to action.

"I'm changing into my suit. Gonna do what you say," Page hollered as Betsy headed down the walkway, balancing her load.

Betsy paused. "Smart cousin. And as a reward for your good judgment, I'll share my snacks —"

"No, no. I'll bring my own." Page hoped her cousin heard.

Page decided to make one call before setting out. She needed to postpone the listing appointment with Gail. Better to keep her schedule flexible. She and Betsy had another mystery to solve.

CHAPTER 18

By the time Page managed to drag her melon-colored chair and matching tote bag down to the beach, Betsy and the Dowager Gertrude were already inseparable. Not wanting to interrupt their time, Page allowed herself the luxury of taking in the ocean's late morning show.

The tide's retreat left a sprinkling of mollusks' homes along the shore. Page watched twin adolescent girls examine their collection of shells' worthiness before dropping them into their buckets. The beach's lure for Page had always been the changing landscape. The ocean was never monotonous or predictable. She hated ho-hum. Stagnation was another word for laziness—something she'd never possessed. Years ago, she came to understand that living in the present moment could reward her with pleasant surprises.

A happy memory came calling as a reminder of that truth. Had Page not paused to sit on a bench with her acceptance letter into a master's program, she'd never met the teaching assistant sitting next to her eating a bag lunch. Six months later, she'd stood at the altar, pledging her love to him. Her Jeff. Life-changing benches come in all shapes and sizes and can appear anywhere if one pauses and observes. Maybe a fresh direction was indeed being orchestrated for her life, and it might be Shell Isle.

"What are you lost in?" Betsy dropped her dog-eared paperback, giving Page her attention.

"Oh, lost in thought mostly and enjoying the dolphins frolicking. They certainly know how to move in joy. See them about two hundred yards out?"

Betsy leaned forward, adjusting her sunglasses, and looked where her cousin directed. "Yes, the dolphins are so adorable. And speaking of adorable, I was wondering if you'd wanna come along later with me to a boutique I spotted near the market? I thought if I bought a size smaller, super sassy beach shift, it might encourage me to drop a few pounds. What do ya think of that idea?"

"That's a great strategy. Maybe we'll do just that," Page said absently. She'd caught sight of Steve and his surfboard moving their way. Just swell. She hadn't finished formulating her plan yet, and here he came. Opportunity was knocking too early.

"Ah, you see our surfing Seal?" Betsy positioned her chair upright and applied sunscreen, daring more freckles to find her arms and legs.

"Listen, I sorta have this plan coming to me. Go along, okay?" pleaded Page.

"Forget your plan unless it's to finagle a date. Hiya, Steve," Betsy tossed out.

"Ladies." Steve stopped, planted his board, and fixed his eyes on Page.

"Hello," Page answered. Great. Is that all she could muster? Why was she fixated on his handsome face? Her plan was doomed if two syllables were her best offering.

"I trust you're both feeling better after last night's sad ordeal?" He slipped out of his sandals, tapped the sand off, and wrapped them in his red striped towel. "Suicide drownings are always tragic. Anyway, I hope you're putting it behind you?"

"We are and determined to cherish our beach day. Right, Page?" Betsy tapped her cousin's arm with her paperback to elicit agreement.

"Yes, a nice beach day," Page managed to get out. Her plan was ebbing with the tide. Whatever was wrong with her? Her eyes remained locked on Steve's. And blast the man, he knew the effect he was having and taking full advantage of her momentarily lapse with the English language.

Steve broke a smile, showing off teeth as white as the cumulus clouds above him.

"A nice beach day is what I chose for myself as well. Excuse me, ladies. The waves are about perfect. I might even get some time in the tube." He grabbed his board.

"Sure. Get out there. Hang ten if that's what surfers still do." Betsy laughed.

Steve paused, waiting for Page's response, which didn't come. He shrugged, hoisted his board above his head, and moved toward the water.

"What's wrong with you, Page? I've never seen you act so loopy before. Ever. Was that your unfolding plan? Coyness?" Betsy leaned over and pulled Page's glasses away to get a closer look.

"No, of course, that wasn't my plan. It fizzled. I fizzled. Sorry. I didn't get much sleep last night. Guess I'm not myself. But, I did register that Steve referred to Catherine's death as a suicide. And you know what that means?" Page asked, relieved her words seemed to be flowing again.

"It means we don't care. That's what it means. That's all it means," Betsy replied emphatically.

"Nope. It means he's lying to us, and I ask you why?"

"Because, Page, maybe the guy doesn't know Catherine had a bullet put in her noggin."

"He knows. And even more puzzling, this morning's newspaper didn't have anything about Catherine's death. This murder is all hush-hush. Again, I ask you why?" Page grabbed a sparkling water from her beach bag and twisted the top. She sipped, forcing herself not to search for Steve among the bobbing surfers. She couldn't care less about his form in the wave's crest or the impressive upper body strength he showed when he lifted his board as if it was as light as her holiday meringues. Geez. Her mind was spinning thoughts like a sixteen-year-old. Page purposely spilled drops of the icy mineral water on her chest. Her senses needed a shock. She noted Betsy in ponder mode.

"I've got one thing to ask and two things to say, so pay attention. Look at my lips and not out at one hot surfer. How do you know what's in the paper? We don't get a paper." Betsy was on point.

"I know that, silly. I kinda borrowed Steve's newspaper." Page looked away.

"What?" Betsy's voice rose ten octaves.

Page sighed. "I told you that I couldn't sleep. I heard the paperboy. His bicycle squeaks. So, I thought, why not—"

"Want me to tell you why not?"

"No need. I heard you yammering in my head when I snatched the paper at five this morning." Page laughed.

"I do not yammer. Just tell me you put it back?" Betsy waited.

"Of course, I put it back. Steve wasn't even home. So there. No problem. What are the two things you want to say?"

Betsy turned her chair to face Page. "Let Steve Tanner lie to us. We don't care. Now, you repeat that back to me."

"Let Steve Tanner lie to us. We don't care," Page parroted. Much better to let Betsy not care for the moment. That would change soon enough. It always did.

"Thank you. My good mood is restored again," declared Betsy.

Page laughed and settled back into her chair. "Read your book."

Betsy stood, re-tying her terry beach cover-up. "Nope, I'm going to the cottage and make us a nice lunch. It's such a perfect day. I want to stay out until late afternoon. You?"

"Sure. Fine, but about lunch…I brought some—"

"Boring peanut butter crackers, I'm betting." Betsy peered into Page's bag. "Yep. There they are. I've got my menu all planned. Be back in a jiff." Betsy slipped on her waterproof sandals and gave a saucy wave.

Page sighed, resigning herself to eating another Betsy concoction with an antacid chaser. But on the plus side, Betsy's love of food had provided Page a window to set an alternate plan in motion despite not being fully thought out. With the surprise of another nudge, she moved into action, pulling her lacey coverup over her head, revealing a figure-flattering one-piece ruched bathing suit. The color matched the sea's dazzling blue-green hues. She watched Steve maneuver his surfboard with ease over a swell. Time to act. Page grabbed Betsy's float and prayed she wasn't heading into deep water. She must tread carefully.

CHAPTER 19

Page waded into the glistening ocean and promptly stepped into a hole, toppling when the next wave washed in. The saltwater she gulped stung her throat, and both knees felt like she'd had dermabrasion done as she righted herself. She resisted the temptation to see if Steve had witnessed her humiliating dunk and trudged back to grab her traitorous float that had ridden the wave to shore.

She paddled out again, appearing carefree despite having precious little time before Betsy and the gut-churning lunch arrived. Page sensed Steve watching her. Yep, the scoundrel knew she was heading his way. He allowed a perfect cresting wave to pass him. That proved it.

"How are the waves forming?" Page asked breathless, pulling alongside him.

Drops of water glistened on his tan body, which provided a stark contrast to the white skin peeping below the swim trunk's waist. "Not bad. Aren't you out pretty far on that raft?"

"Maybe, but I needed to talk to you alone." Page frowned, stealing a glance toward the cottage.

Steve exaggerated his movement of looking around them. "I'd say we're alone, at least on top of the water." He smiled down at the woman clinging to a raft, now obviously losing air.

"Yeah, well, I'd just as soon not acknowledge the sea life right this minute." Just to be sure, Page hopped on her float, grabbing the rope to ride the next swell. She ignored the squishy feel of the raft.

Steve laughed. "Guess you're safe enough on that raft.

What's on your mind?"

Page chose to play dumb about Steve's identity and instead focus on finding Catherine's killer. "I came bringing a proposal for you. I mean, you seemed awfully interested last night in tailing our neighbor. That is, before Betsy and I found her."

Steve ignored the last two statements. "A proposal, huh?" He scooted back on his board.

Page nodded. She felt something brush up against her legs, dangling in the water. She made a quick adjustment and pointed her feet skyward.

An amused Steve noted the maneuver and grabbed the raft, pulling her closer to him. "And just why would I be tailing our neighbor, Miss Drew?" The name referenced a fictional amateur sleuth from the old *"Nancy Drew"* book series geared toward young girls.

Page smirked. "Big ha on the Miss Drew." He'd bit. Time to reel him in. Page paused to gather her words, letting her fingers trail the water, making little circles like an upside-down waterspout. She stole a glance at Steve. He looked anxious. "Oh, I have several theories of why you'd be watching her, but let's skip that part for now."

A wave broke over them, washing Page off her raft. She surfaced only to see Betsy's half-deflated raft speed ride onto the beach. The rat purposely didn't give a warning and let the wave consume her. "Thanks a lot." Page pushed the hair out of her eyes and discreetly repositioned her swimsuit.

Repressed laughter hid behind Steve's eyes. "Here. Grab my hand. You can sit on the board with me."

Page continued to tread water, considering his offer versus further wave humiliation. "You're not very gentlemanly. I don't know."

"I do." Steve leaned over and hoisted her atop his surfboard.

A startled Page grabbed the board, glimpsing another set of big waves forming. So much for her being in control. He'd bested her once again.

"Hang on. I'm paddling out a bit further to get out of the break line."

Page thoroughly regretted her hasty actions of employing Betsy's sub-par raft. Facing Steve felt awkward, and those grey eyes inches away had her going crackers. She'd had her fill of the ocean gods' sense of humor.

"Okay, relax, we're good." Steve scooted back on the board, picking up on the conversation. "You were saying you knew that I was following the woman who drowned."

Page tapped into her dwindling confidence reserve. "You mean the woman, Catherine, who we found murdered?" Her wits returned — finally, a point earned in this matchup.

"Murdered?" he repeated with a raspy voice, eyes firing a warning at the attractive woman straddling his board.

"Bullet hole. Back of her head. Saw it when I covered her with my windbreaker. So, you can stop acting like the woman took her own life. She didn't." Page nonchalantly adjusted her suit's strap and waited to see how he would play this.

Steve let a few seconds pass. "All right, Page. She didn't kill herself, but your knowing this fact changes things, and not in a good way either." His tone was somber.

The furrow between Page's eyes appeared while she pondered his meaning. She let him pull her closer to better balance them on the board. "How so?" Her voice faltered, and her heartbeat ratcheted up from their brief touch.

"Listen, now isn't the time for us to be having this conversation." Steve deftly maneuvered the surfboard to glide over the next wave's crest, noting more white caps forming.

Page held tight, not wanting to invite another dunking. "Okay then, what do you suggest? Betsy will be back at any moment. And trust me, I need to be sitting in my beach chair before she appears."

"Can you slip away from her tonight? Come to my bungalow. We'll talk there," offered Steve.

"Why can't Betsy come too?"

Steve's arm waved in the air, exasperated. "Because I can only deal with one of you, and I choose you. No Betsy."

"Oh, all right, but it'll need to be after she's gone to bed. There's no way I can slip off before that happens. How about midnight?"

"I can make that work. Hang on. Let's get you back to the beach." With that, he started paddling.

Page did an about-face and put a death grip on each side of the board. Slipping off the highly waxed surfboard would not be tolerated by her ego or its owner.

Sensing her anxiety, Page felt Steve wrap his arm around her waist and pull her tighter against him. Her body's betraying response set off an alarm. She was a middle-aged woman, for pity's sake—way past teenage feelings like these. Maybe it was the oysters she'd eaten that had her frisky. She'd be sure to abstain from ordering them again and show her double-crossing body who was in control. Who was in control?

"Will you please sit still?"

Steve's impatient voice penetrated her raging hormones. "Sorry."

"Okay, hop off. You can wade the rest of the way."

Page stood in hip-deep water. "Um, thanks for the ride and the talk."

Steve's tone shifted to that of an investigator. "One more thing, and don't ask me why. Just say okay. You and Betsy stay in the cottage tonight. Got it?"

"But that means I have to eat her cooking and—"

"I don't give a flip if the woman serves you toad on a

stick with flaming red-hot sauce. Stay home. Don't court danger, Page." Steve's gray eyes flashed, and the muscles in his jaw clenched. His body language dared her to offer another protest.

"All right, I'll keep us home…somehow. And if I survive another of Betsy's culinary chokers, count on seeing me at midnight." Page waded to shore. Were she and Betsy really in danger and more worrisome, why?

CHAPTER 20

Page had scarcely dried off and gotten situated in her beach chair before Betsy dropped the cherry red cooler down between them. She gave Page a careful study.

"Hmm...I'd say I've missed something. Care to enlighten me?" Betsy positioned her beach towel on her lounger and settled in, allowing her long legs to dangle off the end.

The sleuth squinted at Betsy. "You've missed my hunger. What's in that cooler? I'm past famished." Page attempted to direct her cousin's attention to food.

Betsy ignored the ploy. "Your hair hiding under the baseball cap looks wet." She glanced out and caught sight of Steve riding a wave. "Page Wright, you didn't."

Page's face wore a sheepish expression. "Yeah, I did. I wanted to tell him we knew Catherine had a bullet in her head. I mean, come on, we are aware the guy is FBI connected. Besides, we have our observations that we need to share—"

"Stop! Need I remind you of the 'we don't care' oath you took just a short time ago?"

Page grabbed the suntan lotion, considering her cousin's words. "We do care, Betsy. Even though Catherine might not have been a nice person, someone much worse took her life. And that's why we care." Page's emotions played across her face. Tears pooled. "We have to care. You know it's what we are called to do. Together."

Betsy let out a breath powerful enough to send three hungry seagulls by their chairs into flight. "Say I admit caring and acknowledge that you've landed us another case. What can we do at this point? I mean, other than telling Mr. Personality out there what we saw and heard? Or did you already share this?" Betsy stared at her cousin, waiting.

"No, I didn't get a chance to tell him anything other than we knew a bullet ended Catherine's life." Page understood why her cousin wasn't happy.

"I see. You cut your swim short because of me. Like I'm not sharp enough to see your wet mop and figure out just what—"

Page grinned. "Trust me. I hadn't planned on getting dunked by a wave or have your lousy raft spring a leak." She pointed at the deflated raft and tucked the traitorous wet tendrils back under her Boston Red Sox cap. Page dared not risk telling Betsy about the midnight rendezvous. Right now, just having her cousin know she talked to Steve, and they had another mystery to solve seemed enough.

Amused at Page's recounting, Betsy peered at the limp float and nodded.

"Besides, I didn't want you to mess up your beach day with sleuthing. I'm considerate that way," Page added, interjecting a dose of humor.

Betsy's upset seemed to evaporate. "Okay, I forgive you, but one day, you'll admit that you can't get away with anything when I'm around. Ask any one of my ex-husbands about my keen observation skills."

"Yep, and you were most cunning with those husbands." Page allowed a giggle. "Let's not waste our lovely afternoon talking about this. Anyway, it's too soon for speculation. I'm much more excited to see what you created for lunch." Page flicked open the cooler's lid. Hanging over her chair's arm, she wrinkled her nose. The aroma hit her hard, and her stomach turned over. The universe appeared bent on proving karma existed.

"That's right…sardines in mustard on toasted multi-grain bagels, with chopped cucumber and fresh raspberries on top. I think this may be my new favorite combination." Betsy placed a sandwich on a daisy-patterned paper plate and handed it to Page. "Spectacular, huh? Lovely omegas, too."

"And colorful...so colorful." Page looked at what the plate held for her. "Come back, seagulls," she mumbled under her breath and questioned how she could stay home tonight for another of Betsy's repasts. She pulled off a small corner of the bagel and put it into her mouth, avoiding the sardines and sensing Betsy's eyes studying her. "So colorful," she repeated.

"Isn't it? Food needs to be a feast for the eyes first and foremost. A cute chef in Iceland taught me that." Betsy took another giant bite, making "Mmm" her latest mantra.

"You know, Betsy, I think I'd truly enjoy having you teach me some of your food-combining tips this evening." Page eyed the first seagull walking her way. She dropped her hand, releasing a whole sardine on the opposite side where Betsy sat. Blessed bird. "I already have an idea of what I want to attempt preparing, but—"

"Oh, I'd be thrilled to help you polish your culinary skills. How fun. We'll need to stay in tonight for you to learn my techniques properly." Betsy warmed to her superior role.

"Sure. We can stay at home. Why not?" Page forced her voice to sound enthusiastic. "And I look forward to the tutorial, and maybe we can find a classic movie on television to close out a peaceful day?"

"Sold." Betsy caught a wayward sardine and dropped it in her mouth. "And best of all, it will be a sleuthing-free night. Eat up."

Page gingerly picked up the sandwich and toasted Betsy. "Here's to our plan. You know, I think I'll take this bagel with me and scoot up to the cottage for a moment." Before Betsy could reply, Page did a quick jaunt with her new feathered friend following on her heels.

She'd freshen up, scoff down a yogurt, and do a fast online search for anything of interest about Catherine Lange. The haunting question stayed with her. Who most wanted her neighbor dead? She bet Steve and Koch had their suspects already targeted and wondered if they might match the ones on her mental list. Those questions would need to wait for midnight.

CHAPTER 21

At eleven forty-five, Page exhaled a sigh of relief when gentle snores echoed from Betsy's room. After two stretched-out hours of unpalatable cooking instruction using Ayurvedic spices in Italian meatballs, Page took back control. She orchestrated the remainder of their evening, designed to keep her cousin engaged in relaxing activities. She even brewed a nice pot of mellowing chamomile tea, ensuring Betsy's cup stayed full. Dimming the lights as they watched a flick whose plot moved slower than a tortoise on a hot day helped, too. Page congratulated herself. The setup had proved perfect for lulling Betsy to sleep. With anticipation on her mind, she slipped out the door.

"You're early. Come on in." Steve stepped aside, allowing Page to pass.

"Yeah, Betsy cooperated better than I could have hoped. Highly unusual." Page paused once inside. The entry's décor didn't offer much for the eye to feast on, except for a grouping of expensive-looking oil paintings showcased on one wall. They depicted one theme…sailing.

"Straight ahead to the great room. Find a seat. Barnacle, get out of my chair. Go on, fellow." Steve waited for Page to settle.

"Hey there, Barn." Page reached down to rub behind the dog's velvet soft ears. "Haven't seen you at the cottage this afternoon."

The dog whined.

"He's been in the crate. Don't ask." Steve put a stare on his companion.

"Well, glad you're out of jail, boy." Barnacle stayed by

Page, enjoying her hand's attention. The room had a distinctive masculine feel, relying on dark espresso-toned furnishings with splashes of pale aqua to invite relaxation. The beach influence was acknowledged by interesting pieces of blown glass urchins resting on a sea chest coffee table. Lamps created from old anchors provided the room's light. The surprise for her was the models of vintage sailing ships displayed on shelves flanking the fireplace. A puzzled Page couldn't resist asking, "Did you put those models together? They're amazing."

"I did. It's sort of morphed into a hobby. The one on the top shelf is the USS Constitution. I finished it last month. Listen, I've got to be somewhere soon, so would you mind if we get started? I'm ready to hear your big proposal. And I have something I want to say, too. You go first. Propose away." Steve's face veiled his thoughts as his body molded to a worn, crackled leather chair, which no doubt had logged some years in his life.

"So first, you need to know I've witnessed some unusual sightings in the last few days involving Catherine Lange." She perceived her host's impatience. "Okay, I'll make this brief for you. My proposal is I'm willing to share my gift to help you solve this case. You see, assisting law enforcement is what I sometimes do. And I'm good at deciphering clues and people's motives. Really good. This case needs me, as you'll soon learn." Page folded her hands, ignoring Barnacle's pleas for more attention.

"You said help me, right?" Steve looked away.

"Yes, of course, help you." Page gathered steam. "I also happen to know who you are, and I surmise you've been tailing some of the murder suspects, along with Catherine, for reasons you'll need to share tonight. If you tell me what you know —"

"Wait a minute. Stop right there. Who exactly do you think I am? I'd like to hear that answer first."

Page expected his intimidating reaction. She'd suffered this before when an investigator experienced her abilities. Still, despite Steve's dashing looks and the late hour, she wouldn't be deterred by his gruff manner. This murder trumped her crazy hormonal body's reactions. She'd take care of that with a change in diet.

"Page? I don't have the luxury of wasting time while your mind wanders off to who knows where."

"Sorry. I was contemplating where to begin. You see, I've developed this keen ability in solving mysteries. It goes back years. I get these inklings, and, voila, I find myself in the middle of helping in a police investigation. That's the condensed version since you don't have time for me to explain my gift in detail.

"And somehow, you're going to connect this for me and explain how this relates to your knowledge of who you think I am exactly?" Steve's hands squeezed the chair's armrest, releasing frustration.

"Of course." Page's exasperation escalated with the man's tone. "As I was saying, I had an inkling the first time I saw Catherine Lange at a travel agency, and, well, she kept showing up in my small world. For that matter, so did you. And your behavior and actions fired up my curious nature. So, I made a call." Page cast her eyes toward the kitchen.

"A call? Honestly, a horse and buggy could get to a point faster than you."

"Not funny." Good manners eluded the guy—not even an offer of a drink. Well, she'd ask. "Um, could I maybe have soda?" She read his expression. "Or, a glass of water would be okay, too."

"Sure. In a minute. Who exactly did you call?"

"Oh, just a friend who's a retired detective. You see, he's running my bookshop while I'm at Shell Isle this summer." Page offered a weak smile, but Steve wasn't having it.

"I see. And this friend told you what about me?" Steve rose and slowly moved toward the refrigerator. Barnacle followed with hopes of a treat.

"Please, you know who you are. You want me to tell you? Fine. It seems you're an FBI type." Page grinned, waiting on the cola to be handed off. He must want her to leave soon, she thought. Not even a napkin or glass. "Thanks." She pulled the tab. "I'll just drink this from the can." Her sarcasm dripped, along with the condensation from the drink on her pants.

Steve nodded. "Okay, so I'm tied in with the FBI." He sat down. "I think I've got a picture of what's in your revved-up mind. You're convinced I'm on this murder investigation, and you have some great information to share. And in exchange, I'm to tell you what I know, keep you informed, and then you're going to get about solving the case for us?" Steve rubbed his clean-shaven jaw.

"Pretty much. Well, let me clarify a bit. Betsy and I will try and solve the murder if you give us reliable information to work with, but we need it as soon as possible. You should know others in law enforcement have said that we make fantastic sleuths because we're non-threatening, like invisible. No one ever pays any attention to us."

"My interest is waning here."

"Not just yet, Tanner. You need to hear more about us. Betsy has a real talent for distracting people while I garner clues, and she's brilliant at getting folks to blab, too. People under her spell give away all kinds of — "

"I've got the picture." Steve's hands moved through his hair, still damp from a recent shower.

Page frowned at her soda can sitting on the wood coffee table. She didn't care if it left a mark as big as a crop circle. This man was starting to infuriate her with his lack of appreciation. "Truly, we can help you," she interjected.

"Look, Page, I appreciate the offer, but we don't need your cousin or your sprinklings or whatever you call them. If you've got pertinent information, out with it." Steve looked at his watch.

"They're inklings—"

"Whatever. We are not going to work together. I can't share my classified information about any investigation with you. Surely you understand that. What I want to make abundantly clear is that you're putting yourself and Betsy in danger if you persist in this amateur sleuthing. The person or people who killed Catherine Lange are capable of doing the same to both of you. *Comprende*?"

"Of course, I *comprende*, but we know how to be careful. As I said, we're seasoned at this. And, we care about justice."

"Please, care from afar. And, once you unload all this information, I can better judge if you two are in jeopardy from your recent shenanigans. I'm hoping that I don't have to task some unlucky officer to watch your cottage. No one deserves that assignment." Steve shook his head in exasperation, but his eyes showed amusement.

Page ignored the last remark. "An officer watching us...totally unnecessary. We've been very covert in our eavesdropping."

"Just tell me what all you observed." Steve's cell phone rang. He silenced it. "Please...before I'm drawing my pension." He grabbed the notebook and pen from the end table next to him.

"Fine. I'll fill you in, but you'll soon see how critical we are to your cracking this case. Then, I will be happy to accept an apology."

Steve held the pen in the air signaling Page his patience was exhausted, and the sparring had ended. Still, he respected the sleuth's spunk.

CHAPTER 22

Page took a long sip, feeling the soda burn her throat. "As I said, I first saw Catherine Lange at the travel agency about a week ago." Page paused, watching the lightning show out the window.

"May I encourage you to continue?"

Page pulled a face at him. "She was trying to make a plane reservation, but what got my attention was her speaking a foreign language on her cell phone. Plus, Catherine had a sense of urgency, telling the agent that she must get her booked on a flight. Oh, and you might be interested that trip departure just so happened to be the night of her murder."

Steve scribbled some notes and waited for Page.

"When the poor agent tried to explain there weren't any seats remaining on the flight, Catherine threatened to have her job and call the agency's owner if she didn't make that ticket reality." Page paused to recall more in the sequence. "Yes, so next, Catherine began counting out one-hundred-dollar bills. Let me tell you, that agent's fingers flew across the keyboard faster than a speeding bullet. Um, that wasn't such a good metaphor."

Steve rolled his eyes. "Did she get a seat?"

"The agent was on the phone trying to finagle something. I believe she succeeded. Our victim was a dominant force when her attention was on someone or something."

Steve managed a grin. "Tell me, if you wouldn't mind, why you were at the travel agency?"

"Me? Well, I was there to surprise someone with a July 4th trip to Shell Isle. Anyway, I left the agency because I had little hope of buying a ticket quickly, with Catherine monopolizing the agent." Page lifted the can, taking another swallow, noting the wet circle discoloring the wood table. Her better manners won out. "Do you perhaps have a coaster?"

"A what?"

Page tapped the wet mark, holding up her drink. Amused, she watched Steve move to the kitchen and grab a stack of paper napkins.

"Sorry." He attempted to hand her the bunch.

"One will do, thanks," she answered, enjoying his chagrin. And she'd wager her favorite gold hoop earrings that feeling rarely visited him. The man had a penchant for being in control of every situation. Even an ocean wave fell under his surfboard's spell. She'd marveled at watching him most of the afternoon anticipate a wave's behavior and use it to his advantage like he was attempting to do with her. And she'd play along until she needed to act. Like Larsen and others, he would come to accept and maybe, in time, respect her gift.

"Boy, the rain is sure pounding on your metal roof." Page squinted at the ceiling's whitewashed wood planks. She pointed at Barnacle, who'd succumbed to sleep under the dining table. Paws pointed in the air.

Steve laughed at the dog's position. "Let's get back to your story. You left Catherine at the agency. Did you re-encounter her?"

"I did. The next chance meeting was at the Bistro, where Catherine and this guy I call Seedy were exchanging words by writing on a paper napkin. So very strange. Why not just talk to each other? Ya know?"

"Yeah, that is weird. Describe Seedy, if you don't mind." Steve held the pen expectantly.

"Hmm...well, for starters, Seedy is someone you already know." Giving Steve that tidbit of information served to hook him. Men were predictable. She allowed her neighbor to think he was running this exchange and repeated her words for effect. "Yep, you know him."

Steve's brow arched. He acknowledged there was something about this woman that he found immensely appealing, besides her excellent genes, which happened to be wearing some sassy jeans. He forced his mind to pick up the interrogation. He grinned. "Really? I know this guy?"

"Seedy's the man you were watching at the Crab Shak. Remember he and the other guy—"

"Ah, that guy. Seedy is a fitting name for that lowlife. I gotta say you're certainly observant and so early into your meddling….um, sleuthing actions with this case. It looks as if you're doing some decent connecting of dots."

Page ignored Steve's fake attempt at complimenting her work. Wait until she laid the rest on his detecting ego-a-plenty self. "Yes, I am observant to a fault, some have said. Want more?" She claimed the empowered moment.

"By all means. I'm hanging on your every utterance."

"So, this Seedy and Catherine are writing notes on a napkin with a lot of nodding back and forth. Confusing behavior. And get this, just before they leave, I observed Seedy pass her a silver pistol under the bistro's table. I'm guessing that's the gun that took her life, too. You know, maybe she pulled the weapon on her killer to try and defend herself and—"

"Could be," Steve jumped in, answering while jotting notes.

Page waited for his attention. "A few minutes after that happened, Betsy conned me into having ice cream. We were parked on a bench with our cones, and guess who appeared?"

"Let's see…Catherine Lange?" said Steve, playing along.

"Ah, a comedian. Yes, Catherine. And she sashays into Garrets Insurance office." Page tucked her legs under her and hugged a tattered throw pillow, evidently a favorite of Barnacle's judging by the dog hair attached. Page grimaced, seeing the deposit of fur on her white jeans.

"Excuse me, but what's the big deal?" Steve asked, confused.

"You're interrupting again. It's what happens later, that's a big deal." She watched Steve rise and motion for her to scoot down on the sofa. Geez, the guy was entering her personal space. A distraction she didn't need at this moment. She needed her wits. Page chose to focus on the small cut gracing his forehead and not on his nearness.

"This is better. We can speak easier. Carry on."

His charming smile alerted Page to his ploy. "Next, Betsy and I watched Catherine come out carrying a manila envelope. She takes a smaller envelope out of her handbag and drops that in a slot at Brakem's office. Do you know him?"

"I do. And you?" Steve could volley with ease.

"Me? Well, Brakem handled the new deed recording of Hibiscus Cottage for me. However, my communication was with his paralegal through mostly email. So, that's what Betsy and I saw that particular afternoon." Page uncrossed her legs and scooted back, gaining six inches more of personal space.

"And that's all you've got for me?" Steve's eyes flashed to the front door.

"No, of course not. Later that evening, Betsy and I go for a beach stroll. When we turned for home, we were in front of the Lange home, and I see Catherine inside talking to three people. You know how easy it is to see people in their homes at night when it's all lit?"

"Hmm. Ms. Wright, you excel at dragging a story. I'm begging you to wrap this up." Steve studied his watch.

"When it's a titillating recap, I like to savor it again myself," Page jousted, delighted with her coveted position in the catbird seat. "Anyway, I pulled Betsy down in the sea oats just as the four of them stepped onto the deck. They were drinking cocktails, and then Catherine starts making demands of Garrett to insure her canary diamond necklace for way more than it's worth. Things got pretty intense from that point.

Page finished that night's recounting. "My eavesdropping makes a case for those three as prime suspects."

"I can see why. There's a hint of a motive in the whole bunch." Steve tapped his pen against the notepad. "What else?"

"Well, just what you already know." Page frowned. Surely, by now, all traces of her lipstick were gone, and she no doubt looked washed out. Steve's voice interrupted her beauty musing.

"Okay, Eve, I'll bite yet again from your apple. Why don't you tell me what I already know?

"You know, you're remarkably transparent for a detective, or whatever your title is nowadays."

Steve shrugged, electing to avoid another bite of her apple. He watched Barnacle head to his food dish.

"Fine. So, I'm compelled to have lunch of all places, the Crab Shak—"

"Another tinkling?" A slight grin found one corner of Steve's mouth.

"Inkling. While Betsy is all up in the air with our waitress's attire and attitude, I observe Ty and Seedy in a heated conversation. I was shocked to see Catherine's houseman…butler…whatever he is associated with Seedy, but no doubt there's an explanation. You'd better look into that."

"Yes, ma'am," Steve replied with a mock salute. "More for me?"

"Your salutes annoy me. Anyway, I know you saw the guys in the Shak's parking lot engrossed over something in a duffle, and they were doing some exchange? Yes?"

He offered her a shrug.

"Come on. I caught you spying on the two guys. Okay, play it that way. I know what I know, mister." Page folded her arms across her chest. Steve could knock himself out, read her body language, and figure out the rest for himself.

"Listen, I admit that I was surveilling, but if you recall, you and your cousin needed assistance. Which meant I had to help you instead of following my two guys." He matched the folded arms pose and raised her an "Oomph."

"Hey, I'm sorry about that fiasco with my vehicle. I knew we messed up your shadowing and then we did it again last night when I followed you and Catherine. I thought that you might be a bad dude, and I needed to know —"

"Me, a bad dude?" Steve howled. "You got off track there."

Page's face flushed crimson. "I admit that. Surely, you see how your stand-offish behavior and your constant dogging — sorry, Barnacle — these people would have us questioning your role and identity." Barnacle appeared by Page's side. Absently, she stroked the dog's head.

"Point made. I had my reasons for tracking Catherine. Let's say she needed to pick nicer people to hang out with in life. Too late now."

"Tell me this, Agent Tanner, if that's what you go by, did you sic Koch on us?"

Steve smiled, from the safety of his chair. He stayed silent, observing.

"Whatever. I get that we were interfering with your tailing and all, but you didn't need to go to that extreme. Koch isn't friendly, and we ended up stuck in that horrid horror movie for almost two hours."

Steve chuckled. "So, Koch informed me. Listen, Page, surely you can grasp that I have a job to do, and I can't have you two amateurs —"

Page let the amateur remark slide. "But we can assist,"

she pleaded. Larsen had told her Steve's analytical mind was legendary at the FBI and that he was called in only for the most entwined type of cases. Larsen relayed that their neighbor was some savant with puzzles. And crimes were, after all, puzzles with fragmented pieces that, once put together, produced a solution.

The sleuth watched him size her up. She didn't mind because she returned the favor. She understood his dilemma. Larsen had the same problem handling Page's insights during their first murder investigation. She had to earn these crime busters' respect by proving her gift was authentic. For now, she'd toss Steve a personal crumb. "My dad retired from the FBI. I get you guys, and besides, surely you can grasp detecting is in my DNA?"

"Your father was with the agency? Interesting. Never mind. I think I've got a decent picture of how this all fits with someone needing to eliminate Mrs. Lange. The motive may fit with Garrett, and Brakem, and a few others. Time will tell."

Page's interest peaked, and she saw that register on Steve's face. "Others? Like who others?" she asked, feeling she had nothing to lose.

"Forget I said that. Listen up, Page. I'm telling, not asking, steer clear of this active investigation. For the moment, I'm relieved you and Betsy haven't piqued others' serious interest. You've not interacted with any of these people, and that gives me some peace."

Page decided she liked him better when he used her given name. Eve was ridiculous. For now, his good looks, physical endowments, and stealth could only tally three points on her scale of a perfect ten in a man. No doubt, any other hidden sterling attributes could raise his score if she cared. She refused to succumb to his brand of temptation. Her single life suited her, and better to give attention to Betsy's idea of a business enterprise and not some hunky guy next door. "Don't worry about us."

"So, I'm going to keep your information between my chief and Koch. That means only five of us will know what you saw and heard. Right, Page?"

She didn't like being treated like a...whatever he was treating her like. She re-engaged and told her mind to shut up. "Totally right. And Betsy and I will not talk. You may rely on us. And if we see someone—"

"No! You will not happen to see a thing. I repeat, no more sleuthing. Your snooping is finito at Shell Isle. Just enjoy your summer vacation." Steve rose, signaling the meeting had ended.

"Oh, all right," mumbled Page, following him to the front door.

"Here, better take my umbrella."

"Thanks." Page opened the door. "Well, I guess we'll be seeing each other, being that we're neighbors and all."

"Expect so." Steve stole a look at his diver's watch. "One more thing. Make sure to enlighten Betsy on the new rules and tell your cousin whatever you want her to know about tonight. The goal here is for you two to be safe and well away from any more involvement with the investigation. That's our new agreement. Agreed?" Steve's eyes locked on Page's.

"Of course, I'll share with her. Good luck tonight, whatever you're about, Tanner." Page turned and walked down the sidewalk, shielded by the umbrella and probably more than she knew. What he didn't understand was that the inklings couldn't be controlled, nor the synchronicities that placed her and Betsy smack in the middle of mysterious doings, but he'd learn. He'd learn.

CHAPTER 23

The sound of a beach services tractor grooming the sand woke Page from a fitful slumber. She welcomed the release from the night's swirling dark dreams, all centered around who'd felt most threatened by Catherine's very being. She turned her focus to the happenings out her window. Fluttering blue umbrellas and matching wooden chairs were called to action by the college-age lifeguard. Her watch said 9 a.m., proving the clandestine meeting with Steve had zapped her energy reserves. Guilt slapped her for keeping the rendezvous from Betsy. She didn't know how best to right the deed, but owning the truth of it was an excellent first step. Grabbing her robe, she went in search of coffee and her cousin.

"And a fine Tuesday mornin' to you. You're starting the day rather later than usual. How'd you sleep?" Betsy poured a second cup of coffee, adding a splash of cream, before scooting the mug across the counter to a subdued Page.

"I slept frightful if you want to call what I did sleep. Too many upsets around here, I suppose." Page stirred her coffee.

"Yeah, me too. It's all so unsettling."

Page noted that Betsy acted antsy, repositioning the sugar and creamer bowls. "Something is troubling you. I know your ways. What's up?"

"Well, for starters, I suppose it's finding that woman's body on the beach and knowing there are people around us capable of hating enough to take a life. It's like I just said...unsettling." Betsy pulled biscuits from the oven and put them in a basket next to a tray of butter, hot pepper jelly, and lavender honey and placed the tray on the breakfast counter. "I know, boring biscuits, but the jelly and honey will jazz them. Feeds your adoration of the honey bees. Have a couple while they're hot."

"Yum. Boring food I like." Page dipped her knife into the butter crock and drizzled lots of sweet bee nectar inside her biscuit.

Betsy smiled, loading on the spicy jelly. "Also, I don't like that we are involved. Not one itsy bit." She took a bite. Butter oozed out and landed on her shift's bodice. She shrugged and squeezed honey over the waiting biscuit. "I wonder if anyone makes stylish adult bibs?"

Page shook her head, smiling at Betsy's ongoing struggle with tidiness. "I know you're not happy about our involvement, and that's why we're going to do something about it. You and me." Page's index finger pointed to each of them for emphasis.

"What kind of something? Nothing that requires me to crouch again." Betsy flexed one leg and adjusted her vivid patterned shift, trying to gather some humor.

Page laughed. "Probably not a crouch. Hey, how many of those beach dress ensembles do you own anyway?"

Betsy had removed the matching tie belt that would fail at flattering her waistline. "Enough to have you ask. And never mind, I still didn't get to that boutique for a smaller size to inspire me. So, what's your grand idea this time, Sherlocka?"

Both women moved with their coffee cups and plated biscuits to the sofa. The sun bathed the yellow walls with a kind of pearl iridescence. The sofa pillows dressed in a subdued sunflower print were meant to cheer any seater. Two flanking chairs were upholstered in a warm sand color, not competing for attention. Aunt Tilly's lifestyle embraced spontaneity, and it followed her into decorating. If she liked something enough, it came to live with her. Page cherished her Tilly memories, but if she kept Hibiscus, some new décor that suited her tastes was needed.

Betsy wiped a drop of jelly from her lap and shrugged once more. "My trademark two drips for the day. Come on. What ya got for us?"

"First, I have a confession." Page's frown testified to her apprehension. How she dreaded telling Betsy that she'd met with Steve on the sly. She'd better spin a good tale and tap into her mother's creative writing genes.

"A confession? You? This ought to be a dandy," replied Betsy with a loud chortle.

"Yeah, it's a dandy, all right. Here goes. I've been talking to Steve a bit more. Actually —"

"More like…actually, you met with him. Well, didn't you?" Betsy leaned in.

Page's eyes widened in surprise. "Well, yeah, I did meet with him. I had to. But, but how did…" Page felt nonplused.

Betsy patted her cousin's shoulder. "There now. And since he's all intense FBI, I bet he didn't give you much choice."

"No, not really." Page let relief come calling. Confession was good for the soul, even if Betsy did the job for her.

"You do know that you could've just told me about this big secret rendezvous. You made me drink cup after cup of that sleepy tea and sit in the dark to watch that awful one-star-rated movie *Unforgivable*." Betsy cracked a grin and succeeded in crossing her leg.

Surprised at her cousin's words, Page replied, "You stinker. You knew?"

Betsy nodded, sipping her coffee, her red lipstick attached to the cup's rim.

"Well, what about that? Who's the sly cousin here? And for the record, you weren't the only one miserable watching that movie. And I had to watch the clock, too." Page laughed.

"Midnight for the big meet, right?"

"Yep, midnight. And I guess those snores..."

"Were to send you on your assignment." Betsy gave another nod. "Next time—"

"Next time, *I* will feign sleep, and you can get grilled by Mr. Manners." Page felt relieved that her cousin wasn't angry but buoyed by besting Page.

"Honestly, was the meeting that awful? Did he act all investigator intimidating like? Fire you up with the grilling?" Betsy's eyes softened with concern.

Page chuckled. "Nah. None of that. Steve's not a bad guy, but a host he's not." Page remembered the soda. "I had to beg a drink from the man and a napkin." She had to support her statement by sharing a little something with her cousin. Ah, but the umbrella, that qualified as somewhat thoughtful. She'd make sure to prop it against his front door later.

"Again, I ask, where are we with this case?" Betsy rose to take her plate to the kitchen sink.

"Okay, let's get you up to speed." Page left nothing out in the telling and included the travel agent encounter but did play down Steve's demand that they avoid any further sleuthing. They'd act extra cautious when clue gathering opportunities presented. Page settled back into her cushion and waited for Betsy to process the latest update.

"Page, I don't see how anything you've just shared translates into steps to catch La-di-da's killer. Whoops, I'm calling her Catherine out of respect from now on."

"You're right. It doesn't translate yet, but I've been mentally mapping out phase one of 'Flush Them Out.' We begin today with our suspects," declared Page.

"I'm not sure..." Betsy fidgeted, making a big deal of setting her watch.

"Hear my scheme before you start throwing up flack. First, I'm going to call Brakem and get an appointment with him to discuss whether I should sell Hibiscus or perhaps make it a vacation rental." Surely, Steve couldn't find any reason to fault her for taking care of personal business.

"What? Rent Hibiscus?" Betsy screeched, scurrying back to the sofa. "You're not going to sell or rent our Hibiscus. I swear I will channel Aunt Tilly down here this minute—"

"Hush, it's nothing more than a ruse to get a meeting at his office."

"Oh, well, in that case..." Betsy relaxed her grip on the sofa's arm and dropped her glare down a notch.

"I'm going to chat him up about Catherine's death happening only a couple of doors from us and how that got me unnerved and thinking about selling."

"Ohhh...I get it now. Very crafty."

"Why, thank you." Page preened, grinning. "We're looking for any Catherine reactions from him. And if need be, you can go into your classic routine, where you're all perplexed how Catherine died. We've got a motley bunch here. Anyway, you know how to perform better than any Tony-winning actor."

"Flattery helps, but I'm still not thrilled you've suckered me again into this murder-solving escapade when I'm desperate for fun and my beach chair. And yes, with all my past performing, I know my script. Still, cautious doesn't feel near convincing enough for how we need to proceed. If Brakem is the one, we sure as Hades don't want him worrying about us, or worse, see us as a problem to..." Betsy gulped. "Remedy."

"Agreed. That's my job to handle. I will laugh and excuse you, like always, if we end up playing things that way. And, if we perform to perfection, we may have baited our first hook." Page emptied her cup and ignored the tiny tremor in her hands. Fear always tested her early in a case.

"Dare I ask if you've planned past this Brakem soirée?"

"Just a few ideas scattering around up here." Page tapped

her forehead. "Nothing definite yet. Though I sense more inklings are coming."

"I swear your blasted inklings, nudges, and intuitings have cast another spell on me. I can't believe what I'm about to say, but I'm in. Make an appointment with Brakem. And I, ol' dependable Betsy, may have an idea for baiting our second hook." She padded toward the bedroom, leaving Page's mouth agape.

CHAPTER 24

While waiting for her cousin to dress, Page's eyes took in the ever-changing ocean's invitation to boats and swimmers this day. Anchored fishing vessels strung like colored beads dotted the horizon. This was the time of day when fishing crews worked with vigor in preparation for the day's run.

The fish population had dwindled over the last decade, forcing the fishers to explore other means of income. Still, the sea remained in the captains' and crews' blood and those of generations before them. They formed a tight group on Shell Isle, these older salty dogs as they called themselves, and were dedicated to fostering and partaking of the ocean's bounty but ever mindful to limit their catch. Their shared hope was that the industry might survive and prosper again if they acted as good stewards of the resources.

Thankfully, Shell Isle's bays remained pristine, unlike the Gulf's, and the price of the fresh catch reflected this fact on the pier's restaurant chalkboard menus. The higher prices helped offset the lower yields for the fishermen, and residents gladly paid to safeguard the island's economy.

Page missed her Aunt Tilly filling her in on local gossip and news. She and Betsy could always count on Tilly educating them during each visit about the island's current happenings. Their aunt had devoted much energy to Shell Isle's environmental projects. Her checkbook always stood ready to support the healthy lifestyle coveted by the locals. New residents came tasked with at least donating time to endeavors meant to enhance the island, or they'd soon find their welcome frosty.

Page forced her musings back to the present, wondering what community role she might play if she kept Hibiscus. Without a doubt, Aunt Tilly would haunt her if she didn't contribute something to the idyllic beach town. And her aunt was a dominant force no matter where her spirit resided. Maybe she'd visit the Chamber of Commerce, especially if she and Betsy came up with a business idea. Page smiled, acknowledging the cottage's pull had sent her mind pondering life there. With a glance at her watch, the sleuth scurried to find her cousin.

~*~

Page took a seat in the chair closest to a waiting Betsy. "Who wants to map out our clue-fishing trip? I've got a two o'clock appointment with Brakem."

"Ya know, I've been wondering what kind of dalliance Catherine had busted this Garrett character on." Betsy placed her cell phone on the nearby table, giving Page her full attention. "So, do we know if this insurance guy is married?"

Page winked. "We do now. Before I fill you in on my detecting, what about that hook of yours?"

Betsy patted her styled auburn hair and freshly applied makeup. Her brown eyes sparkled, helped by the plum eyeshadow. She tilted her nose upward, already getting into character. "Oh, mine is set, too. You see, I'm considering buying a place here. And I want to get some insurance rates and learn about the types of policies needed for residential oceanfront versus one row in. Garrett has me down for three o'clock."

"Well, aren't you something, Miss Thang? Going to buy a beach bungalow and all." Page fanned herself for effect. They both loved the creative part of sleuthing when they had to invent roles to play for gathering information. "Well planned, cousin." Page shook Betsy's offered hand.

"And, I might buy something, you know? The idea sounds quite appealing, especially if you agree to my super-duper proposal that we find something fun to plug into." Betsy scrunched her face at Page. "Never mind. Let's sketch out our spiel for Garrett. I guess buying my smaller size shift can wait until this case is solved. Besides, I'm way too distracted to shop."

Page gave a nod in support and stood up ready to do something, but what?

Betsy supplied the answer to what next. "Let's go down to the beach and relax. I fancy being mindless. Besides, I have another book waiting." Betsy held the paperback up as proof.

"Geez, you have an endless supply of those novels. I'd like to try on mindless. Just let me grab my beach bag."

~*~

The cousins walked crisscrossing around children hard at work. Sandcastles were coming out of the ground while small crabs made introductions. Parents exchanged tips on getting their kids to eat vegetables and tidy up their rooms while the lifeguard's whistle chirped two fearless swimmers to move closer to shore. A typical beach day that many waited all year to experience.

"How about here?" Betsy went to battle with opening her rusting chair.

"Suits me. We'll have to watch the tide's direction being so close to the water." Page hung her beach bag over the chair arm. The breeze blew Page's hair from her face, showcasing a strong jawline, compatible with her determined nature. "Okay by you if I take a walk?"

"Course. Go," replied Betsy, distracted and already digging for a snack.

Page didn't tell her cousin she'd received the nudge to take a walk. She re-tied her sneakers and dropped her sunglasses to her nose. "Be back in a bit."

"Mmm." Betsy offered a weak wave, already munching on pretzels and fiddling with her cell phone.

Gazing out to sea, Page noticed two shrimp boats trolling closer to shore. She thought of the delicious crustaceans, dinner, and Barnacle in that order. She liked Steve's dog, and if Page was honest with herself, she liked his owner even more after last night. Larsen hadn't shared anything personal about Steve, but there were at least three possibilities: divorced, widower, or unmarried. With his type of work, her money settled on divorced. The erratic hours and ongoing danger strained relationships.

The sun tucked behind a billowing cumulus cloud. Seeing the pier up ahead, Page turned back, increasing her walking speed. Time had slipped away from her once again while her mind kept churning thoughts. The nudge returned, growing stronger with each step. She hurried toward what she didn't know.

CHAPTER 25

Page strode closer to the rows of beach residences. Surprise washed over her as she grew parallel with the Lange home. She dropped down on the sand a few yards away as if to sunbathe. The two people standing on the deck didn't notice her, so thankfully, the conversation continued.

"Evan darling, it's so wonderful having the place to ourselves again. That woman made me feel like an interloper in my own brother's home." Gwen's fuchsia flowing dress swayed with her to Evan's side, where she deposited a light kiss on his cheek.

"Again, I say, there's no need to keep carrying on about Catherine. She's gone."

Page noted that Evan was indeed back from New York if he'd even been there. His unimpressive stature forced him to look up at his sister, but more surprising was his gruff, commanding voice. Dressed casually in belted khaki shorts and a nautical polo-style shirt, he portrayed himself as anything but a grieving husband, but more like a vacationer exchanging pleasantries. Page flipped onto her stomach, allowing for an ideal view of the scene.

"Goodness, there you are, Ty. I'm simply parched from this heat." Gwen lifted a beverage from the tray.

"Yes, ma'am," Ty responded before quietly withdrawing back through the glass doors.

Alone once again, Gwen continued, "What's your next move, Evan?" Gwen leaned over and whispered something to her brother.

Page witnessed Evan's body go rigid. She could feel his rage.

He grabbed his sister's arm. "The only matter you need to concern yourself with is finding the contents of my safe. Search Catherine's rooms again. Call the pawn shops. Brakem has instructions to make my other Catherine problems disappear." Evan released his sister's arm and raised the glass that he'd been holding.

"But, of course, I will do my part. I'm confident Brakem will manage things as you wish. He always does. You mustn't worry. Salud, brother dear. And salud your cleverness, I most certainly do." Gwen raised her goblet.

Evan offered a curt nod, then checked his cell phone. "So, tell me, did you contact the name I gave you? Surely, you were capable of handling that simple detail." His expression clouded as he studied Gwen.

"Yes, Catherine's body is being returned home once the medical examiner okays the release." Gwen's voice turned icy from the barbs.

"Excellent. What's troubling is the investigation has intensified. This is an unfortunate complication for me." Evan's sobering words hit their mark.

"Oh, dear." Gwen placed her glass on a table, keeping the wet napkin to press against her cheek. "What have you heard?"

"They're off suicide as the cause of death and compiling a suspect list." Evan released a groan as he checked his watch. "Well, it's time I put on my grieving husband face and meet with this Detective Koch at the local police station."

"Yes, I too must plaster on my sad face for the occasion, though you know it hides my sincere pleasure that the vile woman's gone," replied Gwen. "Enough about Catherine. I have a delightful idea for us. Let me ask Ty to get the yacht ready. We can dine on board tomorrow evening and enjoy a private celebration, as it were. I'm sure all these loose ends will soon be a memory, and things will go the way you expect." Gwen offered a chilling smile.

"They'd better, Gwen. Just make sure to take care of your part." Evan hesitated. "Fine. Have Ty ready the yacht."

Gwen preened. "Wonderful. I'll meet you in the foyer in ten minutes. Let's get this nuisance of police questioning over with."

Page watched the pair go inside. She'd experienced an unfiltered glimpse of the two people linked closest to Catherine. And they cared not a whit about the dead woman. Why?

~*~

"Now things are missing from Evan's safe, too? Are you kidding me?" Betsy jumped up from her chair, hearing what Page had witnessed moments ago.

"Not kidding. All true. Of course, we don't know if the murder and whatever is gone from the safe have any relationship. I guess these two remain suspects, but without a clear motive so far other than disliking Catherine," replied Page, still amused at Betsy's dramatic exit from her beach chair. "This is more proof we've been tapped to help with the investigation. How else can you explain these ongoing encounters?"

Betsy righted her chair, dusting sand off the seat. "I hear you, Page, but I didn't come looking for an adventure. I know. I keep vacillating. Same old Betsy. Am I whining again?"

Page chuckled. "You're whining just a smidge, and I don't blame you one bit. I came here to decide what to do with Hibiscus and enjoy a break from the bookshop's demands. I'm still counting on accomplishing both."

Betsy sighed. "And didn't I just know when you said at the bistro, "How curious," I was doomed to get pulled in again to another mystery to solve? Can we please sit down? The sun's making my head throb." Betsy didn't wait for a reply. She reclined, plopped the waiting straw hat atop her head, and commenced fanning her flushed face with the novel.

"Think of our situation this way: The sooner we figure out who took Catherine's life, the sooner we can enjoy our laid-back beach time. Can we at least agree to proceed with our clue gathering afternoon?" Page was the first to extend a hand for a shake.

Betsy snorted. "Oh, okay. Like I ever really have a choice." She slapped Page's hand. "So, next stop, Braken and Garrett, but until then, I made you a lovely sandwich." Betsy opened the nearby cooler and tossed the foil package onto Page's lap.

"Oh, you shouldn't have troubled yourself." A worried Page peeked inside the wrapping. "Ah, tuna salad. This, I like." Page took an enormous bite and stopped chewing.

"Mock tuna salad, thank you very much. Sans mercury. Eat up." Betsy offered a full smile but not at Page.

"Hi there, ladies. Happy to see you on the beach. I trust this change from meddling is permanent." Steve held the surfboard against his torso.

Betsy reacted first and lifted her chin a few inches.

Page knew indignant words were about to fly. She sent a few jerky head shakes Betsy's way, signaling her cousin to stay mute. It was another failed attempt.

Betsy's voice chimed away. "I'll have you know, Steve Tanner, we do not meddle. What we do is aid the police in solving crimes. You go look up Detective Larsen and ask him. And furthermore, it might interest you to hear we've set some impressive bait —"

"Hold up. Please excuse me a moment, Betsy." Steve's eyes looked like a stormy Nor'easter as they locked on Page. He'd caught her failed warning attempts to stifle Betsy. "Umm, Page, have you developed a tick or something?"

"What?" She sent Betsy an impressive scowl. "No, of

course not. These gnats are so annoying. No nervous ticks here."
She swatted the air, noting Steve's amused eyes were crinkling at
the corners. Blast the man. Must he haunt her every movement?
She noticed Betsy waiting to finish her rant. Bested by both, she
took a bite of the disgusting tofu sandwich.

Ignoring Page's assurance that her motor skills were
dandy, Steve returned his attention to the blabbermouth. "Sorry,
Betsy. You were saying something about bait?" His eyes remained
on Page, monitoring her reaction.

"Bait?" Betsy wrinkled her nose, imagining squirmy
fishing worms, before recalling her reference to the bait. "Oh,
yes. Our bait. Well, you see Page and I…what are you doing?"

Steve lifted Betsy's hand, gently tugging her to rise. "Let's
you and I take a short walk. Have a chat. Page, you enjoy that
sandwich." Steve gave Page a wink, his expression voluntary
and deliberate.

"But, but, Betsy…" Page yammered. What would her
cousin blab? Geez, Steve had done a bang-up job with his style of
baiting and caught a big-mouth fish named Betsy Ross. Resigned,
Page could only reply, "Have a nice walk."

Steve rewarded the sleuth with a wicked grin and laid his
board next to her chair for company. He motioned a too eager
Betsy to lead the way. Page knew her cousin would do precisely
that. Lead the FBI contractor, or whatever he acted as, right to
their plan with Brakem and Garrett. Furious, Page glanced at
Steve's board and considered feeding it to the choppy surf.

CHAPTER 26

Twenty minutes elapsed before the pair returned to a now simmering Page. Babbling Betsy, wearing all smiles, took to her lounger.

Page turned and faced her cousin. "You'd better call both your sons and tell them goodbye. I'm about to kill you on the spot."

"Nah, you don't mean it." Betsy settled back into her chair and laughed while rummaging for her sunscreen. She took her time folding a towel.

"I just may mean every word. I suppose you blabbed all about our afternoon's plans? What do you have to say for yourself?" Page released an exasperated breath.

"I'd have to say the walk was…enlightening." Betsy slathered suntan lotion on her generous arms while watching Steve paddle out past the breaks. Her sandwich waited in her lap.

"Enlightening? By that, I assume you were the one doing all the enlightening? Blast it, Betsy, I'm—"

"You assume wrong. So, I admit that I almost tattled when Steve got all investigator condescending-like with us, but your head bobbing and jerking like a cork on that man's fishing line out there stopped me."

"You didn't tell—"

"Nope. Steve got so frustrated with my senseless drivel that he walked me right back here with only a word of warning to stay out of the police investigation." Betsy shook the bottle of lotion, willing out more liquid. Her legs provided plenty of real estate to protect. Satisfied, she returned to her sandwich.

"You're telling me all you did was conjure up your 'blabber routine' on that stroll? Why, Betsy, that's brilliant. The man detests senseless chatter." Page had underestimated her partner.

"I know, and the guy did so suffer my prattle. Too funny, right? He kept asking me to get to the point, which, of course, I never did. You know, I kinda felt sorry for him."

"No way. Tanner doesn't deserve one second of our pity," huffed Page.

"Well, only a tiny bit, sorry then." Betsy leaned toward Page and whispered, raising the intrigue up another notch. "Wanna hear what I confirmed?" She took a bite and laid the sandwich on a napkin.

"You're kidding? You got him to tell you something? Spill it."

Betsy popped the tab on her ginger ale, took a long sip meant to torment Page. She dropped her voice. "Here goes. It seems the medical examiner confirmed the angle of the bullet to Catherine's head proved that it couldn't have been suicide."

"Duh."

"Yeah, duh, all right. Like we didn't know that. Steve also said Koch was bringing in Evan and Gwen for questioning." Betsy paused.

"Did you tell him we knew?" She wondered if Betsy had failed this temptation.

"Nope. Surprise on you. I surely did not tell him. I only said we assumed that Koch would be interrogating both. After that, I started my jabber because he shifted the questions to me. He was fishing to make sure we weren't behaving like amateur PIs or something."

Page chuckled. "So, then what next routine did you employ on our neighbor? Wait. Let me guess. Umm…how about the one where we let the investigators think our sleuthing has led us down the wrong path, and we've got our clues all mixed up? You know, they believe we've ventured so far away in our thinking that we couldn't possibly be a problem to anyone. That's the one I think would work best on Tanner. Did I pick the right ploy?" asked Page.

"Nope." Betsy stopped chewing to gather momentum and took another sip from her can. "I told him this murder was just the distraction you needed to engage in living life again. And that you'd resorted to buying a classic who-done-it novel and even booked us for an evening next week at the mystery dinner theatre down the coast. Good, huh?"

"You what? Why, Betsy Ross, would you tell that man that I needed to engage in—"

"Because I felt that would sidetrack him from his line of grilling me."

"Well, did it?" Page couldn't help feeling curious about Steve's reaction.

"It sure did. Our inquisitive neighbor asked me why you needed a diversion. And before you throw a hissy fit, I rambled on about your bookshop asking more of you than you'd ever dreamed and how your customers stop by and stay the day. By the time I'd exhausted that topic and not given the poor man a chance to say even a syllable, he was past ready to deposit me back in my lounger. You know, I'm wondering why it is that I must play the ditz so often? I need a more interesting role. I wanna be the sleuth who is crafty and cunning for our next case."

"Well, sure, Betsy, we can work on your role having more..." Page felt at a loss to conjure a word.

"The word is depth. So, how did I do with my ad-lib? Impressive, huh?" Betsy took a bow from her chair.

Page rallied. "I must say you aced that encounter, even if you did make me look pathetic to do so. Well done." Page peered into the cooler for anything to kill the mock tuna taste from her unhappy taste buds. She pulled out a bag of what looked like oatmeal cookies. With Betsy, she couldn't be sure until she tasted one. "I trust these are the real deal?" Page offered one to her cousin.

"Yes, fresh out of a cardboard box. I have a recipe for gluten-free—"

"These are perfect," Page interjected. "Did you learn anything else besides confirming Evan and Gwen are being questioned?" Page glimpsed a wave swallow Steve and felt instant pleasure.

Betsy munched the last piece of cookie. "I saved this tasty tidbit for you. I confirmed Mr. Personality is deeply involved in the case because the tentacles reach further than Shell Isle. And the FBI has been watching Evan for a while now."

"How did you learn that juicy bit of info?"

"He got a call, and I could hear the caller's words and Steve's guarded responses. I put two and two together, and, voila, I bring you more trailing breadcrumbs for us to follow."

"Outstanding job, Betsy. Really outstanding."

"Thanks. I figured that I'd better come back with the goods, so to speak, to redeem myself from my earlier blurting." Betsy put her hand out for another cookie.

"You're redeemed." Page bestowed the whole box on her cousin.

"Then, would this be an auspicious time to make a little request?"

Page frowned. "I suppose so."

"Good. I want to stop by the nursery after our meetings with Brakem and Garrett. Wouldn't it be lovely to plant some bright red hibiscus in the cottage's front yard? It will help imprint the name. The distraction and exercise will be good for us." Betsy offered a thumbs-up to three young girls building a monster-size sand castle nearby.

"Seriously, you want to plant hibiscus?" Page shook her head. "Well, I guess it might add value to the place and make the cottage more attractive to a renter or buyer."

"You're not sellin' or rentin,' my pretty." Betsy's words testified to her determination that Hibiscus would remain their oasis from the world.

Page laughed at the proclamation and chose not to engage since she hadn't found her answer to Hibiscus's future yet. "Sure, let's doll up the cottage's flower beds."

"Excellent. Wait, what time is it?" Betsy held up her cell phone screen displaying the time. "Whoa, time for some sleuthing."

Page suspected Steve spotted them packing up. When they reached the cottage's deck, she frowned, watching him wade into shore.

CHAPTER 27

As Page feared, Steve managed to carve out time to keep an eye on their doings. She and Betsy made a big show of dragging out the gardening tools and even pushed the vintage wheelbarrow around the side yard facing Steve's bungalow. And to put a cherry on top of their ruse, they'd staged a big argument over what plants to buy at the nursery, hoping his open kitchen window captured every word. Page mumbled under her breath to Betsy, "Don't look but Steve's at the kitchen sink. I lay you odds that he's probably standing there, eavesdropping and washing the same clean plate over and over."

Betsy snickered. "I'm not taking that bet. Let's move to our next step on Operation Outfox Tanner and skedaddle."

~*~

The humid afternoon heat kept the tourists off the sidewalks and on the beach. Shell Isle's shops would come alive later in the day. The island's downtown functioned much like towns in Spain, embracing the siesta and savoring long, leisurely lunches.

"Look, there's a great parking spot right in front of Brakem's office." Betsy pointed.

"It's mine." Page parked and killed the engine. "We're a few minutes early, but let's go inside anyway." Within seconds, she opened the impressively carved cypress door at the attorney's office.

Betsy winked as she breezed past.

"May I help you?" asked the twenty-something admin from behind a glass desk that displayed a phone, a legal pad for show, a container of pens, and the most vital thing an office employee needed...a bottle of tomato red nail polish.

The phone intruded, allowing Page to get a read on Brakem's receptionist.

A sheer lemon-yellow knit top plunged as far down as the Grand Canyon, only to meet up with a mini denim skirt that would never touch a knee. The tousled hair looked hurriedly forgotten, likely after some lunch tryst. Where had that thought come from? She hadn't even peeped inside one of Betsy's swashbuckling historical romance novels.

Placing the phone in its cradle, the platinum blond admin turned again to Page. "Sorry. Do you have an appointment or something?" Her voice was laced with a heavy northeastern accent and boredom. The gum popping added more pizazz to the persona.

"Yes, I have a two o'clock meeting with Mr. Brakem. I'm Page Wright, and my cousin seated in the corner is Betsy Ross."

"Hmm...Page Wright, like an author writing a page or something? You two have hilarious names."

"Don't we just. We get teased constantly," answered Betsy, warming up to the admin. She planted herself in a cushy leather chair and snagged a nearby magazine as a prop.

Page took a seat next to her cousin, noting Betsy holding a hunting magazine. With a wink, Page replaced it with a home décor one.

Brakem appeared in the doorway. "Ms. Wright, so nice to finally meet you face to face. He moved to shake Page's hand. "And this is?" the attorney turned his attention to Betsy, expecting a proper introduction.

"This is my cousin, Betsy Ross."

Betsy offered a disinterested nod and returned to her magazine.

Page kept her smile inside, knowing Betsy had settled into

her role.

Brakem repeated Betsy and Page's names and laughed, which both women chose to ignore. He cleared his throat. "Well, why don't you come through Ms. Wright and tell me how I might be of assistance. Lola, please hold my calls." He stepped aside to allow Page to pass.

"Take a chair. I assume this meeting has something to do with Tilly and the cottage she generously bequeathed to you. I trust that the transaction was handled satisfactorily by us?" Brakem swiveled in his chair, grabbing a file from the credenza behind him.

"Yes, the transfer of the deed seemed effortless. I'm sure you're busy, so I'll get right to it, Mr. Brakem. I'd welcome your counsel on whether it makes sense to sell or maybe even rent Hibiscus Cottage. Of course, I plan to talk with Gail, my real estate agent, but I'm seeking an unbiased opinion." Page sat back, allowing her eyes to take in the luxury appointments of Brakem's office.

The décor set out to give the impression that the man enjoyed success in his chosen profession. Page's eyes acknowledged the imposing walnut antique desk that undoubtedly Brakem employed to foster client respect. Paneled walls welcomed impressive floor-to-ceiling bookcases on one side of the room. A ladder with wheels was attached to the shelving, but Page couldn't envision Brakem teetering on it to search for a law book; however, Lola fit the bill. The coffered ceiling with recessed lighting was subdued. Expensive burgundy wingback chairs circled the attorney's desk, with the surprisingly low seats giving Brakem the advantage of looking down on the chairs' occupants. The room's purpose conveyed the mood that a client was chambered and protected by a powerful lawyer. And if not for what Page saw on the opposite wall and the demeanor of the man sitting across from her, she'd have bought the package.

Page sensed Brakem's eyes assessing her while he glanced over the papers. She didn't fault him for trying to read her; after all, it was a talent all skilled attorneys invoked. She'd just keep admiring his expensive and unexpected art collection display while the pretentious man fumbled with her file. She had her talents starting with showing an empty countenance.

He cleared his throat. "Well, I've reviewed the cottage's appraisal done at the time of probate. And the real estate market's valuations haven't shifted much since then, so my advice would lean heavily on your doing an option you didn't give me." Brakem paused to make a few more notes before placing his readers on the desk and focusing on Page.

"Really? I'd like to hear the third option."

"My recommendation is that you keep Hibiscus and make some updates that would be pleasing to you. Then, you may continue enjoying visits with us at Shell Isle, as you have in the past. Additionally, I must share that Tilly was most adamant about not wanting you to sell. I'm conveying those desires now that you have opened this unexpected topic." Barkem laid down the pen and closed the file.

Page read the action. The attorney's interest in their discussion was ebbing. She turned her most charming smile his way. "It seems you and my cousin agree. I'm sure you're right about Aunt Tilly wanting me to keep the cottage. I can almost hear her saying as much."

"Your aunt possessed a strong presence, let us say. As I recall, she felt you could afford to hold the property and with only minor adjustments in your personal lifestyle. I believe that's how she stated it." Brakem's eyes went cold and yet questioning.

Page sat quietly, observing his natural snake-like state while he contemplated adding more.

"Also worth considering, our real estate market might be kinder to your purse if you postpone selling. Renting is not something I would advise in your situation. It can be problematic for owners living away. Anyway, that's the best counsel I can offer." Brakem pushed his chair away from his desk, his piercing eyes observing Page.

"Thank you. I appreciate your honesty. There's just one more aspect of my keeping Hibiscus that's most troubling." Page reached for her handbag.

"Please?" The attorney motioned in the air for Page to continue. Clearly, his curiosity was mildly peaked.

"Well, Mr. Brakem, I must admit hearing a possible murder might have happened just a few doors away involving Catherine Lange is most unsettling. I'm not sure that I feel safe and, honestly, I'm not sure what those people are about, as they don't fit Shell Isle's typical…" Page purposely left the sentence open for the attorney to digest. She didn't like how Brakem stared at her, all slithery and sneaky. She sensed the attorney was questioning her motive for the meeting.

"A murder?" Brakem's voice found a new octave as his fingers gripped the desk's edge.

"Oh, yes. Haven't you heard about poor Catherine?" Page watched the attorney's expression grow as dark as the early morning storm clouds on the ocean's horizon.

Brakem attempted to shield his emotions. "Of course, I'd heard the unfortunate news she'd been found on the beach, but I didn't know the police had changed the cause of death from drowning, maybe a suicide drowning to—"

Page witnessed Brakem's inner struggle to gain control of the conversation. He failed.

The attorney allowed his fingers to tap his forehead for a few seconds before continuing, "Forgive me, Ms. Wright, but I don't see how this happening jeopardizes your safety one iota. A drowning or suicide is unfortunate, but no cause for alarm. Surely, you've garnered some bad information about a murder?"

"Really? Still, if it is murder, I worry it could be some disturbing doings by possibly people involved with the Langes —"

"You mustn't worry. Shell Isle is a safe place with only an occasional little something to warrant the police department's participation." Brakem stood, his coloring now ashen, and the intimidating persona seemed to puddle around him.

Page seized her advantage and fired another volley. "Did you happen to know Catherine Lange? I saw her around town only recently. She appeared the type of woman one didn't miss." Page ignored his outstretched arm, pointing her out to the hallway.

"I knew her slightly." Brakem's voice lacked conviction. "Now, I'm sorry, but I'm running a tight schedule today, and we did work you in, Ms. Wright."

Page extended her hand. "Of course. Thank you for the advising, and I'm truly sorry if I upset you with the news of Mrs. Lange."

Brakem opened his office door. "Ms. Wright, please do take extra care, and good luck to you."

Page nodded and walked toward a waiting Betsy, and signaled her cousin that they were leaving. She didn't like the frigid tone of the attorney's voice nor his veiled parting words.

CHAPTER 28

Once outside, the cousins silenced their words, waiting until a better place to chat presented. The sun had dropped behind the buildings, offering blessed shade. Frozen fruit-ice carts now dotted the street corners, offering quick refreshing treats. Impervious to the sultry temperature, children lined up with money clutched in their hands as they pointed at the colorful syrup choices teasing their eyes.

Before Betsy could claim an ice, Page summoned her. "Come on. Let's pop into the Perk Coffee Shop, where we can talk and get a cup of Joe. We've got time before you meet with Garrett." Page latched onto Betsy's arm, dragging her in the right direction.

"But I wanted something cold." Betsy cast her eyes longingly back to the cart. "Will you slow it down a bit? Guess I'm stuck ordering an iced coffee. Heavy on the ice. I'm already hot as a lit stick of dynamite."

A door chime announced their arrival to a college-age smiling barista behind the shop's counter. The Perk's interior blended intimate conversation niches with technology-friendly work areas. Latte-colored walls displayed local artists' interpretation of life at Shell Isle, while paddle fans moved the roasted beans aroma around, creating the desired effect on a patron's coffee affection. A stand of magazines nearby was meant to enhance and extend a visit and beverage consumption.

Spying the menu options depicted on a giant chalkboard, Betsy read aloud, adding a comment after each one. "That's the one for me." She stopped reciting and turned to the barista. "I want the delightful Sumatra Reserve with just a kiss of hazelnut syrup and iced, but not too much ice, only enough to chill it sufficiently. Give me a cup of ice on the side. Oh, and make the drink size respectable."

"Are you done? Surely you want to add a splash of something else." Page rolled her eyes at Betsy and stepped up to the counter. Page squinted at the menu board. "I'd like a small Matcha My Day Frappe, no whip cream, please. I'm the easy customer."

"Awesome choice. That's my favorite this week." The barista turned to the cash register.

Page opened her wallet. "I've got these."

"Then, I'll pay next time," supplied Betsy, including two chocolate-drenched biscotti to the order.

"Find a seat anywhere. Mickey will bring the drinks over." The barista turned to the espresso machine, waking its hiss.

"Let's go, Miss Easy Customer. You pick the spot." Betsy followed her cousin, offering a wink to the older man sporting a tan fedora embroidered with the name Mickey as they passed by.

He grinned and returned Betsy's wink. His arms laden with bags of coffee beans, Mickey moved toward the display shelves.

"How's this?" Page dropped down in a brown polka dot upholstered club chair. The cushions were cool on her skin, like sea spray had misted them. She yearned for her beach chair and some lovely cozy mystery book to while away a day. Instead, she had a murder of a cold fish to solve.

"This is homey." Betsy settled in a matching chair and grabbed a flyer from the end table to fan herself. "What a scorcher! You hot? No, you're always cool, calm, and collected."

"Wow, did Mickey ever have some instant effect on you." Page's eyes danced, relishing a taste of levity.

"What? Are you kidding me? That clam digger?" Betsy

fluffed her hair, feeling the dreaded frizz on her nape. Her beige linen pants and blouse looked as if an iron had never touched the material.

"I bet Mickey hears and knows a lot about Shell Isle's goings-on." Page's focus narrowed as she watched him stack the bags on the metal shelves and sensed his antennae tuned toward them. Page whispered, "You know, I do believe Mickey might prove useful in a few moments. Follow my lead."

"Yeah, I get your drift. For now, let's talk about our Brakem baiting escapade. Me first." Betsy leaned in.

"Okay, shoot. Sorry. Wrong choice of words."

"Not really. First, Lola isn't a real blond." Betsy grabbed a breath.

"Well, that's sure super important for us to know." Page's sarcastic side came out to play. "Why don't you tell me something valuable like—"

"Hush. I just meant she's plenty wise with what words she lets leave those collagen-infused lips. Forget it. I was thinking about our blond schtick. Anywho, I had to work extra hard on this one." Betsy resumed fanning, noting Mickey's move closer. Time for them to shift to the blond route. She signaled Page.

"Need I remind you that I'm a true blond?" Page pointed to her head, waving a hunk of hair like a duster.

"I know that, silly. And I make allowances for that blond gene. Always have." Merriment danced in Betsy's eyes. She glanced over at the barista, willing her iced coffee to a tray and Mickey's delivering hands.

"Allowances? You make allowances? Let me tell you something if anyone…" Page quieted, keeping her grin hidden.

Mickey appeared wearing a frown. "You gals having a spat or something?" he asked.

Page presented him with a brilliant smile. "Oh, sorry. We're cousins, and, well, sometimes Betsy's outrageous personality—"

"My what?" answered Betsy, straightening in her chair.

"I was starting to explain to Mickey about your strong, stubborn personality…that is so endearing to me," Page replied, reveling in the exchange.

"Now, gals, settle yourselves. I see your coffees on the tray. Let me grab them. Guaranteed to cool things…" Mickey scurried toward the drinks.

Page and Betsy exchanged conspiring looks and continued with their banter.

Betsy served the next volley. "Page Wright, you don't know stubborn. How many times have you refused to introduce your un-neighborly self to the Langes?"

Mickey eyed the pair, gently placing the coffees on the shared end table. "Did you say the Langes? Haven't you heard?"

"Heard what?" both women answered in unison.

Mickey bent down. "Well, it's not official or anything. Didn't make the paper yet, but I heard that snooty Catherine Lange was found with a bullet in her noddle." Mickey's hand turned into a gun to punctuate his words.

"Goodness, how ghastly," replied Betsy. She clutched her chest for added effect.

Page turned to Mickey. "Wow! And isn't it lucky for me that my un-neighborly blond self didn't go calling with some Bundt cake?" Page needed Mickey to remain engaged.

"I'd be inclined to agree." Mickey rubbed his chin, thinking.

"I bet an informed guy like you has a theory as to what happened to Mrs. Lange? I mean, you're in a place where gossip is usually running as often as the espresso machine over there." Betsy rewarded Mickey with another wink.

"Well, that is a fact, all right. Yep, I hear plenty. So much that sometimes I long to be back on a shrimpin' boat where the only noise is the boat engine and my captain's snoring."

"And I wager that you've some fascinating shrimping tales, but we'd love to hear more about Catherine Lange right now, being that we are her neighbors. Gosh, it's sort of concerning," Page slid a metal chair over, hoping Mickey would sit. He bit.

"Hmm." Mickey pressed two fingers above one eye to activate a memory. "She'd stop in here a few times a week for her usual, Turkish coffee with a dollop of cream. You can tell a lot about someone by the coffee they drink. That's a strong cup of java."

"I'll say it is. I'd be awake for a week downing that brew. Was Catherine always alone?" asked Betsy.

"Not if you count her cell phone chattering. She'd sit right where you are and talk really quiet in some foreign tongue. I caught her saying one time the name of what sounded like a Caribbean island that began with a C, but then the rest sounded like mostly gibberish to me," supplied Mickey.

"Could you guess the name?" Betsy touched Mickey's arm to encourage him along.

"Well, I could guess and not be wrong on the island." Mickey leaned over and whispered, "I also heard her say one word over and over when talking. What got me curious was the word is English, too. So, I got my grandson to Google the word's language and match it to an island. Ready for this interesting tidbit? The word was *bang*."

Page smiled. "Most intriguing and clever of you. So, what island and language matched this *bang*?"

"Well, we're fairly sure it's Dutch since they own Curacao and some other islands around there. Yep. Curacao is our pick."

"Mickey, you're ingenious. Isn't he, Betsy?"

"So very ingenious, yes. And did you figure out what the word *bang* means in Dutch?" asked Betsy.

"Mickey, I've got three lattes getting cold over here!" The barista pointed to the waiting mugs.

"Right there, Angie!" Mickey stood up. "The word *bang* means *afraid* in Dutch."

CHAPTER 29

"I knew that Mickey had juicy clues. And of all the words he heard Catherine utter...*bang*. That word proved true for Catherine both in Dutch and English. Troubling." Betsy placed her empty glass on the table.

Amused, Page recalled who had tapped Mickey as a source for information. She allowed Betsy her self-proclaimed 'atta girl.' "Yep, he sure came through for us, but can you please find some new material or I'm dying my hair auburn to match yours? The blond skit is getting tiresome, besides not being based on any truth. It seems we both are craving a fresh character approach in clue gathering. I'm officially nixing any future blond references." Page laughed, enjoying their light exchange.

"But it never fails us. Why mess with...oh, all right, I'll work on some new argument setups. So, can we get back to Lola? I'm busting to squeal." Betsy eyed the ice left in her glass.

"I see Mickey heading out, so I guess we've gotten all we can from him today. Back to Lola." Page used her straw to stir the melted frappe.

"So, our Lola's a Jersey girl and has worked three years for Brakem. Her ego rivals his, let me tell you. She said if not for her expertise overseeing some big clients' foreign investment accounts, Brakem would be 'skewered.' Her word."

"Whoa, you got her to say all of that about her boss?" asked Page incredulously. "Loyalty is sure in short supply nowadays."

"Oh, believe me, I had to stroke her well-endowed ego aplenty." Betsy shook her head. "I can't abide women like Lola. Still, I acted my part."

"I've witnessed your performances, and not just with suspects, I might add," said Page with a teasing tone as she applied fresh lip gloss.

"I've got more." Betsy watched the barista circle wide to avoid them and gather empty cups. Only mildly distracted, she continued, "Lola had two calls while you were with Brakem. One from someone named Armand. She had trouble communicating with him. Kept saying, 'pardon me.' I bet he's tied to one of those foreign doings." Betsy paused to build drama.

"Bet so. And, the second caller?" prompted Page.

"Was from Evan."

"Holy cow. Good stuff, Bets. So, I ask you why a small beach town attorney would have international clients and accounts? And how involved with Evan is Brakem?"

Betsy jumped in. "I can answer one of those questions. Evan's call was to ask about the time of Catherine's will reading. Know what? Being at the beach keeps me thirsty all the time. How many minutes before we need to be at Garrett's?"

Page glanced at her mother's vintage French watch. "Thirty minutes, give or take. Go ahead. Leave me in suspense and get an encore." Page made shooing gestures.

"Be right back." Betsy hurried to the bar.

She returned with a bottled guava juice and continued, "Next, I pretended to make a call so Lola felt freer to speak with Evan. She tells him there's a snag and she can't tell him when the will and other documents unsealing can happen. It must have gotten him majorly fired up because Lola said the words over and over, 'I understand. I will tell Mr. Brakem.'" Betsy took a swig of her juice. "I almost like this taste."

Page grinned. "Hmm. Evan is pushing for this unsealing. We must wonder why the hurry? I assumed he had the money and not Catherine. Or, maybe she had something else of value he wanted? Still, I'm perplexed. She was young and beautiful. Why hitch herself to this Evan dude if not for the moola?"

"I agree. It doesn't add up. And Mickey confirmed Catherine's from — we guess — Curacao, which also plays into her travel agency performance and needing a fast ticket out of the country. Why the hurry?" Betsy grew silent, mulling things.

"We've got quite a collection of whys that need charting on a suspect board," surmised Page. She tapped her fingers on the chair arm, assessing.

"Are you going to insist we buy another dry-erase board for our clues and tracking? I hate having to hide that blasted thing every time we leave to go somewhere. It's so cumbersome." Betsy groaned, rubbing her un-toned biceps, causing her bangle bracelets to clank.

"Certainly, we need a suspect board. Stop whining already. I'll keep it under my bed if need be. What else did Lola say? Hurry, 'cause I still demand my time to tattle."

Betsy set the juice on the table. "So, after Lola rang off with Evan, she dialed someone else. All she said was she had two new 'super richo clients' to share, and Brakem came out. I tell you, if she'd not been a fast-talking Jersey girl, I'd never gotten that much scoop." Betsy's chair creaked. "Serious diet change call to action soon." She fluffed the biscotti crumbs from her lap. "Back to important matters. Your turn to spill, sista. I did my part."

"You earned a gold star. A big, bright, shiny one. Unfortunately, I didn't fare near as well with Brakem." Page allowed her eleven lines to crease between her brows. The case was proving to be an early challenge, especially with possible shenanigans outside of the United States. For starters, she'd need to go to the University of Google and confirm what Mickey shared about Curacao. There didn't seem to be any glue to bind these suspects or a clear motive to Catherine's death. She had a lovely hodgepodge, a sleuth's curse. *One step at a time,* Page thought, admonishing herself for letting her mind run amuck with frustration. Her guidance would come in due course.

"Helloooo? Come on back. What did you learn?" Betsy pleaded, peeking at her watch.

"Sorry, needed a fast mental recalibration. Well, Brakem acted shocked that I knew about Catherine's death but acknowledged he'd heard, too. What's troubling me is he confessed to only knowing her slightly."

"Big *ha* on his slightly," interjected Betsy.

"I called Catherine's death a murder to mess with his head and got rewarded with a most flustered Brakem. Plus, I interjected some general concerns about the Langes not a fit for Shell Isle." She felt a cold shudder each time she said Brakem's name. "I suppose we can assume Evan told him about the death? I pretended concern about our safety at Hibiscus as if there were some sinister doings nearby, and that motivated me to consider selling and meeting with him." Page paused, recalling her impressions.

"More?" prodded Betsy.

"Well, he tepidly tried to assure me that sinister doings weren't worthy of thought, which leads me to speculate the origin of his shock hearing me say she was murdered. Did he react because he truly didn't know she'd been killed? Or, was his surprise that the shot to her head was deemed not to be a suicide? And that, Betsy, is an important piece of unanswered information not to be forgotten. Seems these folks like suicide for the cause of death too much." Page shifted in her seat, weighing her last words.

"The police are keeping pretty quiet. That's puzzling, too. You had to call Steve's bluff to get him to validate that you knew Catherine didn't take her own life. I know your guidance is spot on. Any insights forthcoming?" Betsy drank the last bit of juice.

"Give me a few moments to get centered, and I'll see." The inklings, nudges, and intuiting were a dynamic mixture that, once activated, led her on a merry chase for justice to be served.

Betsy took her leave to the ladies' room, giving Page the opportunity for discernment.

~*~

"Good, you're back. I sense Brakem is flirting with some menacing activities and that the price for this involvement has escalated beyond his control. He's an involved suspect, and we probably need to steer a wide course from him. That's all I have for us now."

Betsy's lips puckered, and she blew exasperated feelings into the air. "I gotta tell you. This is the most fragmented murder case we've landed. At this rate, we may need two charting boards. Come on. It's showtime again. My turn to have the lead role." Betsy grabbed her straw tote bag and ignored her frumpy attire in the window's reflection.

Walking down the sidewalk, Page drew close to Betsy and planted a carefree grin on her face. "Seems we've found ourselves an unwelcome admirer watching from across the street."

CHAPTER 30

"My stars and garters, we've hooked one suspect into our net. That was fast and too easy. I don't like it," Betsy offered, having caught a glimpse of their admirer…Brakem.

"And hooked a lot sooner than I'd like, too. Looks like my words pricked his worry gene. I think it's time we believe Steve's statement these aren't nice people." Page took a step.

"Well, I like the sound of your believing, Steve," said a familiar male voice.

Page and Betsy turned to see their neighbor a mere few feet away. Dressed casually in denim jeans and a shirt advertising the nearby surf shop, no one would guess he was anyone but a local living the laid-back island life.

"Afternoon, ladies. So, how 'bout answering believable Steve two questions?" He didn't pause. "Number one, what exactly do you believe that I've said — ?"

"Hey there, Steve," Page jumped in pleasantly. "Well, just tha — "

"Hold up, Page. You must wait for question two." The amusement in Steve's voice reached his eyes. "And, number two is where have you two been and where are you going next?"

"That's three questions by my count," interjected Betsy, not wanting to be left out.

Steve tendered Betsy with a glare, then quickly settled on Page.

Not deterred by his demeanor, Betsy continued, "Well, I guess you could make it part A and B of question two. Don't you think, Page?"

"Easily, if we were inclined to answer. We're not. Bye, Tanner." Page linked Betsy's arm with hers and started walking away. The man sure knew how to age in slow time. All the muscles showing were too well defined in her opinion. He worked out too hard. Surfed way too much.

Undeterred, Steve jogged ahead, forcing them to stop. "Let me help you since my questions seem not to your liking. For starters, I bet my warning that you stay out of this investigation and any people that might be involved, hasn't been heeded. And now, you have a reason to believe my advice, which leads me to question number two. Part A's answer is that you were at Brakem's office stirring up who knows what mischief, and now the sleazeball is following you. And that fact isn't in your best interest. How'd I do so far?"

Page's anger meter soared. "I'd say you are a talented observer and super annoying interloper. What is your role exactly with this case? An investigator? An agent? What are you called, anyway? I want to know how I'm to address you," inquired a frustrated Page with a fist clenched at her side. The man's interference, along with Brakem's observing them, was too much. Men were bothersome.

"Page, please, we need to go." Betsy looked at the clock at the courthouse.

Steve ignored Betsy. "To answer your question, Page, you may continue to call me Steve. Titles are of no matter to me."

Steve noted the surroundings and Brakem's eyes on them while talking on his cell phone. Engagement was needed to have the creep see Page as a fun and flighty type. He pulled a startled Page into his chest and planted a kiss on her full lips. He didn't have to try and make the act hot enough to melt a glacier. That happened effortlessly. Those too-kissable lips had messed with his head more than once if he were honest. He expected this exercise would banish the desire and give him peace. It didn't.

Steve drew away a few inches to whisper in her ear, "This show is for Brakem. Kiss me back now and make it real steamy if you're capable."

Page saw Betsy's mouth open wider than the Mississippi. She decided right there on the sidewalk in front of everyone and anyone that she'd show this infuriating guy that she'd perfected steamy in high school.

The sleuth stood on her tiptoes and, with one arm, pulled Steve into her lair. She hoped whenever he thought about steamy kissing in the future, her face would flash in his mind, and she meant to imprint it, starting now. Page let her kissing aptitude work its magic. What she didn't count on was his lips returning the favor. The only saving for Page was being the first to push away. She gathered her cool quickly and offered him her best-bored smile that didn't match the passion in her eyes.

Steve hadn't anticipated the effect of this pint-sized, blond spitfire. Words stayed inside him while his betraying body had turned into a nuclear reactor. His sunglasses, now askew, fell off his head and landed on the sidewalk. Anger covered his face, confusing anger.

Not daring to look in Betsy's direction, Page focused on the man still only inches away. "Now, if you'll excuse us, we must talk to our insurance agent about homeowner rates should my cousin decide to buy a place at the beach. Consider question two answered. Close your trap, Betsy. Come on. We're late." Page somehow willed her feet to move. Her hormones begged her to stand in place and do an encore of steamy. She allowed hormones must be trouble at any age. This fact, a fifty-year-old flushed-faced Page, was forced to admit on the streets of Shell Isle while her legs kept walking to their next baiting.

Betsy had moved past shock to dialogue. "My gosh, Bogart and Bacall were frigid next to the two of you. Where's my fan? And what the heck was all that about anyway?" Betsy fumbled in her purse for the fan while trying to keep up.

"Not now. Later. I'll explain later. Is he following us?" Page refused to look back and give her nervy neighbor any satisfaction that she cared what he was doing or had just done. The very cheek of the guy to land a kiss and ask her to deliver another one.

"Nope. Brakem's still sitting on the bench across the street, eyes locked this way. Guess we're safe. He's just watching, for now, at least." Betsy's breathing was labored.

"Not Brakem watching, you ninny, Steve," said Page between clenched teeth. The interaction still had her breathless like her cousin trying to keep pace, albeit for a different reason.

"Ah, Steve. Well, he's standing in the same spot you left him, the poor, poor guy. Look, slow down before I need resuscitation and then a cold shower from this whole experience. Geez, Page, kissing hot on the sidewalk. Whatever supplement you're taking, I want some."

Page burst into laughter. "Thanks, Betsy. I can always count on you to provide comic relief." She shortened her strides, trusting Steve had gotten what he needed. Answers and a tutorial on her version of passionate. What happened to her predictable life of running a mountain village's bookstore? Was she even missing her mountain life? That question needed postponing. Page forced her mind to focus on the present moment. A murderer was out and about, and — horrors — may be surveilling them now.

"Time to get it together. We're close to Garrett's office." Page pointed toward his door.

Betsy set an even slower pace, which allowed for rummaging in her handbag, this time for breath mints. She offered one to Page.

"I could have used this a few minutes ago. Thank you very much." Page tossed the mint into her mouth, enjoying her cousin's shocked face.

"Well, count on me to keep them handy and maybe a hose just in case. And, that 'later' you said, to postpone explaining that kissing spectacle is coming sooner than you think." Betsy opened the door to Garrett's.

A familiar but startling silhouette waited inside the door.

"Garrett, I expect you to handle this problem for me immediately. You know what I need you to do. It's called your job." Gwen breezed past, oblivious to Page and Betsy's presence.

CHAPTER 31

The cousins watched the door close forcibly behind Gwen. When they turned back, Garrett had disappeared into the back-office area, leaving a worried-face receptionist with a short pixie hairstyle sitting behind a desk. A brass nameplate identified her as Ina Funk.

"May I…I assist you?" she asked, flustered.

Betsy stepped forward. "Hello, Ina. I'm Betsy Ross, and I have an appointment with Mr. Garrett."

The past middle-aged receptionist's spirits seemed to lift, and she offered a weak smile. "Yes, seems we both got shortchanged in the name department. My name is pronounced with a short vowel over both letters. Like saying 'in a minute.' What about your friend's name?"

Betsy chuckled. "Oh, she got short-changed too. She's Page Wright. Her mom was a successful book editor with a quirky sense of word humor."

Page made a face at her cousin. "Hi there, Ina. I'm just going to sit over there while the possible descendant of who sewed our beloved Old Glory, speaks with Mr. Garrett."

Ms. Funk hooted, delighting in the women's wit. "You both must be a barrel of laughs with some wine in you. Seems we three like using our maiden names. You remind me of my best friend, Naomi Ziegler. We're always kibitzing about who makes the best brisket. She keeps trying to bribe our butcher to sell me an inferior cut of beef. We can't convince our husbands or friends to vote for which one prepares the most flavorful roast. We've been at a standoff for decades. That Naomi. Full of stunts." Ina's fingers smoothed her chestnut-colored hair.

The receptionist's jovial demeanor encouraged Betsy. "She does sound like a real trickster, your Naomi," agreed Betsy. "Okay if I take a seat, and you can tell Mr. Garrett I'm here?"

Page pretended to be fascinated with a book on touring Shell Isle. She was using the time to think about how to play Ms. Funk. The woman had disappeared to do Betsy's bidding.

"Aren't you the witty one? Descendent from the sewer of our flag," chided Betsy.

Page closed the book. "Well, you might be related distantly."

"Humph. At least Ms. Funk will be easy to pump, unlike Lola. One question should get her yapping. And, so you know, I'm still replaying that X-rated performance you and Steve staged on the sidewalk. I predict that your reputation will be toast by sundown. I can hear Aunt Tilly chastising you for lack of decorum."

"Please, I'm much too old for that kind of reputation." Page punctuated her words with a pop on Betsy's arm.

"We shall see," said Betsy, grinning. "Shush, here comes our Ina."

"Betsy, you can go back. Mr. Garrett's door is the third one on the left." The receptionist returned to her desk.

Page watched Ina staple a few packets and stuff them into envelopes—a task that indeed allowed for some harmless chit-chat. "So, Ms. Funk, tell me how long you have worked at Garrett Insurance? I suspect you're his right arm and leg." Page let the book rest in her lap—time to go to work and hopefully gain some knowledge about the woman's boss.

"Oh, please call me Ina. Let me think. Gosh, it's going on ten years. And you're one smart cookie noticing my role and all so quickly. I tell my husband all of the time Mr. Garrett couldn't find a single form without me."

"I'm sure that's a fact. Your work sounds valuable to him."

"The man hates computers. Refuses to turn his on." Ina lowered her tattling voice. "The one on his desk is just for show."

"That's too funny. I bet you've met some interesting clients, too." Page was warming up.

"You can say that again. I remember one old coot living out of state used to call every morning to ask me if there had been any break-ins reported at his beach house. This business went on for a month until his divorce was final. It seems his wife had threatened to strip the place bare if he didn't pay some significant alimony." Ina refilled the stapler. "Yeah, I've got quite a collection of tales living at Shell Isle and working here."

"Hmm, sounds like that man had a lot of drama around that uncoupling." Page grinned. "Men can be so dumb. Take my neighbor Evan Lange and his much younger wife, Catherine. If ever—"

"Oh, those two are something all right. Talk about conflicting agendas." Ina rolled her eyes.

"Yes, Catherine does love her baubles. I bet Mr. Garrett is busy adding riders to her policies weekly." Page kept her voice light and words matter of fact for the next essential baiting.

"Riders for Catherine?" Ina frowned, thinking. "Not her. You've got the wrong Lange for bauble riders. I probably shouldn't have said that."

Page smiled. Time to shift to a safe topic. "So, it's just you and Mr. Garrett in this office?"

Ina relaxed again. "Yes, we have a part-time bookkeeper that steps in on Friday afternoons so that I can play Maj Jong with the girls. Mr. Garrett insists that he wants to keep me happy working here." Ina stood. "Excuse me. I have some envelopes to weigh in the back room."

"Of course. I'll get back into Shell Isle's delights." Page pulled the book in front of her face and listened to Ina's flats click down the hallway.

She hadn't gleaned much, except Garrett didn't cotton to technology and seemed to rely heavily on Ina Funk. The puzzler was Catherine didn't have jewelry riders, despite her demand of one the other evening. And, more importantly, what did Ina mean when she said Page had the wrong Lange?

Page's worry frown appeared. Wait a Shell Isle moment. Could Ina have meant it was the wrong Lange relation and not another Lange unrelated living on the island? If so, maybe Gwen or Evan were the other Lange. Or, there could be more family of Langes lurking about that hadn't surfaced in Page's sphere yet? Her thinking felt cloudy, and when that happened, she knew to stop forcing. She didn't possess enough information to surmise much of anything other than Garrett acted meek and passive. Now Brakem, he was textbook on aggressive and ego-driven. And what had she said to worry the lawyer enough to be watching them? That question, no doubt, would activate her insomnia.

CHAPTER 32

"The man's a dullard. A real simp. A total waste of fifteen good plant-shopping minutes." Betsy slammed the SUV's door with conviction.

A relieved Page didn't see Tanner or Brakem when they exited the insurance office nor bother to enlighten a flustered Betsy. She started the engine. Upon reflection, the afternoon's sleuthing had been…stimulating. They'd gathered some valuable facts worthy of being on their board. Mickey's sharing was the dividend. "Listen, we can't expect all the suspects to be dark and menacing. There's no challenge there."

"I guess, but I swear that Garrett isn't capable of even providing me an accurate estimate of insurance costs for a small oceanfront cottage. I used Hibiscus as an example for pricing and made a point to tell him I couldn't afford anything palatial like the Lange home. The fool sat in his big executive chair, rocking, mumbling something about beach erosion affecting current insurance rates. But, mind you, he couldn't give me even a percentage of that price increase."

"Wow." Page pondered Betsy's assessment.

"It's like the man's never written a policy. See what I mean? A buffoon," sighed Betsy, running out of Garrett bashing steam. She popped another breath mint.

"I admit it does sound like Garrett has dropped a few notches on our suspect list, but he could also be pretending dumbness? And unfortunately, Ina Funk didn't offer me much either."

Page shared with her cousin the little bit of info garnered

and her puzzlement over another Lange liking jewelry riders.

Both women agreed to let the sleuthing take a siesta while they shopped for hibiscus plants and a suspect board.

~*~

"Didn't we find the most vibrant flame red hibiscus?" Betsy stood admiring the plants lined up like soldiers along the front of the cottage. "I want a lipstick shade the same color."

"You already own a dozen shades of red, you vixen, though I agree the hibiscus plants are a nice addition. Now, if they could only plant themselves," replied Page with a heavy exhale. She'd rather plant mint or parsley. Less exacting on the knees and back. Betsy was the stronger and taller one despite her being out of shape.

"The gardening needs to wait until mañana. My mind's fixed on our take-out dinner." Betsy held the pizza box in the air. "After I devour my half, you'll find me in the hammock. We've had an intense afternoon of baiting, and I'm bushed. Hurry. You set the table."

Page laid the placemats on the white wicker glass table, allowing the pizza box to act as the centerpiece. Lost in thought, she arranged the printed seat cushions. They had suspects that each possessed some interesting and disturbing connections with each other. Maybe putting everyone on the board might indicate the next step. Page relaxed as her eyes glanced over at Steve's bungalow. No doubt Betsy would exact an accounting of their kissing episode before the sun went down.

Page's attention directed next door, somehow manifested Barnacle running for the porch. Within seconds, his paw pounded loudly against the screen door.

"Is that thunder?" yelled Betsy from the kitchen.

"Nope, just our friendly Barnacle's paw acting as a doorbell." Page rose and cracked the door open. "Smelled the pizza, huh?"

The dog gave a deep woof and, wrapped himself around the base of the table and sniffed.

"Let me guess. He's hoping for droppings?" offered Betsy, parking two glasses with layers of colored liquid by each plate.

Page eyed the concoction. Admittedly, her cousin could ruin ice tea. "Yep, we've got a pizza lover here. Sooo, what's in my glass?" Page dipped her index finger into the liquid and placed a few tiny drops to her lips.

"Doesn't it make a lovely presentation? The bottom layer is espresso. Next, we have strawberry syrup, whipped cashew milk, and that's frothy pineapple juice looking sunny on the top. Hurry and look in case the layers sink to the bottom." Betsy put the straw to her lips and sipped.

"Sunny pineapple juice?" Page's stomach fluttered. She glanced at Barnacle, knowing he'd be of no help this go around. She placed the straw at the bottom of the glass and hoped what came up was pure coffee.

"Oh, aren't you smart, drinking one layer at a time? And, I was going to stir mine." Betsy pushed her straw further down.

"Yes, smart me." Page grabbed a giant slice of pizza and broke another slice into pieces for Barnacle, who figured the napkin on the floor had his name on it. "Here you go, Barn. This treat is to make up for my last disastrous food toss," Page whispered.

"So, Barnacle here is a reminder that you owe me an explanation for the sidewalk spectacle between his owner and you. I've waited long enough." Betsy re-positioned the pepperoni to her liking and took a huge bite.

Page shifted her tone to lighthearted. "It's not that big of a deal. The spectacle, as you call it, was Steve's way of trying to throw Brakem off from thinking I had any real interest or aptitude for murder doings. You know, play up the fact that I had more fun things to focus on. Anyway, Steve whispered to play along and kiss him back. Ridiculous plan. Even more, ridiculous man."

If you ask me, you both were showcasing your baser desires. The man is certainly not lacking in that department," Betsy snickered. "Next time, I'd be happy to stand in for you."

"Remember, Ms. Ross. You are off all males. A nice long hiatus from relationships. Besides, there won't be a need for another performance." Page almost felt regret wrap around those words.

~*~

"Holler when you want my input on the board. I know how you like to get things recorded before you invite me to play name-that-clue," said Betsy, turning a page in her novel.

"You and Gertrude keep enjoying each other's company. This project is going to take a while."

"Okay, but first one question. Which suspect's name gets to be red? That always tells me who has your attention." Betsy pointed to the marker in her cousin's hand.

"Not sure. I haven't a hint of the murderer's identity. So, I guess no red yet." Page laid the marker to the side, releasing a frustrated sigh.

"Heads up, Page. Here comes the master of Barnacle and kissing."

Neither Page nor her body desired another encounter with Steve Tanner this day. Her blood pressure number still felt questionable. She darted behind the drapes out of sight. "Deal with him. I'm busy."

"My pleasure. Hiya, Steve. Come on in." Betsy kept her grin in place.

"Is he...yes, he is. Barnacle, come." Steve held the door open and pointed.

Barnacle, head down, streaked past them.

"Sorry. It seems he's conquered the screen door latch at my place."

"Not a problem. We were gonna bring him home once we drew straws," replied an amused Betsy.

Steve caught Betsy glancing at her waiting novel and understood. "Well, be seeing you. Oh, and tell Ms. Drew, hiding behind the door and likely listening, I expect you both to steer clear of anyone involved with the Langes. This is not optional." Steve let the door slam.

"I'll tell her. By the way, Barnacle's had dinner." Betsy latched the screen door.

"Dinner?" Steve looked back, perplexed.

"Italian," shouted Betsy with a wave.

~*~

"Betsy, say goodnight to Dowager Gertrude and come inside," Page called out, hoping their discussion might illuminate something helpful to the case.

"Goodnight, Dowager. Don't fret about your stolen jewels. Sir Pincher will find them, that is, if he wasn't the one who stole them." She tossed the book on the table.

Betsy entered the room where Page waited crossed-legged on the area rug and collapsed down next to her. "Begin post haste. Let's make some progress." Betsy tried and failed to tuck her legs but instead opted for a large cushion to sit on.

Page lifted an eyebrow. "Settled, princess? Suspects first. Evan, Garrett, Brakem, Ty, Gwen, and I threw Seedy in at this stage. Agreed?"

"Yip." Betsy nodded, focused on the board's entries.

"Next up is the motive. All we've got is Catherine threatening Garrett with blackmail. We're clueless about any other strong motive than dislike. Agreed?"

"Yip."

"You sound like Barnacle. Okay, info bullets next and not in order. Do you want to get something to drink before I go on? I hear you smacking, which usually means—"

"That double pepperoni pizza is messing with me." Betsy returned from the kitchen with a bottle of mineral water. "I'm ready for bullets. Fire away."

"Almost funny. Here's what we know: Catherine was desperate to book a flight for the night she was murdered. She took a large manilla envelope from Garrett's office and dropped a smaller envelope in Brakem's box, all hours before the three met at her home. With me?" asked Page.

"Every step."

"Again, we know that Gwen, Garrett, and possibly Brakem loathed Catherine. I'm not sure how Evan felt about his wife, but that's something to unearth. His emotions could run from mild caring to strong hate. We know that Ty was her do-boy and is acquainted with Seedy. No idea how these two heavies felt about Catherine. We know that the police are investigating the Langes and others unknown to us. Also, Garrett was asked to falsify a jewelry rider. Next, we know Evan's upset about items or papers missing from his safe." Page pointed to each bullet, tapping the board with her marker.

"Actually, we know quite a bit this early in the investigation. I think our deducing skills are pretty decent all considering," offered Betsy. "What else?"

"Well, we know that Catherine wanted Evan's will tweaked by Brakem. And it's plausible he's dealing with both shady business accounts and people. Remember, he was aware of Catherine's death but acted surprised when I said the word 'murdered.' What else? Help me finish." Page laid the marker in the board's tray, letting frustration take control.

"Well, we have Mickey overhearing Catherine speak the word 'bang,' meaning afraid in Dutch and ironically the sound of a gun firing in our native tongue," supplied Betsy.

"That's right." Page wrote on the board. "Give me more on today."

"We have Lola telling Evan there are problems with getting his hands on some documents and the will. And Armand, the caller we suspect might be tied to Brakem in shady foreign dealings. Plus, Lola called someone and informed them she had two rich clients' names to share. That may or may not relate to the murder. And Ina Funk said you had the wrong Lange asking for riders. No idea what to make of that yet. Good so far?"

"Very good. We can't forget hearing Gwen and Evan talk about having Catherine shipped home and having to pretend to be sad. They're to dine maybe tomorrow evening on the yacht to celebrate." Page wrote her words as she spoke them to Betsy. "Whatever we missed, we can fill in later. Why don't we let this simmer 'cause I'm not seeing obvious connections? Let's hope the three necessities of motive, means, and opportunity will present soon."

"Sounds good to me. I'm ready to tuck in." Betsy yawned and stood.

They each moved silently to turn out lights and secure the doors. Betsy wandered to her room while Page went to close the kitchen blind and got an inkling to look out. Parked under the street lamp, Brakem sat crouched in his luxury sedan.

Page tapped on Betsy's bedroom door. "Brakem's parked outside. Make sure your blinds are closed. Nighty."

Betsy cracked open her door. "What's with this guy showing up at Hibiscus? And all you've got to say is 'nighty'? Boy, am I glad Steve Tanner lives next door."

"Don't start fretting. I bet Steve knows he's out there, too. Brakem is a fool, a scared fool. Sleep well." Page smiled when she heard Betsy releasing the blind cord and cussing a tangle. She expected more intuiting would greet her the next day, but for tonight, she'd try and release the worry of Brakem watching. Steve's kissing ruse must have failed, at least with the attorney.

CHAPTER 33

Humpday morning held promise to Page's eyes. The promise of a peaceful time gardening with Betsy and that an inkling might unlock the next door she needed to walk through.

While Catherine Lange certainly wasn't beloved, her life still mattered. The desperate person who judged that not true would be identified soon enough. And Page had learned to trust in that outcome. She paused at her cousin's bedroom. All quiet meant Betsy hadn't stirred herself or, thankfully, any skillet.

The clap of distant thunder hurried Page to the front door with Larson's birthday card in hand. She'd check with him later to make sure the bookshop hadn't morphed into a meeting place for the local Mountain Brook Trout Club. That thought brought a smile and surprise that she wasn't missing her shop.

Page lingered on the cottage's front porch, taking pleasure in her surroundings. She gazed at the sky, noting the storm clouds moving away at an impressive clip. The rain missing them meant hibiscus planting awaited. The sleuth watched a group of young boys pulling a wagon with fishing gear in the direction of the pier. The senior couple who lived in the newly restored bungalow on the other side of Hibiscus waved as they set sprinklers to welcome an expanding family of marigolds.

Again, she wondered if Shell Isle could offer her a new path. She'd forever miss the love shared with her husband, but dormant emotions seemed to be stirring. Was now the time to chart a course away from her mountain life and bookstore? She gave the gnawing question free rein and admitted the beach had always been the place where she drew joy and contentment.

Was she game to embrace becoming a full-time beach resident? Perhaps. But how might she fill her days? She'd learned long ago, when answers didn't present, to wait for them to come in the perfect moment. Let the rhythms of life play her song, and she'd keep listening.

Page cast her ever-watchful eyes around once more. Relieved to see Brakem gone and Steve's SUV tucked into his parking place, she sauntered out to her mailbox, depositing the birthday card. The urge for a short walk dropped into her mind. Taking note of the sneakers on her feet, she shrugged and turned on the sidewalk toward the direction of the Lange home.

"What are you about at eight o'clock in the morning?" Steve closed the SUV's hatch and stood, arms folded, watching her approach.

"Geez. You scared the puddin' out of me. Must you always act so stealthy?" Page halted.

Steve chuckled. "Again, I ask where are you headed and why?"

Page blew out an annoyed breath and raised her sunglasses to make direct eye contact with her too-nosey neighbor. She chose to ignore that he looked like a shower recently claimed him and a razor awakened to show off his finely chiseled jaw. "It's called a morning walk. A simple walk. No motive at all, except if you want to count the need for exercise and appreciating some quiet moments away from Betsy." Page took a step.

Steve touched Page's arm. "Hold on. I was about to take a walk myself. I'll join you." He whistled for Barnacle.

"What? Seriously, I don't want a walking buddy. I want solitude. Hey there, Barn." Page bent down to hug the dog.

"Oh, I can be silent, or perhaps you can tell me all about life in the mountain village you call home." Steve and Barnacle joined her, setting the pace.

Page released an exasperated breath. "I guess I don't have

a choice of your company." She clipped her hair back, trying to ignore the man's proximity and the way his forearm kept flexing as he adjusted Barnacle's leash. Page finally understood what a manly smell meant, all citrusy and way too masculine — blasted pheromones. This guy spelled lethal in all the right ways. Another inkling interrupted her hormone's rampage. Alerted, she went silent as they approached the Lange home.

The two caught the movement at the same instant. Steve dragged Page behind a parked car. "Quiet. I need to watch this," He touched Barnacle's muzzle, signaling the dog.

Page crouched, still able to observe the scene unfolding. Steve's arm found her waist. "What are you doing?" she hissed, trying to push his arm away.

"Be still. I'm steadying you," Steve replied, never letting his eyes leave the two men in conversation.

Page accepted his answer and the steadying. She was far more interested in the heated exchange of words happening between Garrett and Evan.

A nervous Garrett dialed a number on his cell. Evan grabbed the phone, disconnecting the caller, and then used the phone to punctuate his next words on Garrett's chest. The insurance agent tried to back away, but Evan advanced menacingly.

"Listen up, you spineless excuse for a man. We were robbed, and I want a claim filed by noon. My safe was emptied, and if you don't take action, I'll be emptying that useless brain of yours into a garbage dumpster. Getting the picture?" Evan shoved Garrett against his vehicle and pivoted toward the house.

Garrett found his voice. "I'll…I'll take care of this just as you directed, Mr. Lange," the insurance agent stammered back. Garrett found his handkerchief and mopped up enough sweat to fill a tidal pool.

"That's our manly Garrett, all right," mumbled Page. "Oh my gosh. Detective Koch is pulling into the Lange driveway. He's blocked Garrett's escape. Lucky me, I get to witness this."

Steve's face registered entertainment. "I'm betting you're here because you got one of those hunches." Steve propelled Page to a standing position. "Go on with your walk. I need to join Koch."

"Come on, Tanner. I know how to conduct myself around an active investigation. Let me tag along and prove my worth." Page planted her feet. "Wait a sec, did you know the Langes were robbed?" prodded Page.

"Of course, I knew about the theft. We're also pursuing the burglary investigation since it occurred the night Catherine died. Listen, Page, it's too dangerous for you to be seen by another suspect. You've already got Brakem flustered. Do me a favor and take Barnacle on your walk, and I might give that sleuthing head of yours an update later." Steve grinned and motioned her toward the sidewalk.

"Oh, all right. And depending on what information you share with me, I may be inclined to apprise you with a few interesting snippets of my own. Come on, Barnacle. It's only a matter of a day or so before your owner wises up and begs for my help." Page grabbed the leash, leaving Steve to digest her words.

CHAPTER 34

Steve sighed, watching Page's retreat, and forced his attention on the two men up ahead. "Koch," said Steve with a curt nod. "Mind if I join in?"

"Join away. I've got some questions for Garrett. I just left his office with Ina telling me where to find him. Glad to have you add your brand of interrogating," said Koch with a sneer directed at a flustered Garrett.

The insurance agent's eyes darted between both imposing men a mere foot away. Garrett's hand found his handkerchief again. "Look, I need to go. I've...I've got back-to-back appointments and clients waiting at the office."

Steve blocked Garrett's move toward the vehicle's door. "Tell you what, Mr. Garrett. You give us the right answers, and we'll let you be on your way. Of course, if the heat is too much for you, we can all take a nice ride down to the station. Koch's office has plenty of AC. Right, Koch?"

Koch chuckled. "Yep, I've got air conditioning that I'm happy to share."

"Okay, okay, guys, but can we at least move our vehicles away from Evan's home? I don't need him witnessing your grilling me. And maybe you could act friendly now like we're friends or something? I'm sure he's watching. Help me out here."

Koch and Steve made a show of laughing and shaking hands. Garrett patted Koch on the back and nodded to Steve, smiling.

"Enough of this buddy business. Tell you what, Garrett, I'm going to slip inside and talk with Evan. Why don't you and

Tanner meet at the pier and continue this little visit? Work for you, Steve?" asked Koch.

"Yep, Garrett and I will head on to the pier. Do offer our condolences again to poor distraught Evan. I will drop by the office later and update you on my progress."

Koch grabbed his laptop from the passenger seat and headed toward the front door.

"Move, Garrett. I thought you wanted to do this elsewhere and get to your office."

"I...I do. Thanks. Right behind you, mister...agent... detective...?" stammered Garrett.

Steve ignored him and jogged next door to get his SUV.

~*~

The inkling came as soon as Page walked away from Steve. She'd done the fastest power walk ever. Poor Barnacle was panting from the heat and effort. She rewarded the dog with water from her bottle. She glanced at her watch, guessing she'd left Hibiscus no more than fifteen minutes ago, and hoped Betsy was still asleep.

Page pivoted, recognizing the reason for the nudge. "Come on, Barn. Duty calls." She covered the few yards unobserved while her smart canine companion stayed mute. She'd find the dog a good reward for his cooperation.

A smile plastered, Page spoke. "Steve, it's about time you arrived. Barnacle and I have been positively baking out here waiting for our boat ride." Page cozied up to her neighbor.

Steve's eyes turned fiery, but his words hid the anger. "Sorry, babe, I'm running a bit late. I need a few more minutes to chat with Mr. Garrett here."

The insurance agent wore his baffled look well—a state he seemed to reside in by all observations.

"Hello, Mr. Garrett. We met yesterday." Page extended her hand only to let it fall by her side when Garrett didn't move.

"Remember? I came to your office with my cousin Betsy Ross. She had an appointment with you."

"Yes, yes. Of course. Your cousin is interested in buying a beach place." Garrett's cell phone rang. He silenced it along with himself.

"Listen, Garrett, I have one more question, and you can be on your way. "Where were you Sunday night between the hours of, say, nine and eleven? Just need to establish everyone's whereabouts." Steve turned his focus on Garret's body language.

The insurance agent's handkerchief worked overtime. "Why, I was home working in my study. I had some new forms that needed completion. I hate to keep my clients waiting. Always want them happy, you know?" Garrett fidgeted.

Page feigned a bored look.

"Can anyone verify you were home?" Steve pushed.

"My...my wife was there. Yes, Beverly was most certainly home, but then she is most evenings."

"Okay, I think that's about all for now. You can go." Steve shot Page a glance.

"Umm, detective, why question me when it was a burglary gone wrong? I'm just the Langes' insurance agent." Garrett, realizing the questioning was over, seemed to find some gumption.

Steve leaned into Garrett's face. "I never said anything about a burglary. Have yourself a safe day out there, Mr. Garrett, and do call us if you can think of anything that would be of help."

Garrett tugged on his collar. "Yes, sir. I surely will." He turned and hurried to his sedan.

Steve's eyes, full of amusement, landed on Page. "Boat ride, huh? Well, let's go if that's what your heart desires, Page Wright. I aim to please. And while we're enjoying our time sailing about, you can enlighten me. Starting with why were you and my dog at the pier waiting? What information are you keeping

from me? Should make for an interesting sail, don't you think?"
Steve crossed his arms, waiting for the sleuth's reply.

CHAPTER 35

"Sorry, Captain Tanner, I don't have time for a sailing excursion. Betsy's probably having fits wondering about my whereabouts. Though, I'd appreciate a ride back to Hibiscus. And I definitely feel inclined for a mutual information exchange soon." Page motioned Barnacle to the back seat and hopped in the passenger side. She'd let Steve noodle awhile about what led her to witness the conversation between him and the weasel Garrett.

Steve settled behind the wheel. "You're stomping all over my patience and good mood. Okay, let's get you back to that cousin, who I can only hope has prepared you a spicy karmic pancake in your absence." Steve laughed, then added, "And I'm giving you a raincheck on sailing with me."

Page ignored the sailing taunt. Other things bothered her far more.

Barnacle's owner maneuvered around the vacationers, emptying their vehicles of beach gear in the parking lot. Steve glanced over to see if the discerning woman sitting next to him caught Brakem watching them. He'd pay the attorney a little visit and see why he was so fascinated with their doings and encourage him to find other ways to occupy his time.

"Hibiscus Cottage. Out you go, Page. Good luck with the culinary delights waiting for you." Steve's eyes glinted.

"I'd invite you to join us, but know you have suspects to check on...like our persistent friend Brakem parked at the pier. Give him my warmest regards." Page closed the SUV's door and walked around to Steve's side to deliver one final jab. "And if I were you, I'd pay a visit to our insurance agent's wife. Garrett lied to you."

"How do you know Garrett's lying?" Steve hollered back.

Page turned and shrugged, disappearing through the cottage's door.

"Where have you been, Page Wright? I came out to the kitchen, and the coffee maker was cold." Betsy appeared dressed for gardening. Worn denim pedal pushers and a faded oversized man's shirt showed her earnest desire to dig. The signature straw bonnet rested on the kitchen island next to a bottle of sunscreen. "So, what ya been up to, kiddo?"

"I acted on an inkling that took me on an amazing walk. I will explain while we eat. I'm famished. What do I smell in the oven?" Page moved warily toward the cooker, peering inside the oven's window. Is that a casserole bubbling away? For breakfast?"

"Yes, for breakfast." Betsy grabbed the oven mitt. "Go seat yourself, and I'll bring your plate, Sherlocka."

Page's panic awoke when Betsy claimed a large metal spatula. "Whoa, make my serving small…really small." She felt plenty leery of a breakfast casserole, especially if Betsy birthed it. Blast Tanner. The man had called this latest culinary debacle to her.

"There you go. Tuck in." Betsy placed both their plates on the counter and took a seat. "You're going to beg for this recipe." Uncharacteristically, she waited for Page to take her first bite. "Well?"

"Hmm. This is delicious. Is this like baked hash browns with onions, peppers, and tomato chunks? And what is this creamy cheese lacing the top?" Page savored another surprise taste of good karma. "Outstanding, Betsy."

Betsy paused to preen. "A winner, huh? The cheese is smoked gouda. I coaxed the recipe from a chef in Norway. He was such a cutie pie in that white cap of his. Where ya going?" asked Betsy, craning her neck around.

"To get more, of course. I need extra sustenance if we're going to be planting bushes later."

~*~

Shovel in hand, Page lifted the sand out of the first hole. She'd just detailed to Betsy the morning's events with Steve as their gardening day unfolded. "Don't you see? Somehow, we've got to break inside this case. We're on the outside and not privy to the suspects targeted and clues the police are working. Evan's reported a theft. What role, if any, did a burglary play on the night of Catherine's death? Maybe Evan took advantage of Catherine's death and added another ingredient to the mix. Money. I mean, there's so much chatter about jewelry riders and such. Maybe the break-in was staged to get some insurance money. And then, there's the strong possibility her death is tied to some bad guys in Curacao and the theft was a ruse. Or, there could have been incriminating papers of some sort. I don't see this guy Armand making our suspect board yet. He's the unknown."

Betsy pursed her lips as if a persimmon had landed in her mouth. "Too many dastardly people and actions are weaving into our clues. I'm confounded."

"You're right, Bets. This confounding case feels like a maze. And guessing wastes our energy and time. We need to find a way to gain access to the investigation. Tanner did promise to exchange some info, but I'm expecting it to be one-sided. He's not proving helpful, only annoying."

"Agreed, but Koch and Tanner think we're nothing more than eavesdroppers and bumblers. How can we impress them with your special gift and our abilities to solve crimes?" Betsy frowned, not liking how she'd labeled them.

"Put the hibiscus in this hole, will ya?" Page waited for her cousin to maneuver the wheelbarrow closer. "I'm thinking on what you just said. Pretty insightful and, alas, truthful too."

"The part about us being eavesdroppers and bumblers?

Because I'm rethinking…"

"Hush. We aren't like that. I'm talking about how it's time we prove ourselves as talented sleuths. I need a sign, another inkling, or a nudge to direct me. I can't intuit without those doors opening first." Page felt the unwelcome frustration envelop her thinking while she shoveled dirt in the hole and onto her new sneakers. Page released an impressive string of expletives.

"Ah, Page, don't despair. You'll be shown something soon. I just know —"

"Ladies. Am I interrupting gardening time?" Steve noticed the remaining bushes waiting for planting.

"As a matter of fact," Betsy quieted, seeing the shovel taken from Page's hand.

"Tell you what. I'm going to prove how neighborly I can be. I'll plant these three remaining hibiscuses, and then I'm going to deliver on my earlier promise to you, Page."

Betsy could read men, even this complex one. Hanging on to them was her failing. She kept her laughter stowed. "What promise is our helpful neighbor talking about, dear cousin?"

Steve jumped in before Page could throw up flack. "Oh, I promised Page a sail on my sloop. There's no chop today, so how about you walk over to my place around five o'clock? Bring your beach bag and appetite."

Page struggled to find words to decline the outing and whatever type of appetite he was alluding to her bringing. "I'm sure sailing —"

"What Page means to say is she's sure sailing and a tasty meal will be sublime, and she thanks you for the invite and help with planting. Right, Page?" replied Betsy, the traitor.

"I suppose." Page shot Betsy the fiercest dagger looks she could manifest, which were ignored. She pushed the wheelbarrow containing the bags of fertilizer and plant food toward the infuriating man who'd bamboozled her into an evening alone with him. Page wondered about his motive. There had to be one. The inkling hit. Page needed to be on that sailboat. She intuited something significant to the case was imminent.

CHAPTER 36

Betsy stood outside Page's bedroom door wearing a Cheshire grin. "Aunt Tilly's maddening cuckoo clock just announced five o'clock. Time for your big sailing date. No more stalling. Get out here and show me how you prettied up for our handsome, personality-starved neighbor."

Page cracked the door open. "Would you please stop acting like this is some romantic date? I told you Steve's trying to play me for information. Trust me. This outing will become a double play, meaning I'm not coming home without some titillating facts for our suspect board." For now, she elected to keep the latest sensing to herself.

"Don't forget your fancy diamond earrings that I left displayed on your nightstand." Betsy moved toward the porch, bringing her expectations.

"So now you're a dresser?" Page stepped onto the porch. Slim white jeans grabbed her flattering curves. A gauzy pale mint-colored blouse revealed a saucy black bathing suit underneath. Canvas deck sneakers testified to Page's experience boating. The classic diamond studs caught the afternoon sun, while the sparkle in her eyes reflected something long absent…attraction.

"Good golly hot Molly. You look—"

"Yes, she does," offered Steve, pausing at the screen door, his eyes appreciating his sailing mate. "Sorry, but when you didn't walk over to my place, I thought I'd bop over and make sure you hadn't…"

"Bailed?" supplied Page. "Not at all. I was heading your way." The beach bag hung on her arm, affirming the words.

"Enjoy your evening with Gertrude."

Steve opened the door wider to allow Page passage. His charcoal grey swim trunks offered no competition for his Navy Seal t-shirt emblazoned with the blue and gold emblem. "Who's Gertrude?" he asked, confusion mirrored on his face.

Betsy snickered, taking up residence in the hammock. "Oh, no one you're ever likely to meet. Happy sailing, you two. Do you need a curfew because I can provide…"

"Bye, Betsy," they said in unison, grinning.

~*~

The sun's late afternoon rays painted the marina in varying hues of orange and violet. Page let her eyes feast on Mother Nature's beauty as she exited Steve's vehicle. She wondered if her companion noticed the glorious landscape. After all, the guy missed little.

"Beautiful, isn't it?" Steve stood next to Page, admiring the color show.

"It is, and you picked the perfect time for our excursion." Page watched him effortlessly hoist a duffle bag over his broad shoulders as if filled with feathers. The cooler found his free hand. She peered into the SUV's cargo area and reached for a grocery bag she surmised must hold dinner makings. Page felt awash in surprise as, until this moment, his hosting manners hadn't impressed. She recalled the soda offered without even a glass or napkin. "Unpredictable man," she muttered to herself. "I'm grabbing this bag. Oh, that delicious seafood aroma wafting my way from those cartons has me—"

"No peeking in my sack; however, I accept the offer to tote. Can you manage one more?"

"Yep, just let me drape my beach bag further back on my arm." Page shadowed Steve along the dock, admiring the lonely sailboats moored, waiting for their owners' return. Hungry pelicans perched, staking out their real estate claim on the posts bordering the fish-cleaning stations. Tired fishers wearing weathered faces tossed a few morsels to the birds. Page spun to catch the wind's direction and noticed a stiffness that replaced the breeze's earlier gentleness. Seasoned sailors understood the winds' nuances as their movements dressed the ocean's surface. Page stopped short, aware Steve's pace had slowed.

"That's my sloop on the left. Let me board first, then I'll give you a hand. Do you sail?" Steve asked, helping Page step onto the bobbing deck.

"I know enough to stay out of the way and help in a pinch." Page's spirits lifted as she took in the sloop's lines. "She's a thirty-footer with a Bermuda rigged main and a headsail. Very good for sailing into the wind, right?" Page stroked the mast like a fine filly who'd won a race.

"Right, you are." Steve's face registered genuine pleasure and surprise at Page's sailing knowledge. "She's plenty enough for me to handle and maintain. We have a long but interesting history, you might say." His expression shifted to melancholy.

"I'd like to hear that story." The soft tone of her voice showed sincerity.

Steve studied her face. How much was he willing to share? He leaned against the railing. "My dad bought me this boat when I was seventeen. He was a Navy guy and loved sailing. I guess he wanted to instill that passion in me early, and he succeeded. My older brother, dad, and I had some great times on this sloop."

Page sensed this telling carried some pain not yet revealed. "I'm sure those memories remain special for you; however, I think there's more to your history. Am I right?" Page moved next to him.

"Yes." Steve looked away but continued, "When my dad got sick, we needed money to cover medical costs for experimental treatments. I told my mom to sell the boat, which she begrudgingly did. The procedure bought my dad a couple of years, and for that, I'm glad. He and my mom used the time to travel. My brother and I were away at college, so that gave them the freedom to enjoy some wonderful experiences, just the two of them. I marveled how they were able to put aside his imminent death and enjoy life." He turned to Page, his grey eyes full of emotion.

"Steve, their love must have been that uncommon type that transcends time. How great that they made each day incredible. In a way, maybe it was a gift, knowing his time was limited. That gave them the chance to have an amazing finale as mates in this life. Still, parting with your boat and, ultimately, your dad had to be so difficult for you. I'm so sorry. Please, won't you share the rest?" Page drew on her kindness easily.

His countenance lightened. "Thank you for what you said. I've never thought of things in that way."

"You might want to reframe your story."

Steve nodded and continued, "So, when I joined the Navy, I got stationed on a cutter in Key West. Lucky me. The Florida Keys are incredible. Anyway, one afternoon, we got a call that a sloop had radioed for help. The boat was becalmed with a woman on board going into labor. Don't even ask me to explain why she'd gone out sailing with her husband and another couple, never mind on a sailboat not outfitted with an aux engine. When we approached them, I recognized the sloop right off as mine. Pretty insane, I know." Steve reached out and ran his hands along the railing.

"Seriously, they owned this very boat? That's not even close to being a coincidence. That's providential." Page felt excited about the young man's find all those years ago.

"Yep. Crazy. It was my sailboat, all right. When we got back to port, I asked the owner for their phone number. I waited a month before I called inquiring if they'd be willing to sell me the sloop? I told my story, and with the new baby's arrival, they'd pretty much decided owning a sailboat wasn't for them. The following week, I gave them my check, and on that incredible day, I made her mine once more, and mine she'll stay. You know the happiness of our reunion has never left me." Pride shone in his eyes.

"What an extraordinary story. I'd say you two are a perfect match. You take care of each other, don't you?" Page could feel their bond.

Steve's face registered surprise that Page understood the attachment. "Introduce yourselves. I'll be right back." He disappeared below to stow the things they'd brought on board.

Page noted the boat's tidiness. The deck gleamed, the teak and handrails polished to a high sheen, and the sails were wrapped with a type of reverence. She smiled at the different nautical knots used to tie off lines. The guy's Navy heart was evident wherever her eyes landed. One fact had escaped before she boarded, and now was her opportunity to get the answer. She hung over the bow and laughed. "Perfect choice."

"Yeah?" replied the familiar, baritone voice standing a few feet behind her.

Page turned, wearing a smile bright enough to illuminate the cabin below. "Carpe diem," she said aloud, feeling her heart flutter. The Roman poet Horace's work "Odes" awakened her memory. The words had defined her take on life since college. "You named her?"

"I did." Steve returned the smile. "I know you may find this puzzling for an ex-Navy Seal, but my favorite movie is *Dead Poets Society*. And carpe diem sort of defines my take on life."

She felt a jolt as he'd repeated her same thoughts.

"Come on. Where better to *seize the day* than when you're sailing? No other name fits."

"Funny happenstance, Steve Tanner. That movie holds a top place with me, too, and carpe diem happens to be my mantra, too." She chose not to delve into their extraordinary linking.

"Then, Page Wright, let's get about seizing the rest of this day together." Steve reached for her arm and did the unexpected. He kissed her hand with a sweetness that surprised them both.

CHAPTER 37

The often-fickle sailors' wind decided to charm Carpe's sails, allowing Steve to tack out of the bay and not engage the engine to maneuver them around other boats. Page watched, admiring how deftly he and the sloop communicated. Once out in the ocean, he set the sails to capture every bit of breeze. The boat skimmed across the water with the rudder pointing them to a nearby, tiny, deserted island.

"How ya doing? Ready to take a turn steering?" Steve grinned, motioning for Page to join him.

"Gee, I don't know about taking that wheel. I mean I was fine to help with the sails and tying off, but I'm directionally challenged. The whole tiller and rudder business…and turning opposite of where you want to go. I'm gonna pass, but thanks for the offer." She was having fun—and with Steve Tanner. Surprise on her.

"Maybe Carpe will entice you later to know her better."

Page nodded. "Tell me about that little island you're sailing toward." She donned her white bucket hat befitting of a sailor and joined Steve.

"That island is a great place to throw anchor, enjoy a swim, and get off sea legs for a bit. For some reason, boats seldom stop there but instead go another half mile to the bigger Conch Island. Me, I like this one for privacy and peace. "Drop your head. We're coming about."

Moments later, with sails lowered and the anchor securing their spot, Steve returned to Page's side wearing only his swim trunks and a rakish grin that any pirate would claim. "Thanks for the help, first mate. Outstanding crewing. Would you like to take a swim and explore the island?"

"Thanks for the compliment. I'll keep it, and yes, I'd love to have you introduce me to the island." Page had exchanged her jeans and top earlier for a beach coverup. She tossed it on the nearby seat, kicked off her deck shoes, and bent over the starboard side. Peering into the clear aqua water, she felt relieved to see nothing but a few colorful fish investigating the sloop and any possible food falling their way. "Guess I'm ready, but you jump in first just in case there are any rays around. After all, you're the fearless Seal. Rays creep me out."

Steve laughed. "Okay, I'll be the chum, but you'd better be following me." He offered his characteristic salute before diving overboard.

Page thought his salute charming, and before she let her mind explain that shift in thinking, she jumped over the side, missing her captain by inches.

Steve righted them both. "Lady, you know how to make a splash."

Embarrassed at her miscalculation, Page could only manage, "Ooops. Big sorry there, Tanner."

"Tanner, huh? Well, Wright, I'll race you to the beach and even give you a few strokes head start." Steve treaded water, watching Page's swim strokes reach long. He grinned, understanding her competitive spirit, and if he was honest with himself, enjoyed her company more than any woman's in a long time. He'd closed off that part of his heart, and with good reason.

~*~

They took pleasure in a short hike around the island, appreciating where the birds called home and marveling at the impressively sized mangroves—their curved roots like living wood sculptures wrapped around most of the island. Small fish surfaced in a cove's cognac-colored water, capturing the Halobate insects for dinner, proving habitats possessed a unique ambiance for life forms co-existing.

Steve dropped down on the sand, welcoming the sun's warmth. He patted the place next to him for Page to sit. "So, now that you've met this beguiling island, what do you think?"

Page joined him. "I think you've found the ideal place to escape for a few hours. I love your island. By the way, does it have a name?" Page frowned as her fingers touched her wet ponytail and released the clip, letting her hair fall away. She glanced at Steve and caught his eyes fixed on her movements, and unable to resist, she returned the favor watching him turn on his side facing her. Attraction was a potent emotion, and Page sensed they'd been doused. "About that island name?" she asked, bringing them to the mundane.

"Umm, the island's name is…well…it's Calypso." Steve's face reddened, and he cleared his throat, finding a grin. He sat up. "Calypso…a man's downfall."

"Ah, Calypso. She recalled the mythology of the nymph, representing a temptation to Odysseus. Page sensed the call of the island's charms, mainly because of who sat next to her. "I think this island has a kind of bewitching force field true to its name." She felt butterflies fluttering inside and willed her body to behave. Butterflies didn't visit women in her decade of life. She scooted a smidge further from Steve before speaking. "Odysseus sure succumbed to Calypso's temptations and for like seven years." Her smile telegraphed their almost awkward moment had passed.

Steve kept his focus on Page's flushed face, smiling at her chatter attempt, meant to diffuse things. "Not exactly a force field, but probably something else like female wiles come to life." His eyes danced in merriment.

Page wanted her wits back. She'd analyze her wayward thoughts later in the safety of her bedroom. "Never mind, wiles,

I'm sure Odysseus would understand why no one dares set foot on this beach."

"Especially if you're male. Enchantresses get us men every time. You, Page Wright, bear watching." Steve laughed, noting Page's expression shift to confusion.

"I bear watching? Ha. You're nuts. Oh, forget it, Tanner," countered an exasperated Page. "I'm ready to get back to the sloop and see what tasty fare awaits, and I'm even more hungry for some tidbits on the Lange case."

Steve moved to the water's edge before offering any reply. "Perhaps you'd like another chance to beat me back to Carpe?"

"No encore needed. Thank you very much," Page tossed over her shoulder as she swam toward the sailboat. The water droplets felt cool on her skin as she flipped on her back to take in the sky. She noticed the clouds overhead had an unusual tint outlining them, and it wasn't a silver lining but an unattractive, lifeless shade of charcoal. The inkling swished over her body like the last swell. "Please, not yet. Portend me later."

~*~

Back on board, Page checked the time. "Gosh, it's already gone seven o'clock. I'd like to get dry. Mind if I change out of my suit before I lend a hand with dinner?"

"Go ahead. I'm going to peek at the radar to make sure the weather is holding true this evening. Pop-up storms can annoy this sloop." Steve scowled at the same mystifying clouds Page had witnessed but said nothing.

Page jumped in. "Besides these unusual clouds hanging out with us, the sky's hues are all coral and crimson on the horizon. What's the saying? Red sky in morning, sailors take warning. Red sky at night, sailors delight? I see delight."

Steve's expression softened. "Right, you are, mate. I see delight, too, but I'm still going to do a radar check."

Page disappeared, humming an old sailing song. The

outing had succeeded at propelling them to act more relaxed with each other. He behaved less adversarial, which boded well for her gaining his trust. Time to focus on obtaining information from her host while he acted obligingly.

CHAPTER 38

"Our dinner awaits literally on the deck if you'll pour the green tea." Steve pointed to the two trays placed on a folded blue canvas tarp. He'd employed life vest cushions to serve as their seats. "Improvise with me and think Japanese style."

"You're an impressively fast Captain at putting dinner together." Page settled on the cushion and lifted the brightly colored striped pitcher, filling their glasses. "Sushi and salad, I see." She unwrapped the chopsticks and tucked a bamboo-patterned paper napkin in her lap. He'd chosen well, not knowing Japanese cuisine scored in her top three favorites. She liked the clean eating approach with interesting flavors and unexpected balanced food combinations. Betsy could benefit from the Asian influence in the kitchen. "Love the tempura roll."

"Glad you're a fan of sushi. I gambled. If you see a roll that isn't to your liking, you can bargain with me. I'm easy with food." Steve nabbed his first piece. "Sushi toast," he said, touching his roll to hers, smiling.

"Here's to solving Catherine's murder very soon." Page arranged her rolls while allowing her mind to guide the conversation. "This salmon roll is outstanding too." She dropped her eel roll on his plate and snagged his remaining tempura, and cut a sassy grin. "No need to bargain. I'm the guest." She paused, caving to the nosey voice inside her. "Umm, Steve, would you be open to a personal question? You can ask me one in return."

"Try me."

"I'm curious. Have you been married?" Page dropped her head, not wanting to make eye contact. She feared she'd ventured into the too personal territory for this aloof man, but the words were out. She'd have to see if they caused damage or opened them to more personal sharing.

"Well, that wasn't the question I anticipated, but sure, I'll answer. You'd eventually go detecting and find out." He laughed and took a sip of tea. "Yes, I was married during my time as a Seal. Unfortunately, that service doesn't make for a great husband. I'd get called away on a mission with no way of telling Sue when or if I'd be home. When our son came along, well, let's say I missed out on too many of his milestones. Milestones I can't get back. I didn't blame Sue for wanting a husband she could count on. We divorced, and I've not remarried. My life's easier unencumbered. So, did I satisfy your curiosity gene?" Steve tapped his chopsticks against his plate.

"You did. I can understand both sides. You had a call to serve our country, and your wife tried to support that and find balance in a marriage. It sounds like you both strived to make things work, which shows how much you cared. How about a part B question since we seem to like those?" Page grinned, recalling their sidewalk exchange.

"Shoot."

"What about your son now?"

"That's an easy answer. He's a Seal based out of California and married to the team. No serious girl in his life…yet. He learned from his parents' mistakes."

"You must be so pleased with his accomplishments and that he followed you as a Seal." Page was surprised by Steve's willingness to trust her. Another sign of at least a budding friendship with her neighbor. She liked that idea. Friendship felt right. Safe.

"I'm extremely proud of Adam. I hear he's a great addition to the team. My turn. You get the same question with a part B if applicable. Spill it, Wright." Steve relaxed.

"Okay, sure. I married a terrific guy that I met in college. Jeff was a teaching assistant working on his Ph.D. in Archeology while I was focused on getting my MFA."

"An Indiana Jones type of guy," responded Steve, showing admiration.

"Yep, Jeff exhibited those traits when in the field. He led the explorations that others shunned. His last work focused on the study of the relationship between dogs and man 15,000 years ago in Israel. I've read studies now suggesting that at least some Late Pleistocene humans may have established a devoted attachment to their dogs. So fascinating. If Jeff were alive, he'd be immersed in these exciting findings. Unfortunately, the last dig about four years ago cost him his life when a cave collapsed." Page looked off, waiting for the usual sadness to consume her, but tonight, the feeling stayed away, and so did the tears.

"That's a loss I can't imagine dealing with, Page. Your Jeff sounds like a brilliant guy. There must be some comfort knowing he left doing what brought him happiness; at least, I hope so." Steve allowed his hand to cover Page's for a moment.

"That's true, and what I've reminded myself countless times." Page's voice changed to a lighter tone. "I do have a part B answer for you."

"Excellent." Steve sat back relaxed.

Page's expression softened. "I have one daughter, Hannah, who's living the corporate life and eschews marriage like Adam. Truthfully, I think she's afraid to care. Losing her dad took a toll despite her being older. They were super close. You know. Daddy's little girl forever." Page smiled away the remembrance. "Still, I remain hopeful one day, a guy will come along that she will trust her heart to. She's the reason I was at the travel agency that day I saw Catherine. I wanted to purchase a ticket for Hannah to visit me. Her birthday is July fourth. So, that's the scoop on me."

Steve paused, his eyes reading Page. He decided to shift the subject. "Shall we?" He activated the chopsticks, signaling his attention was going back to the plate in front of him.

~*~

Page set her tray to the side. "So, so good. Thank you for feeding me. So, how about we bargain for an info exchange?"

Steve tossed his napkin aside before answering. "I'm a gentleman, after you. And, maybe start sharing what you and Betsy uncovered snooping about town at Brakem and Garrett's offices." Steve stacked his tray atop Page's. "Oh, and I'd especially enjoy hearing why you said Garrett was lying to me about being home the night of the murder." The sailor in him remained ever alert to conditions around them on the water. He turned back to Page.

"Well, I'll begin by naming the suspects we have on our board." Page wanted to share in a logical order.

"A board?" The furrows on Steve's forehead displayed confusion.

"Our suspect board. You know. To help us keep everything and everyone in order." Page plunged on. "We've got Brakem, Garrett, Gwen, Ty, Evan, and Seedy's names plastered up, but truthfully, we are weak on motive, except for plenty of Catherine hate going around most of the group and her possible blackmailing." Page uncrossed her legs and stood. "Could we maybe sit on the benches? My back muscles are chatty."

Steve followed Page to the seat she preferred. "I agree with your named suspects, and as for the blackmail, well, it's been going on a while, but not by Catherine."

"Not her? But then who?" Page asked, intrigued.

"Not yet, Ms. Wright. You still have the stage."

"Fine, but your correcting me on the blackmailer direction has thrown me off course a bit." Page recounted what she and Betsy had garnered from visiting Brakem, Garrett, and their two admins. "Anyway, Betsy and I determined Brakem fit the shady type, and he's possibly up to something with his questionable client dealings."

"Yeah? What about that causes you to jump to sketchy dealings?"

Page chose to spell it out for him and hoped he'd give some reaction to let her know if she was on track. "Well, for starters, I'm not counting Brakem watching and worrying about us. Number one, we have Catherine moving envelopes around Brakem and Garrett's offices after receiving a pistol from Seedy. We have her demanding the attorney make changes to Evan's will and, of course, the call Lola took from someone with a thick accent called Armand. I checked the origin of the name, Armand."

"And?" Steve prodded, leaning closer.

"Later, Tanner." Page paused, "It's not much of a leap to see a connection with Armand and this motley bunch, and that's without me having enough Brakem puzzle pieces yet. Brakem has dirty dealings that will surface. You already know this stuff. And then we have Garrett, the blockhead, who can be intimidated by a church mouse scurrying near him. Catherine exploited her knowledge of Garrett having his little dalliance by telling him to inflate the jewelry's value on a rider. That's a form of blackmail. The why I haven't figured out." Page gave Steve's shoulder a shove. "Come on, Tanner. At least let your face give me some indication of how you're assessing my deduction skills."

"Too soon. Keep building on the suspects and motives for me." Steve moved to grab two sodas from the nearby cooler and offered Page a can.

"Still no glass or napkin, huh?"

"Excuse me?"

"Skip it. This is fine." She popped the tab and took a long swallow. "Back to the blockhead. Garrett's having an affair. A dalliance, as Catherine called it. He's capable of being dishonest, to what degree I don't know. Falsifying riders, given a good reason, wouldn't be too much of a stretch for this guy if he even knows how. Ina covers for his ineptitude, but I don't see her colluding. That's my take on Garrett." Page wiped the can's drips from her hand on her jeans.

"I find myself in agreement with you on…what did you call him?" laughed Steve.

"Tonight, a blockhead. But he's also the classic sap. Take your pick," said Page, adding her laughter with his. "And, what type of woman would consider an affair with him? My answer is a gold digger, which leads me to my next question." Page always enjoyed setting up smug detective types, even if she'd grown to like this one.

"Don't leave me hanging?" Steve's growing respect for the sleuth was evident. Page's mind analyzed human nature as well as any private detectives he'd been around. "Come on, what's that next question."

"Okay. A gold digger is after something, and I'm asking, where's Garrett getting his gold?" Page settled back on the bench. Time for Tanner to give up something.

"You're definitely on Garrett's scent, but before I supply you answers on our investigation, there's one more question about Garrett I need you to answer. What did you mean earlier today when you said he was lying to me about being home the night Catherine was found and the theft occurred?"

Page let the waves lapping against the boat's hull help her ponder the reply. Was she ready to explain more about her gift? Could she trust him not to judge her harshly? Maybe he'd feel willing to help her find Catherine's killer? "Tell me, investigator, have you had experience with other deduction methods that aren't in traditional textbooks?"

Steve's expression gave nothing away, nor did he reply.

Page sighed. He wasn't making this easy. "Let me provide

an example. Are you open to the concept of someone's intuition being formidable and valid with investigations? We've touched on my inklings before." Her hands trembled, waiting to hear the response from the man she'd come to admire and value this day.

Steve took one more read on Page and covered her hands with his. "I am open and highly respectful of the ability when the person intuiting has proven themselves worthy and authentic. Why? Page, are you trying to tell me that part of your sleuthing involves this heightened type of perception? Your inklings have proven reliable?"

The expression that had colored Page's face with anxiety softened as she released the held breath. She matched the intensity of his eyes. "Yes."

CHAPTER 39

"I suppose this would be the appropriate time to bow to your sleuthing prowess and admit I had you figured all wrong. As for Betsy..." Steve paused. "Probably not." Laughter escaped with the shake of his head. "That Betsy is a force."

Page joined in the laughter. "Yeah, you've got Betsy's number, so to speak, but her worth is solid. She's invaluable to me with my work, and, as my cousin, trusts in my gift." Page felt grateful that the nudge to share her ability with Steve had proven right. She watched with amusement as Steve began pacing the sloop's short deck while digesting only a single serving of her admission. Expounding on the way her insights came needed to wait. "Does walking back and forth help you process?" chided Page.

"Not this time." Giving up the exercise, Steve crouched down at Page's feet, meeting her eye to eye. "Thank you for trusting me. I'm beginning to understand why you've been so meddlesome with this case. Want to tell me how you intuit?"

"I think maybe another time, Steve. Let's move on with the info exchange. I sense time isn't to be frittered right now. Something is about to be asked of us."

Steve nodded and shifted tone. "Wow, okay, then. I believe in your ability, and it changes everything. And, so you know, I've seen some branches of law enforcement leverage intuitives to assist with investigations with effective outcomes."

"Does this mean you're keen to include us in the investigation? Betsy and I might be crucial to helping solve this murder. You'll soon appreciate our usefulness." Page wondered if she'd said enough or too little.

Steve smiled. "I'm cautiously prepared to collaborate while I have you on the boat, unable to get into mischief. See this as your maiden voyage to see if you're seaworthy. If you prove to me over the next, say, twenty-four hours that you and Betsy can stay out of harm's way, we'll negotiate a role for you two — a minor role. Minor, I say again. I need to bring Koch and my FBI chief into this arrangement first thing tomorrow. Agreed?" Steve extended his hand.

"Sure. Agreed." Page shook his hand.

"Hold on. I'm worried. That was too easy. No arguing? No defending your right to snoop anytime or anywhere?" asked Steve, frowning.

"Nope. We're good. I'm in your trust door and gaining respect by the minute. You'll be calling on us soon enough." Page knew the drill. Their first case with Larsen demanded she and Betsy prove their unusual knack for solving crimes. Then reliance by both sides to pool information followed. However, the request to stay out of trouble always proved their Achilles heel, despite striving for caution. Often people who committed crimes acted rabid and unpredictable. Page knew to rely on her repertoire of inklings, nudges, and intuiting insights to guide her. The person or persons who took Catherine's life needed to worry. She saw Steve's left eyebrow still arched, meaning skepticism reigned. "I'm telling you that we're good here. No worries."

"I'm not a buyer just yet of this 'we're good,' but I do want to hear the rest of your assessment of the suspects and interactions. So, I believe we left off with you alluding to the fact that Garrett hadn't been home the night of the murder? You were right. I enjoyed a rather brief exchange with his wife Beverly earlier this afternoon." Steve's fingers tapped on the railing as he gazed out to sea.

"What did she say?" Page felt the first flush of anticipation move through her body. Steve's respect for her gift meant forthcoming info.

"For starters, she's a lush…a real doll, this one. I'm a sailor, and her language embarrassed Barnacle and me. The woman confessed to waking up on the family room floor around eleven that night. She blamed it on bad grapes."

"The old story of a bad vino corkage. That's one of my favorites. Poor woman," offered Page with a heavy dose of sarcasm.

"Well, she managed to get herself upright and told me when she passed by her husband's bedroom, the door was ajar, and the bed still made. Our blockhead wasn't home. Guess Garrett counted on his wife's nightly pattern of passing out early. His alibi is rubbish. Have any thoughts?" Steve asked.

"Oodles. First, on the surface, it looks like he certainly had the means, motive, and opportunity to murder Catherine. Despite his being a sap, Garrett remains a strong suspect on my board. Plenty of saps find the gumption to kill when something rises inside of them that matters. That's the means part. Catherine was threatening to expose his affair if he didn't do her bidding, and that checks motive. A small-town insurance guy can't afford to have his clients take a markdown on his weakness. I find opportunity often challenges a killer, but in Garrett's case, he must have felt confident in Beverly providing an alibi. That's the crack you uncovered. It's the *what* or *who* that matters to him that leads to the next clue." Page inhaled, letting the salt air invigorate her.

"Like maybe a gold digger?" supplied Steve.

"Yep, like maybe a gold digger. We need to find out her identity. It shouldn't be hard. Betsy and I can—"

"Hold up. We had a deal. You and Betsy are to stay out of harm's—"

"I know…stay out of harm's way. We will. I'm sure

tomorrow we can learn the hussy's name. This bit of detecting doesn't interfere with your case and doesn't flirt with danger. Come on. Surely, you see finding out some guy's side honey isn't perilous."

"Wright, you can wear a man down. Okay, you've got an assignment to find out who she is, and that's all you and Betsy can poke your noses into. Got it?"

"Aye, aye, Captain. All right, back to our discussion. Our other suspects of Evan, Gwen, Ty, and Seedy have us cloudy. Obviously, Gwen hated Catherine, which gives her motive, but only if that hate carries enough evil to kill. Ty and Seedy have shown support to Catherine, but that doesn't mean they're loyal. What do you think?"

"I think plenty of murders are unplanned. We aren't sure this falls into that category. The gun was fired from a few feet back and not close range. We're only speculating until the autopsy results come back. Having that info should clear up some of the postulating we've been doing. We still haven't found the weapon. Do you have anything else to impart from your excursion around town yesterday?" Steve glanced at his watch.

"You betcha," said Page, surprising herself by scooting closer to Steve. "We stopped at the Perk Coffee Shop and had a rather enlightening exchange with Mickey. Know him?"

"I do. He's a bigger gossip than the two of you."

"That kind of response doesn't inspire me to share a very juicy piece of Mickey-garnered intelligence with you. Let's have a do-over. Do you know Mickey?" Page enjoyed the banter.

"Yes, Ms. Wright, I do know Mickey. Koch and I find him to be a reliable source. Please, won't you tell me what your clever sleuthing skills got from Mickey?"

Page laughed. "I'd be happy to share. Mickey divulged to us that Catherine was a regular customer who appreciated a strong Turkish roast. What's important, though, is he overheard her speaking a foreign language to someone on her cell phone the same day she died. Catherine kept repeating one word, *bang*, to the other person. Mickey felt troubled. He had his grandson jump on the internet to find the word, its meaning, and what language. Pertinent knowledge to consider, I'd say."

"Only if you enlighten me too." Steve grabbed a white bag from the cooler and returned to their bench. "Tell me, and I'll share a tasty reward." He sniffed inside the bag and winked.

"Not fair. I possess a penchant for sweets." Page wondered what temptation the male version of Calypso offered. "The place Catherine hails from is likely Curacao, and they speak—"

"Dutch," finished Steve, pulling out two containers, each holding a decadent slice of dark chocolate torte. "And the word's meaning besides the obvious in English?" He waived a slice in front of her.

"Smells divine. The word means 'afraid' in Dutch. Listen, we need to find out who or what had Catherine afraid and desperate to flee. Remember the travel agency story I shared? Catherine didn't just want a ticket out of the country. She needed it. Give me that fork."

Steve passed the fork to Page's waiting hand. "You've earned a slice of torte. Eat up."

They paused to devour the dessert, each digesting the rich treat and the pooled facts of the case.

CHAPTER 40

Page dangled her legs off Carpe Diem's bow, letting thoughts keep her company while Steve tended the sloop. The outing had been a surprise on all fronts. Despite feeling devoid of any real knowledge about Steve's life at Shell Isle, she had the impression the place represented his haven from what, she'd only be guessing. His affiliation with the FBI kept him working, albeit contractually. Larsen said her neighbor's analytical skills were stellar and the bureau tapped Steve for cases complementing those skills. What mattered most was that they worked together to find Catherine's murderer. And "keeping company with a man," as Aunt Tilly used to say, should be nothing more than "an enjoyable excursion on life's journey." Page smiled, recalling Tilly had lived by that creed, eschewing marriage. I hear you, Tilly. I've been given a case, and must maintain my focus and keep these Steve excursions to a minimum. Easy as a bird finding a tasty worm after a spring rain. Well, maybe not so easy this time.

Page's mind admitted the brief interruption from Betsy's company felt like a gift. Poor Betsy. She'd forgotten about her cousin sitting alone at Hibiscus, probably bored with only a book to occupy her. She moved gracefully toward the hatch, stepping over coiled ropes. "Ahoy, down there? What time is it? I left my beach bag and cell phone in your cabin."

"Ahoy, yourself. It's almost 20:30." Steve appeared from the access with a dish towel slung over his shoulder.

"20:30? Can you translate that into non-military time?" Page counted on her fingers.

Steve chuckled. "That's 8:30 p.m. You got a hot date or something?"

"Not this evening," said Page, inflicting a bit of emotional trifling. "It's just Betsy's probably worrying. We've been away for hours. Maybe I should ring her." Page tried to pass Steve on the narrow steps.

"Hold up there. You're about to send us both tumbling." Steve turned sideways. "Remember, Betsy offered us a curfew, but we declined. I'll grab my satellite phone for you. You'll have a reliable signal."

Page stood rooted on the step above him, taken aback by another kindness.

"You're going to need to decide between heading up or down. Adjustments need to be made soon. I'm teetering with one foot on this step."

Page burst into laughter, realizing Steve's precarious position. "Ah, come on, a strapping Seal can't conquer maneuvering through a sloop's hatch? What would the guys say? Never mind. Grab me that phone."

In a few ticks, Page scurried deck side, phone in hand. "Hey, Betsy. I'm checking in. I got you on speaker. Are you bored silly yet? Wait, what's that noise?"

"No, I'm not bored one bit. I'm getting some exercise. All's fine."

"Betsy, exactly, where are you?" Page rolled her eyes at Steve as he sat down next to her.

"I'm at the Island Bowling Lanes. And I must go 'cause it's my turn to bowl next. I'm coming Team Mermaids. See ya later, Page."

Page handed the phone to Steve. "This news defies understanding—Betsy's bowling. I've never known her to do anything the slightest bit physical. She even managed to get excused out of PE in high school, claiming grass allergies bothered her every season. How in all that's sane did Betsy end up at a bowling alley?"

"With the Mermaids," added Steve, chuckling. "Guess you'll get that mystery solved soon enough. The important thing is she's experiencing a new adventure. And if she strikes out..."

"Stop being clever. Strikes out. Geez. I liked you better, dark and stealthy." Page wished she could pull those last words back into her mouth. Whatever made her make such a proclamation?

"Dark and stealthy, huh? I can certainly shift—"

"Forget it. That came out wrong. Let's get back to this vital info exchange. And, Tanner, I think it's your turn to enlighten me." Page pulled paper and a pen from her back pocket. "Always prepared."

"I can see. But remember, this information's meant for you to analyze and not to activate the snooping. Right?" Steve lifted Page's chin, forcing her to meet his eyes. "Here's where you say 'right.'"

Page shifted and stared skyward, considering. "Right... mostly," the last word she mumbled under her breath, preserving future opportunities. A good sleuth never closed doors to clue drops when they appeared, and she'd felt starved long enough. Tanner needed to deliver soon, as Page sensed the players in this investigation were getting anxious.

"So, I'd say you've got a good bead on Garrett and Brakem. Pun most intended. "Continuing, I can tell you we're looking into Garrett's business dealings. As for Brakem's shadiness, I've been watching him for the last month. He's choking on debt from liking the ponies, but something concerns me more."

"And that is?" asked Page, relishing any useful insights. Brakem's behavior and actions had seemed irrational.

"He's laundering and not his shirts. We've been trying without much success to connect him to various syndicates under surveillance. Tailing him hasn't produced any results except watching the chump make bad bets and get rejected by women. We've also got a tap on his phone. Some untraceable calls with cryptic messages have come from men with heavy accents. I suspect he's involved with more shell companies than there are shells on our beach."

Page grinned. "And you've not been able to decipher the meaning?"

"Not yet, Page. They give him a string of numbers followed by a date and hang up. I think it's to offshore accounts and the time for him to act, but the numbers don't jive with banks we have as contacts. At any rate, this represents the type of cases the FBI involves me in. It's my specialty to crack these ciphers, and I will. Whether Brakem's actions intersect Catherine's with murder, I remain open to that possibility. And, no, I can't tell you why...yet."

"Does Brakem know you're interested in him? Does he know you freelance for the FBI?"

Page received an inkling.

"Oh, he's clear I've got some interest in him. I've messed with his head a couple of times. Enough said there." Steve's serious expression gave nothing away.

"My latest impression says Brakem wasn't watching Betsy and me. He was watching you." Page released a breath, feeling relief she and Betsy weren't noteworthy. "It's only a fluke. We live next door to you. Brakem was parked the other night outside our houses, and I believe it focused on your doings. And, on the sidewalk, when you made me kiss —"

"Hold that thought." He clicked the cell phone button. "Tanner. Well, isn't that fascinating? As luck would have it, I'm anchored off the island. Yep, I sure am." Steve's laugh held confidence. "Oh, have zero doubts. Leave it to me. Later." Steve lay the phone aside, noting darkness was settling around them. "Okay, back to us and the hot kissing," replied Steve, his eyes relaxing on the sleuth.

Page chose not to question the phone call. "Tanner, that was make-believe hot. Nothing more. So, do you or do you not agree Brakem is focused on you?"

"I agree the kissing exercise tested him. If Brakem followed you and Betsy on to your next snooping appointment, I'd know you'd jangled him, saying God knows what in that meeting. Instead, he hung back with me, which proved—"

"You were the apple of his eye. You used me."

"Hold up. I used you to know how best to protect you." Steve touched her forearm to further his meaning. "At least I could ease up keeping tabs on you two that night. Okay?"

"Okay, I guess. What about the rest of our suspects? What ya got?" Page wanted to glean as much as possible before he sailed them back home. "I'd like to finish this exchange..." Another alert hit her.

CHAPTER 41

"Listen, Page, we'll continue this later, but right now, I have something to do."

"I know," said Page.

"You got some flash or something?" asked Steve, struggling to grasp how Page's insights worked.

"Sorta. How can I help?"

"Are you ready to play the role of my girlfriend again? That was Koch saying he got a tip from one of his wharf stoolies that Evan and Gwen are aboard their yacht and about to throw anchor nearby. It seems the mock mourning twosome are dining on board in celebration of Catherine's demise." Steve shook his head in disbelief and disgust.

"I overheard them on their deck planning this outing and hadn't gotten around to filling you in."

Steve stiffened. "That was important—"

"Honestly, it kinda slipped my mind. Of course, I had no idea where they planned to go just that it might happen nearby, which I just intuited. Even though that information clues us to what despicable people they are, let's act on this chance to... what's your plan?"

Steve sighed. "Making a case for your eavesdropping again?" He heard the yacht's diesel engine before the bow tip appeared.

"That must be our new friends," whispered Page, aware that voices traveled easily across the water.

"Yep, that's their anchor chain dropping. Fortunately, the yacht drifted back, so they can't see us in the cove. Now, let's hope we can hear them talking. Quick, help me tie down this clanging rigging. We must operate with stealth. As I recall, you prefer me—"

"Stop with the stealth talk," Page moaned. She pulled slack from the line. "Rope secured around the cleat, Captain." Anticipation coursed through her.

Steve did a swift check of the sloop. "Think we're buttoned. Time to eavesdrop. Your specialty."

Page overlooked the jab and moved to the boat's stern, pulling Steve with her. "I just heard a man's voice say, 'Join me.' I think we should."

"Not yet, party girl. Here, plant yourself." Steve wiped the salt spray from the seat.

They settled into uncomfortable positions to listen.

"Darling, Evan, I'd like to propose the first toast with this delightful vintage champagne from our cellar. It was Mother's favorite, and she had impeccable taste in everything," declared Gwen, her voice sounding almost giddy.

"Very well. Make your toast," Evan's voice wrapped bored around each word.

"To us. May your marriage faux pas, now rectified, bring us the freedom and fortune we deserve."

Glasses clanked, followed by silence.

"Most satisfactory, Ty. The entrée looks lovely," offered Gwen. "Evan?"

"Yes, yes, quite nice. Ty, give us some privacy. We'll summon you should we need anything." Evan's condescending tone booked no response.

Steve winked. "Should get rousing now."

Page smiled, nodding.

"How's your lobster, darling? I do hope I've pleased you with this menu." Gwen's voice sounded pleading, as if a compliment was a rare visitor.

"What would please me is your finding Mother's stolen jewelry. Did you make the calls to the pawn shops like I directed?" Evan vied for control.

"Of course. No one claimed to have seen the pieces I described, but we know these businesses are notorious for not reporting everything they purchase daily to the police. Maybe you should accept that they're gone as you told me to do when you lavished the suite of Mother's cherished canary diamond pieces on that Catherine. Oh, what's the point of talking about this upsetting occurrence? It's all history. Besides, I stopped by and woke up that useless Garrett to begin filing the claims—"

"Are you really that brainless? You take after that idiot father of yours. Why our mother married him first…oh what does that matter? What matters are those jewels and other pieces. Not that I owe you any explanations, but the Canaries were to keep Catherine quiet about something she overheard me saying on a business call. Furthermore, the riders from Garrett won't cover the jewelry's true value. Nor did I insure every piece. The policy cost was too prohibitive. We're in a dire situation thanks to your ineptitude, you senseless woman."

"Dear, oh dear, Evan. This does sound quite dire for you."

"Aren't you comprehending? Dire for us. Want to know what has me breaking into flop sweat?" Evan's speech shifted from an intimidator to a poor me.

The insults didn't find any caring nerve in Gwen. "Goodness, but you must tell me, brother. I've never seen you in such a rattled state."

"Well, I've never let myself get so deeply involved with the Members before. In the safe containing Mother's pieces, along with Catherine's hush jewels, were a bag of rare Russian alexandrite stones and two museum Fabergé Eggs that belonged to one of the Members. If he gets wind of the burglary and that his pieces are missing, my life won't be worth what this champagne cost. If you care about this lifestyle you've come to depend on through my generosity, you'll find those valuables tomorrow. Tomorrow, I say again. Involve Ty. He's connected and discreet. Do whatever it takes, but find those pieces, Gwen."

"Evan, dear, of course, I shall make another grand effort. This news is most disturbing. I don't understand why you'd have possession of a Member's priceless treasures?" Gwen's utterance was deficient in concern.

"Because, Sister, they had a mission to procure something the Members needed. My trip to New York settled the terms and time for the exchange. Come Friday night, Gwen, I'm either going to be dead or a whole lot richer. And you had better awaken any stray caring gene you possess to see that I live, or the Members might see fit to include you in my earthly farewell." Evan coughed.

"Me?" Gwen's voice hit a high octave. "I don't know any of these people. I'm nothing to them. Still, I will enlist Ty on this search first thing tomorrow. He has plenty of lowlife connections, no doubt. Why don't we put aside your worry and enjoy our celebration? I think this might be the sweetest lobster to touch my lips. Do you need more lemon, dear?"

The brother and sister ate in silence, providing Page and Steve an opening to discuss in whispers the Langes' exchange.

"Holy smokes. Evan's a dead man walking, and his sister doesn't give a flying flip," declared Page, clipping her blond hair back. The saltwater had left her mop looking like a bowl of limp spaghetti had been dumped on her head.

"No, Gwen doesn't appear the least concerned over his predicament. And Evan just confirmed he's involved with a syndicate, which is a moot point for me. I don't know what Catherine had on him, but it might have fueled her rush to flee the country. I think she feared for her life. And Koch shared with me a worrisome tidbit that Evan's flight landed before the murder, which allowed him to solve one of his problems…Catherine. Evan moves higher on my suspect list." Steve released the lock on a chest.

"And, having his wife around was no longer desirable, and Gwen may fall into that category if she's not careful. So many twists with this case. It feels like a maze. And I can't move past the fact that they're on that yacht celebrating Catherine's death. What horrible—" Voices interrupted Page.

"A most delectable dinner. Shall we discuss my moving back into the main house? I detest that wing I've been exiled to since your marriage. That vile creature with her doctor-perfected body has made my last eighteen months unbearable. I'll never understand your agreeing to marry to get her citizenship here." Gwen's words dripped with hatred.

"And I've told you repeatedly that marrying her wasn't an option for me. I had a favor repayment called due. At least I can celebrate now that that's settled and some peace is back in my home without you two constantly warring. Move back over if you wish. I've got bigger worries than where you lay that simple head of yours."

Gwen overlooked the snide remark. "Lovely. Tomorrow, I return to my rightful place in charge of the household—another thing to rejoice. As a show of this positive reception, I've one of your much-loved desserts to surprise you with now. Ty? Ty?"

"Ma'am?" answered an indifferent-sounding Ty.

"There you are. Please prepare my brother's sweet and serve it exactly as I instructed."

"Of course. I'll return in a few moments, Mr. Lange," replied Ty, making a point to exclude Gwen.

"Excuse me, Evan dear; I must freshen up."

~*~

Steve had shaped his plan while the Langes dined. Time to act. "Page, sit tight. I'll be back in a few minutes."

"What! Where are you going? I'm coming—"

"No, you're not. I need you to stay on the boat. I'm about to deliver an invitation."

Before Page could protest again, Steve dove overboard into the ocean's inky darkness, clasping something she couldn't make out.

CHAPTER 42

The silence engulfed Page as she paced the deck. Being alone on a sailboat at night woke up fearful nerves, and what-if alarms sounded with every boat creak. A half-hour ticked by with no Steve. Her mind became busily engaged with all sorts of conjured scenarios involving his doings, and worse, what if he didn't return? She allowed confidence in his covertness to eclipse worry; after all, Seals were steeped in moving invisibly and safely. Page willed her thoughts to focus on the sounds and movements around her.

Flapping blue and yellow telltales peeking out of wrapped sails signaled a change in the wind. The ocean chop had increased Carpe's movement on the water, which Page understood made swimming a challenge for Steve. A wave of queasiness took her by surprise — *no seasickness, Page Wright.* Pushing the feeling aside, she concentrated on welcoming the rising full moon, which lit the water with a cerulean essence. She gazed off the port side. "Was that a shark fin? That's not the kind of distraction I need right now. And why isn't anyone talking on the yacht?" she mumbled. The answer to her last question came.

"Evan, did you sincerely enjoy my surprise confection for you? I'm so glad I asked Ty to serve it in the solarium. I think Crepe Suzettes deserves a formal setting. Pour me another splash of brandy, won't you, darling brother?"

"Yes, the dessert was satisfactory, but as I said, crepes have never been my favorite. They're yours. Still the ever-self-indulgent sister," rebuffed Evan. "We both know that you never do anything that doesn't first benefit you. Take notice. You might want to begin preparing yourself, as things in your world are about to change. Drastically."

"Change, you say?" questioned Gwen, her voice tinged with disdain. "I quite agree, brother. Yes, I concur significant changes are coming very soon for us both."

The sudden chill in Gwen's tone and words ushered complete silence on the yacht.

"Could they be any more despicable? Not a single caring bone in either body," Page declared to the night, releasing a sigh. How does someone get to a place in their conscience where caring about another ceases? Page never understood total self-obsession, though she'd witnessed it often enough.

"Miss me?" Steve climbed the ladder attached to the sloop's bow. Water droplets cascaded down a face pleased with his mission.

Page jumped up. "Thank Neptune, you're back. I was close to losing my sanity grip alone on this boat. Too many unknown sounds, and there was a shark here just moments ago." Page peered over the side. "You were down there...with him." She straightened and wrapped her arms tightly around Steve's torso. The spontaneous gesture surprised her.

"Hey, I'm fine. I saw your friend swimming, but we decided not to tangle this night. However, I'm considering jumping back in if it gets me another one of those hugs."

"Stop teasing. Besides, one hug is my limit. By the way, I think the Langes' last menacing exchange has cast a pall on their celebration. Tell me, what's been happening on your end?"

"Well, I expect the diesel engine to fire up anytime."

"I thought we had to attend their celebration?" asked Page, disappointed in not getting to meet the Langes.

"Have faith. Hear that? Engine's running. Time for us to act."

"What can I do?" Page stepped back.

"Put your party face on. I'm going to use my boat's auxiliary engine to make maneuvering easier. Excuse me. I need to get to the winch." Steve reached around her and pushed the button to lift the anchor.

"Won't they hear us?" whispered Page, leaning out of Steve's way. She felt confused about why they were abandoning hush-hush.

"Party face, Page. Just a party face. Follow my lead. This is your chance to show me how nimble you can act when clue gathering." Steve's countenance grew somber.

Once Carpe's winch's motor quieted, Steve and Page could hear agitated voices erupting from the yacht.

"What's happening, Ty? Don't you know how to handle my yacht? Why do inept and brainless people always surround me? Do you have the intelligence to handle this?" Evan's tone oozed rancor.

Steve winked at Page's growing amusement and understanding.

"Yes, sir, I'm capable of piloting a bigger boat than this, but we've got an engine stall," answered Ty.

Gwen joined with her dithering. "Oh dear. I have some pressing matters to attend yet this evening. Ty, you must remedy whatever is wrong immediately and get me home."

"Ah, I get it. We've turned into party rescuers," surmised Page, chuckling. "You've done something to their motor, making them needy. Steve Tanner, you scare me."

Steve smiled. "Who knew how powerful a bit of rope on a propeller could be. Take a seat. We're heading over to introduce ourselves now." He steered the sloop out of the cove with running lights announcing their arrival.

The two men's heated discussion ceased as they caught sight of the sailboat's rapid approach.

"Ahoy there. We were heading back to the marina and

heard your engine fail. Need some help? Name's Tanner, and this is my girlfriend, Page." Steve used his foot to keep the sides of the boat from making contact.

Catching Steve's nod, Page turned on her smile.

Ty approached them first. "Thanks, man. Appreciate your coming our way. Name's Ty."

Evan sized up Steve before deciding to join them. Desperate emotions colored Evan's non-descript features, except for a bulbous nose that'd taken a few punches. Sallow skin hugged a weak jawline while his eyes illumined the coldness beating within his heart. He turned to assume command of his tricky situation. "I'm Evan Lange. I'll make it worth your while if you'll give my sister and me a lift back to the marina. Ty can remain on board and radio for a tow. Gwen? If you want off the yacht, now's your chance," bellowed Evan, clearly presupposing he and no one else would determine the terms of help.

Steve anticipated Evan's reaction would be to jump ship. A trait that likely represented how the man lived his life when unpleasant things closed in. Steve pretended to consider Evan's decree before agreeing. "Sure. I guess we could drop you, but I don't need any payment."

Gwen appeared with her designer tote and plastic smile aimed toward Page. "This is so fortuitous. How do you suggest I get on your…your…dinghy?" She tilted her bobbed nose.

"Actually, it's an impressively outfitted thirty-foot sloop," replied Page, matching Gwen's condescending tone. "Give me your hand and step here. Gwen, isn't it?" How could this snooty woman succeed at infuriating her within seconds? Just swell. She'd already lost her party face and caught a glare from Steve.

"I'm Ms. Lange. Take my tote." The older woman stepped gingerly onto the sailboat's moving deck. "Where's a comfortable seat?"

Page bit her lip, allowing the pain to help her course

correct with the grating Gwen. "Why don't you and I sit on the cushioned bench on the port side? I'd love to find out who does your nails. They're lovely, and the polish shade is divine," said a feigned simpering Page. She'd play this woman like a fine Stradivarius and show Tanner she was trophy-worthy.

Gwen lifted her hands, admiring her nails. "Well, I don't usually share the people who serve me, but I guess since you have rescued us from dreadful hours of waiting for a tow, I can make an exception this once."

Page softened her tone to sound affable. "You can trust me. I understand the desire to keep one's beauty secrets, and don't we women cleave to our secrets?"

The sleuth pointed to the three men struggling to finalize plans. "They're making such a fuss over the simplest of tasks. I find males so tiresome, and we women, thankfully, do seem to have the edge in the mental arena. There stands our proof." Page warmed to her role. She'd see if Gwen's ego felt hungry enough to bite and if the generous imbibing of champagne loosened her acid tongue. Page made sure to tuck her hair back to flash the two-carat diamond stud earrings Jeff had surprised her with on their last anniversary together.

Gwen noticed the stones. "You and I seem to be kindred spirits. I agree men define foolish. Even my brother, Evan, qualifies. No, typifies." Gwen offered a smile that could never reach her eyes as she smoothed a wrinkle from the charcoal linen pants.

"How interesting your brother didn't inherit your obvious astute mind." *Okay*, Page thought. *Time to bait a much-anticipated hook.* The latest inner guidance had rewarded her in spades. "Forgive my lack of manners. May I offer you some sparkling lime water? Alas, Steve isn't known for his selection of beverages." Page looked his way. Good. Steve was occupying Ty with inner engine workings while Evan grew unhinged with the mechanical chatter.

"Guess I must accept if you don't have anything stronger." Gwen's slightly slurred words mirrored her more draped form on the cushions.

"This should help." Page returned, handing the chilled bottle to her prey. She paused for effect. "My goodness, this meeting is happenstantial. I just this moment realized we're neighbors. You see, I own Hibiscus Cottage a few doors down. Social graces demand that I offer my condolences at the loss of your sister-in-law," said Page, now trolling.

"You knew Catherine?" Gwen's face registered interest.

"Oh, yes, do forgive what I'm about to say. I was raised brash and to speak my truth. Catherine and I overlapped around town too many times for my liking. Let's say I witnessed how difficult and, dare I say, spoiled she could behave. Sharing a home with another woman who didn't belong in your sphere surely must have been so intolerable. I tip my cap to you." Page punctuated her words with the gesture. Nervous that she'd spoken too many unkind things, Page hoped, wherever Catherine had ended up, the dead woman would forgive and understand her motives.

"Well, you certainly seem to have a clear grasp of my situation. How refreshing to encounter someone sympathetic." Gwen leaned in; her breath confirmed that she'd indeed enjoyed an ample amount of champagne's mellowing effect. "I'm gratified that creature's gone. All she cared about was getting my foolish brother to provide her with expensive jewelry and a steady stream of money. I happen to know Catherine's ultimate objective was to get hold of every piece of our mother's jewelry. Every piece," seethed Gwen.

"Simply appalling." Page scooted back a few inches.

"Oh yes, and I recently saw her wearing my mother's most treasured canary diamond necklace and earrings," Gwen studied

Page, gauging her reaction.

"How torturous for you to witness Catherine prancing around draped in your mother's cherished jewelry." Page intentionally stoked the other woman's ire.

Gwen's hands made tight fists, her nails biting into her skin. Her crimson face showed she was reliving the scene. She said nothing.

Page pressed on, "And, I also heard even more upsetting news that in addition to her untimely death, you've been burgled. Please tell me those precious pieces weren't nabbed, too? I can't imagine—"

"Imagine this fact if you can." Gwen's garbled speech didn't diminish her ignited fury. "My horrid mother left me nothing— not one piece of her exquisite collection of jewels. Instead, she gave everything to Evan. Everything. Oh, pardon me, except for her adding a magnanimous stipulation that he should look after my needs as he sees fit. That's my lot to endure." Loathing wrapped Gwen's words.

"Truly unbearable and so unfair." Page shook her head, pretending sympathy.

"Yes, and that, my dear, is why I must tolerate so much from my brother...half-brother." Gwen's expression froze, realizing her weakness for alcohol had caused her to spill too much.

Page read the panic and touched the woman's hand. She needed to calm the tempest brewing. "Gwen, I can't fathom your mother's cruelness to such a sensitive and brilliant daughter as you. No doubt it's your inner strength that you've relied on in the past and will continue to do so. I'm sure these recent unfortunate happenings will provide you with an opportunity to chart a new course that suits you." Page smiled, acknowledging her play on words meant to assuage the moment.

Gwen straightened, finding her rigid persona once more.

"Why, yes, I've most definitely set a new course. I want some time alone." Gwen stood and teetered to the starboard side.

Steve noticed the exchange between the two women had ended.

The sleuth caught his eye and saluted to let him know she'd completed her mission—nothing more to garner from a withdrawn Gwen. Analyzing the woman's emotional health remained a task better left for an expert. She hoped Steve's time with the two men had rewarded him. Plainly, they didn't know his identity, which gave him the advantage for the moment.

Steve led the way for Evan to board Carpe. Very few words accompanied them.

Page disappeared below to allow Evan and his sister a chance to settle while Steve readied the boat to leave. Questions swirled in her mind, much like the ocean currents around them. Would Steve sail back to the marina or rely on the sloop's small engine? The wind gusts were stronger and ready to fill the sails, but maybe Steve wanted a slower trip back to the dock. Perhaps he'd use the time to question his captives. And, more importantly, what role did he want her to play in this next phase? The thought of having to interact with that snake, Evan, caused her skin to get goosebumpy. Before the next question could come calling, Page heard footsteps moving toward the hatch.

"Ahoy, first mate, I need you on deck. Time to unfurl the main and jib."

CHAPTER 43

"Are you telling me we're sailing back? Maybe I'm better off waiting on a tow. I detest sailing," said Evan, grabbing hold of the handrail trying to decide whether to jump ship again.

"This sloop may not have your yacht's high horsepower engine, but she's at least dependable. And, unlike your boat, we have two sources of power," replied Steve, unable to resist landing a jab. "We'll make the marina in less than a half hour, relying on the wind."

Evan Lange grunted and took out his cell phone to make a call. "Brakem, I want you at my home in an hour. Bring what I asked for." Evan hung up, not waiting for a reply.

Gwen approached. "Don't tell me you've got that attorney coming to our home tonight?"

"My home, Gwen. He's coming to my home." Evan walked to the opposite side of the sailboat, seeking distance from everyone.

A fuming Gwen clenched her jaw and watched a passing shrimper drop his nets.

Page drew near. "Is there anything else I can do, Gwen?"

"Not unless you can make this sailboat go any faster. Otherwise, leave me alone." Gwen's eyes remained on the other vessel. She'd revived her disagreeable self.

Steve caught the exchange and motioned for Page to join him. "Take the wheel. Once I get the sails full of wind, I need to ruffle up Evan. And don't you object to guiding Carpe toward the marina. When you tied that knot earlier, I knew you were a capable first mate. Make me proud." He gave her back an encouraging pat.

"Oh, all right, but you'd better keep a close eye on me. I'm not as adept as you think. It's been a few years since I sailed with friends," replied Page, taking over. Inhaling, she mustered her sailing skills by holding their course and letting the winds do their magic. She felt the exhilaration rush through her body as the mainsail luffed. Sailing set her spirit free like nothing else, and she vowed to repeat this experience often while at Shell Isle. Perhaps she'd investigate renting a small sailboat. There was a unifying with nature and body when surfing down big waves and the spray flying toward her face. Under Page's steady hands, Carpe Diem skimmed the water with ease as if Poseidon had blessed their voyage. Page favored a nod to a watchful Steve.

Satisfied with his first mate's able sailing skills, Steve returned to his male passenger's side and offered a soda. "You know, Evan, we've got something in common."

"That's highly unlikely, but I'll take the cola." Evan tossed his jacket over the rigging and took a long swallow. He pivoted, looking out to sea, signaling idle talk wasn't welcome.

The tactic amused Steve. "I beg to differ. In fact, we're neighbors. I own the bungalow next door to you. Please accept my sympathy about the tragic loss of Mrs. Lange. Rest assured, Detective Koch and other law enforcement will find out what happened to your wife and reasonably soon."

Evan's face registered surprise. "I don't care to talk to you about any of that. Just get us to the marina."

"That's too bad. I could've maybe saved you a trip to the station for a chat with me tomorrow. You see, Mr. Lange, I'm one of the investigators, and I've got some questions, starting with your reported burglary."

"Again, I'm not going to discuss anything with you. I could care less that we're neighbors. Call my attorney and make an appointment."

Undeterred, Steve moved on. "For instance, according to the report I read, the safe didn't show actual evidence of tampering. I'm wondering who all had the combination? Then there's the unknown entry point of this burglar, and your security system wasn't on. Why was that? Certainly, you'd agree that burglary and the murder of your wife on the beach near your home on the same night casts suspicion? Were they related or coincidental? Those bothersome questions give me pause, Mr. Lange. Why not relieve my mind with a few answers before we reach the dock? Watch your head." Steve adjusted the rigging tighter. "You see, Detective Koch and I like to wrap cases up fast and tidy just like I sail my sloop. Now would be an excellent time for you to cooperate."

Evan spun to face Steve. Rage filled his body. "You aren't a very adept thinker as an investigator. I have two words to answer your absurd confusion about no evidence of tampering—a safecracker. It wasn't a complicated safe to breach. I meant to replace it. My security system is being upgraded due to sensor and camera malfunctioning. It's unfortunate timing. As for who shot my wife, she was associated with people who got angry when promises weren't kept. I have nothing more to add to this conversation except to do your job and focus on finding my stolen valuables. My wife's killer is of no importance to me. She's gone, but the safe's contents are alive and well somewhere. Impress me and bring my property back by Friday morning, and we'll get you some extra investigator training. And, might I add that training is not a bribe but a necessity." Evan's pigeon chest puffed as he mistakenly perceived dominant position.

Steve's body grew rigid. "Let me offer some advice. You'd do well and live a healthier life if you'd refrain from angering the investigator who happens to have you as a prime suspect in your wife's death. You see, Mr. Lange, you possess the three elements that all murderers afford themselves." Steve moved within inches of the portly man, eyeballing his anxious face.

Evan gathered some gumption. "Please, by all means, enlighten me with your genius."

"Happy to oblige. You, Evan Lange, are in possession of means, motive, and opportunity," supplied Steve, tapping the center of Evan's chest as he named each one. "That earns you a high ranking on my suspect list."

Evan's beady brown eyes squinted at Steve. "Ah, again, your inability shows. I didn't have an opportunity. I was on a flight from New York when my wife was found," answered a smug Evan, still vying for the advantage.

"As you would have us believe, however, I looked at the CC cameras at the airport. And what do you think I discovered?" Steve didn't wait for a reply but did toss Page a wink. "I discovered that you must have something to worry about. Why would a man who's legit and law-abiding book himself a flight using another name and then a later flight using his given name? See what I mean? My list of questions is very entangled, and I detest tangles, be it my lines on this sloop or a case," finished Steve, watching Evan's smugness evaporate like a stick of cotton candy on a humid day. "As I said, you're a man with means, motive, and opportunity. And the spouse is always awarded top rank in a murder."

Page watched, enthralled by the two men sparring but secretly proud of how Steve took the insults and parlayed them into the surprise sucker punch. Seeing the arrogant Evan nonplussed was an unexpected reward, but the clue gathering mattered most. Page noted Gwen was standing off to the side, pretending indifference.

Evan pitched the empty soda can toward Steve. "For the record, you're wasting time looking at me. Find my valuables." He moved away, telegraphing he had nothing further to say.

Steve had to raise his voice to be heard over the wind

whipping the canvas sails as he tied off the slack. "You're welcome for the drink and the lift. You may not have anything else to say, but I do. Be at Koch's office tomorrow morning at eleven sharp. You and I will most definitely continue with this interrogation. Feel free to bring your attorney, Brakem. I'm interested in him as well."

Evan didn't reply nor engage with his sister a few feet away.

Steve returned to Page's side, offering a nod. "I assume you gathered some helpful information. I'll take the wheel now. I noticed and liked that you and Carpe seem to get each other. Find a place to relax for a few minutes. I'm going to need your eyes once we get close to the marina."

"Of course, 'Oh captain, my captain,'" answered Page, drawing on the famous line from their favorite movie, *Dead Poets Society*. She disappeared below deck to gather her belongings and do a final straightening of the galley from their meal. She was already anticipating Betsy's reaction when given the full evening's recounting...sans the hand kissing.

CHAPTER 44

The moon slipped behind the clouds, extinguishing the light on the ocean and bathing the sloop in darkness as it grew close to the marina. Steve fired up Carpe's engine, allowing him to dock the boat effortlessly.

Page popped her head up from the hatch and, getting Steve's nod, assumed her first mate role, securing the rope to the pier's cleats. Her job completed, she took a moment to note Gwen's lack of interaction, as if returning to land had sobered her.

Steve offered a hand to the silent pair as they stepped off the boat. "Remember, Evan. I expect you at the station tomorrow morning. And, Gwen, you're invited, too. This little get-together isn't optional, folks, and I imagine you'll see other guests you know." Steve's solemn tone promised anything but a lighthearted gathering.

"Total waste of our time. You make sure you find the items stolen from my safe and soon," demanded Evan once again. "Gwen, get moving."

Page half expected Gwen to bid her a token goodbye wave, but that expectation wasn't rewarded. Instead, they watched the Langes make a hasty retreat. "I wonder what Brakem's toting to our Evan tonight?"

"No doubt something felonious. Let's see if we can find out." Steve grinned.

"But how...?" Page mumbled as they headed for his SUV.

"Koch. We're back at the marina, having just sent our happy pair home. Listen, are you free to put one of our search warrants to use and intercept Brakem on his way to Evan's? Great. The attorney's carrying something I think we'd benefit in seeing. By the way, I extended the party invitation to both Langes for tomorrow morning. That takes care of everyone for our meeting, but one." Steve accorded Page with a shake of his head. "Let's exclude him for now." He tucked the phone away.

"Impressive and fast work, Tanner." Page high-fived him.

"Thanks. Listen, Page, before we leave, I want to shift to something, umm, personal. And, fair warning, I'm not good with personal. Cut me a bit of slack here."

She smiled encouragement. "Okay."

Steve's eyes rested on Page. "I had a good time tonight, particularly before the Langes interfered. And Carpe responded to you, too. That's a sign that we should go sailing again sometime. A friendly sail."

She studied the man in front of her. "Maybe we should," she answered, with a tentativeness wrapped around her three words.

"Great. Come on, then. Let's get you home to Betsy and the two-way grilling."

~*~

"Well, well, who do we have coming in the door from— I'm betting—a scientific sleuthing mission on the wild seas. Tell me, what did you discover while I was beating it to get the skinny on one of our suspects? No. Let me guess," said Betsy, stifling any response from an amused Page and Steve standing before her. "Umm, I bet you discovered why some shrimp run at night."

Page shook her head and laughed as she set the beach bag on a nearby chair.

"No? Then, it must be you uncovered what makes all jellies migrate at the same time of year? Never mind, I give up. Join me in the living room with my chosen invigorating tea while I detail what this exercised-to-the-max sleuth hit upon this night.

And, please, let's not be staying up into the wees to debrief."

Steve and Page followed and dropped on the sofa next to each other, anxious to hear what scuttle had Betsy ready to bust from her always snug buttons.

"Bet you want to know first how I ended up at a bowling alley, of all places?" The teapot sat on a decorative tray with three matching mugs circling it. Betsy poured rich orange-colored tea into the first cup.

"Umm, Betsy, think I'll pass on a cup of that..." Steve hesitated, letting his index finger point to the teapot.

"No brew? Well, Tanner, you're missing out on my latest tea recipes that is purely sublime. I think that will be my name for this. Here you go, Page. Take a sip." Betsy blew in her cup, waiting for her compliment.

Page gingerly put her lips to the cup and took the tiniest of tastes while she observed Steve trying to mask his mirth. "Packs a pow. It's raspberry but with a hit of...India."

"It's turmeric, Page. We must work on your spice identification soon. Isn't the color intoxicating? Now, on to my story, and don't you two dare interrupt and cause me to lose my telling sequence," threatened Betsy.

"Get to it." Page placed the mug on the nearby table. As far as she was concerned, it could remain there.

"So, after you two left on your maiden voyage, I went to the market to shop for tomorrow's supper, and I ran into Ina. We exchanged a few pleasantries, and she told me one of the girls in her bowling league had to rush home to Philly to see about her ailing father. The next thing I know, Ina's introducing me to the other two members of the team, and I had rented shoes on my feet, a ball in my hand, and a too-small Mermaid Team shirt that I could only drape around my shoulders, with three females shouting, "Put it down the middle!"

Steve and Page burst into laughter, providing Betsy with

the attention she craved.

"Anyway, after the game, Ina and I shared a brew in the alley's lounge. I weaseled my way into her confidence, thanks to the suds' effect, and got her to squeal like a sow about Garrett. Or is it squeal like a pig? Whatever, the woman can blab. Here's the scoop. Ina's worried because Garrett's having her prepare fewer insurance riders for him. She said the change happened after she questioned some of his valuations not jiving with the jewelry appraisals. He brushed her off and said he'd seen other evaluations which satisfied him. Ina's worried Garrett may have crossed over the ethical line with some of his dealings. She doesn't know how exactly but senses trouble brewing with some demanding clients."

"The Langes, for example?" asked Steve.

"Oh yeah, them for sure, but it's Garrett's marriage that she feels might motivate him to do unethical and illegal stuff," replied Betsy. "Ina says Garrett's marriage is a joke because of his wife being soused most all the time and he's lonely and vulnerable to another woman's wiles. Ready for whose wiles snagged the sap? Brakem's admin, Lola. Yep, Lola. Close your mouth." Betsy laughed.

"Lola? Are you kidding me? What does that little hussy see in Garrett?" asked a baffled Page.

"She sees lots of lovely dollar signs. Ina suspects our hussy is feeding Garrett clients. How, you ask?" smiled Betsy. "By cherry-picking wealthy clients of Brakem's who need special insurance on their baubles and referring them to her boyfriend. And, besides inflating the jewelry value, I can't help but wonder if some of those gems might be synthetic or what they call paste?"

Steve chuckled and joined in. "Paste?"

"Listen up, Tanner; I had a girlfriend once whose husband lavished a bauble on her every time he strayed. It wasn't until she decided the jerk would never rehabilitate his wandering eye that she went to sell some of the pieces to fund her new life. Well, the jeweler informed her she'd been adorning herself with imitation diamonds. Anyway, it makes sense that a legit appraiser wouldn't put any value on fakes or inflate the worth of genuine pieces. Get my drift? This little scheme of theirs could go in many directions. Who knows? Garrett could have the real stones replaced by synthetics. Lots of ways to steal. Plus, I expect Lola to take a cut. She's in this for some green. What do you two think? I scored big and for the Mermaids' competition, too."

"Holy smokes, Betsy. We don't need to find out who Garrett is dallying with, thanks to your skills. You hit the motherlode tonight, and your deducing is sound. Right, Captain?" She gave a playful jab to his ribs.

Steve ignored the poke and sat quietly, absorbing Betsy's telling and more pieces to the puzzle.

"Out with it. What ya got to say about our sleuthing abilities now, Tanner?" Betsy took a long sip of her brew.

Steve leaned forward, rewarding Betsy with his full attention. "Well, Ms. Ross, I'd say tonight has been pretty illuminating, both in the information we've all gathered and in setting this investigator straight on the competence of the two sleuths in my present company. It seems Larsen's advice steered me right about giving credence to anything passed by you two."

"Larsen?" cried Page. "Please, tell me you didn't talk to him." Her right eye twitched, threatening a migraine. No doubt her bookstore sitter would be crashing into her morning with a phone call and plenty of protesting. "Did you call him, or did he call you?" She massaged her temples.

"Wait a second. Don't get all amped. I haven't gotten to bask in Tanner's compliment," pouted Betsy.

Steve ignored the newest Mermaid. "Relax, he called me, Page. Don't worry. I covered things nicely. Told him I'd shut you two snoops down, and you were focused on reading books, igniting my dog's stomach, and checking out the surfers." Steve's expression displayed his teasing.

Accepting the subject had shifted away from her exploits and accomplishments, Betsy fetched the brandy and poured a splash into Page's mug. "Drink this to calm yourself after you explain what he means by igniting Barnacle's stomach? I will, however, agree to the accuracy of the other two statements, but a dog's digestive system?" Betsy returned to her seat but kept her eyebrow raised.

Page beat Steve with the answer. "Oh, it's nothing. I made the mistake of giving Barn a slice of my pizza. You remember." Page's one non-twitching eye managed to shoot Steve daggers. Betsy need never be enlightened about the chili pepper French toast escapade.

Steve's next words moved to support Page's ploy. "No more feeding my dog, ladies. Pizza isn't for Barnacle. Let's get this settled now. I take care of his food. You may, however, bestow love on him at will. We good here?" Steve looked at each woman, showing his grin.

"Yeah, we're good," replied a still baffled Betsy.

Page downed her mug's concoction, ignoring the vile taste but eager for any numbing effect the brandy could offer her frayed nerves and painful head. The day had delivered her a wallop of insights into this case and its suspects. Tonight's intuition of meeting the Langes had sealed the night's success. The puzzle pieces were taking shape and asking for a home on the suspect board. Page looked around the room with a devilish grin, realizing her cousin had secreted it away somewhere.

Betsy punctured the silence. "Back to this case. Pizza-eating dogs with weak digestion hold no interest for me. Do you know what I think? I think Garrett and Lola robbed the Langes. They knew about the jewelry and its value. How about that scenario, kids?"

"I think that's plausible, Betsy. But how'd they get into the safe? How does Catherine's death fit into this, or does it?" Steve rubbed his chin. His dark five o'clock shadow in full view only added to his attractiveness.

Page pounced first. "Betsy's theory is one worth considering. Maybe they had someone involved who knows safes. Maybe that person did the burgling. Evan said the safe wasn't complicated."

"Yeah," Betsy tossed in.

"And maybe they're in some ring involved with stealing and fencing their client's expensive jewelry, along with creating fake inflated riders to milk the insurance companies for stolen pieces. Or maybe some of their clients are bringing fake jewelry to get riders. Garett and Lola go along and oversee the claims, and they all split the insurance money. Like Betsy said earlier, there are many ways to scheme." Page paused to assess her scenarios.

"Yes, I did say that. I'm smart that way." Betsy poured more tea into her cup.

Page smiled and continued, "After all, we heard Catherine demanding that Garrett falsify the jewelry values for her. You can bet Aunt Tilly's cuckoo clock that Catherine had a reason and a plan. Hold up a sec. Have there been any robberies reported at Shell Isle of late?" asked Page, building on her cousin's notion.

Steve nodded, mulling the two women's assessments. "I gotta say your analytical aptitude is growing on me. Koch told me we had a few professional-appearing break-ins in the last months. One woman reported approximately thirty grand in jewelry and cash taken from her wall safe. The burglars pulled the whole safe out and left a mess, but no prints. Another break-in involved bags of silver coins, some collector St. Gaudin gold pieces, and various pieces of jewelry. They were hidden in a floor safe, which the burglars opened. That particular lot was impossible to value without a rare coin expert. None of the valuables have been recovered."

"Might be a connection here to the Lange loss," added Page.

"Possibly," replied Steve. "The owners told Koch that Garrett had written riders on the jewelry but not the coins. So many ways for things to intersect or not. The only fact we're sure of is the desire for money wraps around the riders and actions. But Garrett doesn't seem to have the grit for being the mastermind. As far as his involvement in Catherine's death—"

Page jumped in. "Listen, don't forget we know that Garrett's alibi about being home the night Catherine was murdered proved a lie."

"Not fair, you guys. You haven't told me any of this," exclaimed Betsy. "I'm postulating at a disadvantage here." She threw her arms in the air.

Steve cracked a grin. "I'm sure Page has every intention of detailing our eventful sailing adventure, which she can do now." Steve glanced at his diver's watch. "I need to cut out. Betsy, I'll leave you with this bit of news. Tomorrow morning at eleven, we'll have Garrett, Brakem, Ty, Gwen, and Evan at the station for another round of interrogation. For now, Seedy, as you refer to him, is excluded as his whereabouts are unknown. We've got enough suspicion now to push each suspect to high anxiety. Page, you wanted to add something?"

"Yes, I'm getting confirmation that one or more in this contemptible bunch did indeed involve themselves in the death of Catherine Lange. I concur it's time to choke down on each of them."

CHAPTER 45

"Well, cousin, I don't know which story I'm more enthusiastic to hear. The evening's doings around you and our neighbor, or what intelligence you gleaned about our case." Betsy locked the front door. She peeked out the window, watching Steve cross the yard to his bungalow. "He's growing on me."

Page laughed. "Guess I'll confess to finding myself liking this guy more than I probably should. Tonight, showed me an authentic version of who he is, and we can trust him implicitly. He's one solid man, Betsy. For now, I'd like to leave it at that and pick up where the real action began. I am busting to report my adventures on the high seas, as you referenced earlier." Page ended her report recommending that they not drag out the suspect board, but instead find their beds.

"I second the bedtime, and I figured we'd turn up trumps tonight. I'm telling you, bowling with Team Mermaid asked a lot of these underused muscles. From the day I arrived, being with you has been one long workout." Betsy moved her right arm and grimaced.

Page patted her cousin's sore bowling arm as she passed. "You did an amazing job with Ina. But now, I'd like to partake of one of your aspirins. Acting as the first mate for Steve's sloop flexed more than you can imagine."

~*~

The morning started late for Page and Betsy. Nine cuckoos were enough to roust them from their slumber. The grey sky hung over the island as if to warn of imposing trouble. Even the children venturing out to the beach seemed subdued. The line of royal blue closed umbrellas stood like soldiers, with the lifeguard nearby trying to assess whether to bother opening them. The waves looked off-putting to the single surfer, watching their form fall away.

Page observed this beach scene from her bedroom window. A fitful few hours of sleep left her still with a migraine and a list of suspects who each might possess the mettle to take Catherine's life. She and Betsy stewed over who placed first and could only agree that Ty should appear last on the board if for no other reason than lack of info on him. Page went to the suspect board and, with a fresh mind, reviewed their efforts and leanings. With a heavy sigh, she realized the morning offered nothing new to solving the case. And where was the gun that killed Catherine? Steve had told her they'd been unsuccessful in locating it. An inkling flashed into her mind's eye married to that day at the Bistro when Seedy passed the small pistol to Catherine.

"What ya doing, cuz?" asked Betsy, appearing beside Page. She glanced at the board and groaned. "Too early for that. Let's feed our brains something self-indulgent with lots of fake energy-empowering sugar."

"For once, I'm aligned with your taste buds," offered Page with a weak smile that struggled to awaken her dimple. "What are the options?"

"Only one. We're going to the Pancake Place. Each Thursday, they offer my favorite flavor. Yep, I'm having pumpkin spice and pecan cakes with lots of whipped cream, a large order of crisp bacon, and a chai latte with more whipped cream. Got my keys." Betsy slid her feet into the ever-present flip-flops and plopped her sunbonnet atop her head. She paused. "Not a word about the diet fizzle or shift shopping. I'm postponing my monastic eating until after we solve this murder."

Page gave a wink. "Pancake Place it is, then. I'm feeling some love for a stack of blueberry ones, and I'll raise your bacon with an order of their famous country ham. Maybe I should bump up my protein for extra strength. Something tells me I'm going to need it." Page closed the cottage's front door.

Steve pulled his SUV into Page's driveway and dropped his window, motioning for the sleuth to come his way. "To further prove what a great guy I am, I spoke to Koch about your…talents, and we'd like to invite you to the interrogation happening with our five illustrious suspects this morning. Of course, you'll be behind the glass mirror where they can't see you. We're hoping you might pick up something to help wrap the investigation faster. Interested, Ms. Wright?" His face evidenced no weariness from the night before.

Mind racing, Page hit a snag. "Wow, this is super, you bringing me an invite and all, but what about Betsy? I can't just leave her to the Pancake Place. We're a team. She's got her talents, as exhibited to you last evening. Remember, she became a Mermaid for the greater good."

Steve laughed. "You're one loyal sleuth, Page Wright, and I respect that rare character trait. I told Koch you'd try and shove Betsy into the mix. Can you control that yap of hers?" Steve caught sight of an approaching and waving Betsy.

"She'll be fine. We really can be of value. Come on, Betsy. Change of plans," hollered Page, not waiting for Steve's reply. She hopped in the passenger side of Steve's SUV with her cousin following.

"Okay, I'm buckled in, and I'm starving. Pancakes are all that's on my mind. Are you buying breakfast?" Betsy asked from the backseat.

"See, what I mean? A real chatterbox," declared Steve. "Betsy, you're going where an unlimited supply of donuts and coffee await. Page will explain. I've got to make a call, so you two whisper amongst yourselves. You know how to whisper, right, Betsy?"

"Yeah, Lauren Bacall taught me in one of her movies with Bogart. You put your lips together and…something," explained Betsy, pleased with her witty response.

"Lauren was teaching Bogie how to whistle, not whisper," explained Page, twisting in the seat to look at her cousin wearing a confused expression. "Never mind. We're going to the station to observe the suspects getting interrogated. And a new inkling is going with us. Big doings today, cousin. Big doings."

CHAPTER 46

Page and Betsy felt protected, tucked away in the adjoining room with cups of coffee and a box of strawberry jelly donuts staring at them. Steve supplied each sleuth with a pen and paper for observation notes.

The interrogation room chairs were placed in a semi-circle, awaiting the five suspects in Catherine Lange's murder. An oak table closed the circle. The grey walls with two fist holes that were never repaired did nothing to soothe nerves. Uncomfortable wooden chairs served to encourage talk and bother each body enough to hasten the occupant's departure. The efficient chair layout allowed the investigators to observe everyone and still maintain authority and an intimidation stance.

"Everyone, take a seat. Excuse the ruckus down the hall. Our recent guests have found their accommodations not to their liking, and breakfast hash has never been a favorite at the jail. Anyway, Investigator Tanner and I appreciate your coming in as a group. We find this approach moves our discovery phase along effectively." Koch stepped aside and let Steve take center stage.

The suspects sat mute but full of anxiety. Evan glared at Steve while Garrett fidgeted, causing coins in his pocket to jingle, annoying Brakem. Gwen's attention centered on her polished nails. And Ty found a fly's movement fascinating.

Steve allowed them this pretense. "Okay, folks, I want to begin by stating we are pursuing some significant leads on the Lange murder and theft. It seems our laid-back little beach community has some unseemly types doing business here and, of course, the typical local bunch of petty thieves, which today's focus isn't on. I'll get right to it. Despite not finding any prints on the Lange safe, we did find Ty, Catherine, Gwen, and Evan's fingerprints all over the den. Those were expected."

Steve took a pause to let the information settle on the group. "Additionally, we learned of some troubling connections with most of you here today. For the time being, I'm going to defer discussing other active investigations that may or may not tie in with this case; however, those of you in this room should not forego worry."

"What does that mean? I'm a respected attorney in this community, and I resent your implications. I may even go so far as to say I'm inclined to see a lawsuit in the making. Tread carefully, Tanner. The Langes are my clients as well." Brakem nodded to Evan.

"Well, Mr. Brakem, let me assure you that I'm well versed in criminal law, having a JD myself. So, since you were the first to engage me, let's start with you. Why don't you begin by telling us where you were the night Catherine was shot?"

Shock at learning Steve possessed a law degree dissolved any advantage Brakem sought. His voice wavered. "That's easy. I was home enjoying a cognac, a fine cigar, and the Braves game on television in no particular order." Brakem crossed his arms over his chest.

"Did you happen to place a winning bet, for a change, on that game?" Tanner countered.

"What do you mean? I don't—"

"Brakem, you're a gambler with two bad problems that I'm going to spell out for you. One, you're a lousy gambler. My twelve-year-old niece could pick more winners than you. And second, which should concern you most, are the guys to whom you owe money. My information states they're plotting all kinds of dastardly acts to perpetrate on that self-important person of yours." Steve turned away and grabbed the file from the table, winking at Koch. "Tell me, Brakem. Who did the Braves play, and what was the final score?"

"I...I can't recall now." The attorney tugged on his designer tie.

Steve's smile lacked emotion. He bent down at eye level with the attorney. "The Cardinals won handily, and your lousy alibi is concerning me."

"Ty, same question. Where were you the night Catherine was found?" asked Steve pleasantly.

"I've already told Detective Koch. Why do I have to repeat my statement? I shouldn't even be here." Ty needed two chairs to handle his size.

"Yes, you have provided Koch with your account, but I'm an investigator with preferences. I like to hear it directly from a suspect and not read it in this file." Steve held up a different folder. "Let's hear it."

"As I said, it was my evening off. I went for a drive down the coast. I had things on my mind. Driving helps me get stuff straight. Know what I mean?" Ty's accent slipped out, proving his nervousness at being questioned.

Steve nodded, choosing to ignore questioning his country of origin. "I'm like that too. So, Ty, I'm curious. What things had you troubled?"

"Just business matters. Everything worked out."

"Happy to hear it. What time did you get back to the Langes'?" Tanner's tone shifted to a hardline.

"Koch knows when I got back. I came long after the police had arrived with the news about Mrs. Lange being found dead on the beach. Like I said before, why would I want to kill Mrs. Lange and risk being out of a job?" Ty shifted, spilling over more in his chair to make eye contact with Evan.

"Thank you, Ty. I don't have any further questions for now." Tanner tossed the file on the table. Seeing Ty had relaxed,

Steve turned back and delivered a jab. "Well, except for the fact that Ty Richards didn't exist two years ago. Our database shows you appeared on the scene with a North Carolina driver's license in hand. We're puzzled. Can you possibly clear this up, Mr. Richards?"

Ty cast his eyes downward, avoiding Tanner's gaze. "Man, I don't know. That's my name. Must be some glitch on your end."

Tanner looked at each suspect and nodded. "Could be, but I don't think so. Don't worry, Ty, we'll get it sorted out very soon." Steve returned to Koch and the stack of files. "Who's next detective?"

"Let's move to Gwen Lange." Koch's phone dinged. "Excuse me, folks. The autopsy report just came in." The detective moved purposely to the door.

"Okay, back to business. Ms. Lange, I had the pleasure of your company last evening, but we didn't get to chat about your sister-in-law's death. Let's see if we can establish your alibi now. Where were you that night?" Steve pulled up an empty chair and sat down to face the woman.

Gwen dressed her part well in a black dress, hair in a tight bun, and pale lipstick. "First, I want to say how distraught my brother and I are about the loss of Catherine. Simply tragic. We're hardly able to speak of this, but for you, I will try to hold my emotions inside for a few moments." Gwen pulled a tissue from her handbag and dabbed dry eyes.

"Again, please accept my condolences. Now, if you'd answer my question?" Tanner jotted something in the file.

"I had one of my terrible headaches. They're quite incapacitating. I took a strong painkiller and retired early. Anyway, the drug knocks me out for hours. I'm oblivious." Gwen touched her temples for effect and offered a simpering smile.

"I see. So, you heard no intruders. No screams. Nothing at

all to awaken you?"

"Sorry, no. My rooms are on a far wing. If only I had been awake. Maybe I could have spared my brother the loss of our valuables and jewelry." Gwen twisted the tissue in mock despair.

Evan jumped up, face flushed in anger. "Gwen, for the love of...the jewelry is not *ours*. It's mine. Just mine."

"Mr. Lange, please sit down and contain yourself," commanded Steve. "Gwen, it sounds to me like you're more concerned about the theft than Catherine's murder. Perhaps you can tell me when and who told you of your sister-in-law's death?"

"I'm fuzzy about that. Maybe Ty or Evan came to my rooms. It's a blur. This talk is all too upsetting. Please, move on to my brother."

Brakem and Gwen shared a subtle nod.

"Of course, Ms. Lange. I understand how difficult this must be, but I have one more question for you. Why did Garrett issue you four jewelry insurance riders on the same pieces Catherine had listed on a document as belonging to her?"

"What do you mean Gwen has riders? In her name?" spewed Evan. "My sister doesn't have any ownership rights."

"Evan, for goodness sakes, calm down. Garrett is an imbecile. He made a mistake and issued the policies incorrectly. They were, of course, going to have your name listed. I know that I haven't any rights to the gems, though we both know Mother made an error in judgment leaving them to you." Gwen's body went rigid as she fought to contain her anger.

Garett piped up. "Hold on. I'm no imbecile unless you want to count my being involved with you two pains in my backside. Gwen and Catherine demanded I prepare those riders, and legally, I can if a client is willing to cough up the dough, but only one claim gets filed...I think. Ina knows and takes care of all of that," said Garrett, fizzling out.

"No one gets any money for what was stolen but me. See

to the claims, Garrett, or I may need to make some phone calls to your corporate office," threatened Evan.

Steve's hands found his hips. "All of you shut up. I've heard enough. You can get your questionable affairs in order outside this station." Steve returned to the table, stifling a grin. He'd managed, and with little effort, to get them turning on each other like a pack of wolves. He snagged another file, returned to the group, and scooted the empty chair over to face Evan.

"Mr. Lange, thank you for attending our little soirée today. I want to resume where we left off last evening. I'm still quite confused as to why you booked two flights home from New York using an alias for the first flight and your given name for the later flight. The airport cameras show someone resembling you disembarked from that earlier flight, and even though the passenger roster shows you boarded the second flight, the camera didn't reveal a passenger who matched your appearance. Time to clear up this confusion for us. Now!" Steve shouted the last word, causing Evan to flinch.

"I...I had someone in New York book me on two first-class flights, as I wasn't sure when my meetings would end. I can't explain why she made a mistake with the names. I didn't bother to verify the tickets." Evan stood and moved toward a water pitcher. He poured a cup and sat on the opposite corner of the table and glanced at his watch.

Steve approached Evan. "And which flight did you board? I advise you to tell the truth. I already have my answer. Your answer is merely for the record, Mr. Lange."

Evan studied the investigator. "Okay, fine, I took the first flight home. Someone else must have used my second ticket. So what?"

"Return to your seat, Mr. Lange," instructed Tanner. He waited for Evan to settle. "All right. I'm going to need your alibi now that we've established you were back at Shell Isle before your wife's murder and the theft occurred as well."

"Fine. I had business to conduct before returning to my home that evening. I received a call from Ty, I think, alerting me that there had been a break-in. Catherine's body was found after that, as I recall. No, maybe I was first alerted about her." Evan's voice faltered.

"Mr. Lange, you've not been paying attention this morning, but I have. Ty just told us he came home after Catherine's body was discovered. You knew before Ty, and he didn't call you, but someone else did. Someone in this room. Who?" Steve walked by each suspect with his questioning face. "I think that fact is telling to this case. And I have the means to find out by checking everyone's call history, which annoys me to waste time doing. I will do this today unless Evan and the unknown caller wise up and answer." Steve stood in the middle of the room, counting ten seconds in his mind.

No one spoke.

Betsy patted a silent Page's hand and mouthed, "Good stuff."

"Yep, this is helpful. Shh, there's Koch," whispered Page.

Koch entered the interrogation room, puncturing the silence. "Quiet group you got here, Tanner." He loped across the room to stand next to Steve.

"Yes, they are all contemplating their future and whether it includes some time spent at the state's facility in Raleigh. I don't see any of this group fitting in with the likes there." Steve chuckled. "What ya got, Koch? Maybe if you share, someone will feel inclined to talk to us."

"Well, the ME's report is pretty interesting. There's one fact I think is pertinent to our folks' hearing. Mrs. Lange wasn't alive when she got tossed in the ocean. No water in her lungs. Plus, her skin didn't show any long exposure to the salt water. Someone wanted us to think she was shot on a boat. Or perhaps that she drowned after being shot? She did not. Add to the fact that Mrs. Lange was wearing high heels, which isn't what I consider beach or boating attire. This is what my daughter calls a conundrum." Koch handed the report over to Tanner and grinned at the squirming suspects.

"Thanks, Detective Koch." Steve turned back to the five. "I'm going to give you all one more opportunity to confess who spoke to Evan that night, or perhaps Evan, you killed your wife and didn't need the call?"

"What? That's preposterous. I didn't kill her. I wasn't home to kill her. Furthermore, why would I rob myself?" Evan grew more agitated. "Brakem called me. There. Big deal." Evan shot his eyes the attorney's way. "Tell them."

"So, I called my client and let him know what was happening at his home." Brakem appeared unruffled.

"Okay, Mr. Brakem. You must tell us how you came to know while engrossed in the baseball game and your fine cigar," Steve pivoted toward the attorney. "You all should have your own family tree. So much co-mingling," offered Tanner with a dose of sarcasm. "Mr. Brakem? I regret that I'm not known for my patience."

Brakem smirked. "I heard the news on my police radio. Heard Koch here say you all wanted to keep it hush-hush, but I figured Evan needed to know what was waiting for him."

"Next time, Brakem, we'd thank you for staying out of police matters," interjected Koch.

Tanner walked around the room. "I think Mr. Brakem understands his screw-up. So, Evan, you got the call from Brakem that I assume enlightened you about your wife's death and the theft?"

"Yes, I told Evan about Catherine's death. I had no way of knowing about the burglary. That fact wasn't reported on the scanner. Come on, Evan, get your facts straight," demanded an agitated Brakem.

"All right, Mr. Lange, so Brakem clued you in on your wife. Did you come right home from this business you were attending to?" Tanner grabbed a pen and wrote more. "Listen, Evan. I want the facts of where you were, who you were with, and when you received Brakem's call. Either talk now, or I'm charging you —"

"You've got nothing on me," declared Evan, starting to rise.

"Keep your seat, Lange. I have enough to secure you a cell down the hall, but I'm not ready to activate your reservation. Answer my questions."

"I can't tell you who my business associates are. They wouldn't take kindly to me divulging that information or where we met." Evan stared off. "Brakem called me. That's all I've got for you."

"As your attorney, I'm advising you not to say anything more. They're bluffing on charging you. Relax." Brakem folded his arms in his customary manner and placed a self-satisfied grin on his face.

"Koch, he's all yours. You've got my list of counts to book this guy. Let's start with obstructing and suspicion. The other illegal activities we're on to him about can wait a while longer." Tanner stood.

"Can they arrest me, Brakem? Do something. I have an important meeting on Friday night that I can't miss. Take care of this problem now," Evan demanded as the detective approached him.

"Go along. I'll see about getting bail posted," replied Brakem, not hiding his pleasure in seeing Evan Lange cuffed.

"Come with me, Mr. Lange. I've got a nice cell picked out for you with a roommate you're sure to enjoy. His friends call him Bruiser. I'm even going to read you an early bedtime story called Mirandizing a Chump." A chuckling Koch shoved a dazed

Evan out the door and past the sleuths' room.

"Get a load of that, will ya, Page?" Betsy leaned in to whisper. "The man's sniveling like a child."

Page's face lit with amusement at the sight. "Right now, Evan's worried about making friends with Bruiser." Page turned her focus to the interrogator. "My inkling says Evan's not guilty of killing his wife or robbing the house safe, but I bet Tanner's got him on money laundering and other things. He's using Evan for some other purpose. Whoa, Gwen wants to talk again."

"My brother has been under great strain of late with his business dealings. He should have cooperated. This interview is quite overwhelming. My nerves are snapping. I really must leave now and call my doctor."

Steve picked up Garrett's file and crossed the room to Gwen. "I appreciate your understanding about Mr. Lange, but I'm sure you also understand I need you to remain until Mr. Garrett shares his alibi. You wouldn't want to miss this. I can have one of the female detectives drive you to your doctor as soon as we wrap up." Steve appreciated the opportunity to expose a 'cry wolf' type. Both Langes majored in the worn behavior.

"That won't be necessary. Please continue with this charade." Gwen's voice returned to its normal combustive state. She crossed a leg with a vigor surprising for her age.

Steve showed no interest in the woman's acerbic tongue. "Now, I come to you, Mr. Garrett. I find myself hungry for lunch with two delightful and most law-abiding ladies, so I'm going to get right to the point. Your wife has disputed your alibi of being home that evening. Without sharing your marital issues with the others here, would you tell me where you were that evening?"

"Did Steve just say he's taking us to lunch? These stale donuts wouldn't live on a day-old bakery shelf. I'm past starving," declared Betsy.

"I believe he did. Stifle your hunger talk and listen," said

Page.

"Last chance, Garrett," threatened Steve while glancing at the clock.

Garrett grimaced. "Not in front of everyone. This is personal, and I can't risk—"

"Garrett, for the love of all that is holy, we all know you're getting it on with Lola. I have an important appointment. Spill it already." Brakem took his turn at the water pitcher.

"Sure, I'll be happy to spill it, starting with the fact that your important date is with the ponies. At least I'm with a real woman and not pinning my hopes on the last lap," Garrett spat at Brakem's back. "I was with a woman named Lola until around two in the morning, and I'd appreciate this fact not getting shared with my wife." Garrett took a measure of the people surrounding him. His trusty handkerchief came out.

"Thank you, Mr. Garrett. And, so you know, I have someone speaking with your side honey in a nearby room. So, let's hope her story jives with yours. As far as your proclivity in writing what appears to be excessive amounts of jewelry riders, we're looking into that for you as well. I want to ensure, forgive the pun, that you're operating your business properly. I'd hate to see you back here for another chat," said Steve, landing a jab on this suspect. The robberies still had him on alert with Garrett and Lola's possible involvement. "Anything else, Mr. Garrett, that you'd like us to know regarding this case?"

"I didn't have anything to do with Mrs. Lange's death, and neither did Lola. And she'll confirm I was with her that evening because it's the truth, so help me." Garrett raised his right hand as if taking an oath.

Steve dropped Garrett's file atop the rest. "I still think Catherine's threat of blackmail worried you. Maybe enough to kill her. Okay, everyone, thank you for coming in. Let me remind you that no one is to leave Shell Isle without express consent from us, and that consent won't be forthcoming. Any questions?" Steve paused. "No? Well, the officer standing at the door will show you out."

The solemn faces of Gwen, Garrett, and Ty filed out. Brakem was the caboose.

"Hey, Brakem, aren't you going to file the papers on Evan's behalf before you leave?" asked Steve.

"I'm not in any hurry. The guy's a jerk, and I've got somewhere to be." Brakem kept walking.

Fifteen minutes later, Steve poked his head into the room where Page and Betsy waited. "Ladies, you doing okay?" He offered them each a smile.

"I'm ravenous and ready for that lunch you promised us," answered Betsy.

"I'm ravenous too, but for hearing your thoughts and information update after this interrogation. Tanner, you're a force," finished Page with a firm slap planted on the investigator's shoulder.

Steve chuckled. "How do you all feel about lunch at the Crab Shak?"

"The Shak. Why the Shak?" asked a confused Page. That wasn't exactly the kind of place she'd envisioned Steve treating them to.

"Color me there. The Shak's cakes have been calling to me since our last visit. Hurry up, kids." Betsy scurried out the door.

Page pulled Steve back. "Why the Crab Shak?"

"Just got a tip." He touched Page's waist, ushering her out.

CHAPTER 47

"I can't believe we got Velma as a waitress again. Anyway, I'm ready to listen to whatever you want to tell us, Tanner." Betsy placed her napkin in her lap, anticipating what was coming.

"How about I start with asking if you gleaned anything from this morning's exchange?" Steve took a long sip of his iced tea, discarding the lemon. "They're dangerous whenever I fool with them. I'm sparing you two a squirting," he explained, laughing.

Page jumped in. "Well, I eliminated Garrett and Evan as murderers, but that's not to say they're not involved in some manner. Garrett could still have played a part in a burglary gone wrong. He stayed mute on the theft. And back to the murdering part—the guy's not strong enough to carry a bowl of sugar."

"Unless he had a helper with muscle," added Betsy. "Nah, he's low on my list, too."

"Why not Evan?" asked Steve.

Page smiled. "Easy. Even though he didn't provide names to validate that meeting, he didn't pull the trigger. His associates might be capable of that, though, given reason. Remember, Catherine was afraid and trying to get out of the country. Do you agree with my assessment?" Page studied the man she'd come to respect. Watching him interrogate today only amplified the attraction.

Steve grinned. "I agree to a point. We've got a case of money laundering that the Bureau believes is close to being ready for prosecution. I've enough surveillance proof and one guy on the inside to guarantee Evan an extended stay with a secure steel door, compliments of the taxpayers. Whether these Members, as they call themselves, wanted to whack Catherine, we haven't yet determined. It's possible what she overheard from Evan did frighten her enough to want to leave town that night." Tanner signaled the waitress for a refill.

Page craved more information. "What did Koch find last night when he stopped Brakem on his way to Evan's?"

Velma took her time pouring Steve's tea. Her eyes failed at making the connection she'd hoped with him. She gave a huff and sauntered off.

Betsy laughed. "Thought Velma was hot for bikers. It seems she's casting her net wider to include you, Tanner."

"Sorry, she's not my type." Steve glanced around before answering Page. "Brakem must have seen the officer following his vehicle. We found nothing and got nothing out of the attorney, except Brakem, stating he only wanted to check in with his client, who was back in town. We know Brakem has connections with Evan and the Members. He made the mistake of accepting a loan from this group to pay his gambling debts. Now, he's into some tough guys for six figures."

"Brakem makes bad choices and ignores his clients. He chose to take off to place a bet rather than see to Evan's release. Swell guy," declared Betsy with a huff.

"That's the hold and insanity of addiction, Betsy." Steve shrugged and checked his cell phone.

"So, how about this? Brakem could have killed Catherine and taken the jewelry to offset his debt? That theory works, right?" Betsy moved the bottle of ketchup closer and tucked a paper napkin in her lap.

"How'd he get into the safe?" asked Steve.

"Right, the safe again, which Evan states he alone possessed the combo." Betsy eyed Velma, tormenting her and making a slow pass with a full tray of desserts.

Page decided to enter the conversation. "We haven't talked much about Ty. What can you tell us about him, Steve? Other than Ty's probably not his real name."

"I should know more about this too-quiet suspect very soon. I had the lab guys lift fingerprints off Ty's chair after he left today. Ty is an enigma, but not for much longer. I've got some ideas, but I'm not at liberty to share them."

"Don't forget he's got an accent. Page and I caught that when you were grilling him," interjected Betsy.

"Oh, I think Ty and Catherine hail from the same place." Page expected a response from that snippet.

"Another intuiting? Do they usually come this often?" asked Steve, fascinated with the sleuth's gifts.

"They do when we're getting close to cracking a case. This is good news to celebrate, Tanner," explained Betsy.

Ignoring their exchange, Page stood. "Please, excuse me for a moment while I go freshen up." She walked away before they could question her sudden departure.

The nudge sent her into an empty bathroom stall just before another woman entered. Page stood on the seat, crouched as silent as an alley cat, ready to pounce on an unsuspecting mouse.

"Listen, Garrett, I told them we were together the other night, but nothing about the duplicate riders or the claims. And, if you want me to keep mute about a lot of other things, my cut needs to be half now. Are you serious? Don't go all clingy on me. I don't love you. I don't even like you. Are you kidding me? I have no desire to run off anywhere with you. You know what? Change of plans. Drop off my cut from that last referral. You and I...we're done."

Page waited for Lola to leave the ladies' room. She splashed cold water on her face and went to enlighten Steve and Betsy. As Page entered the dining room, she noticed Lola had taken a booth near the door.

"Are you okay?" asked Betsy. She studied her cousin's flushed face. "Ahh, Page has something for us."

"I do. Sorry, I got the nudge and had to act fast. Lola came into the bathroom and had a phone chat with Garrett. She not only asked for half of her cut but ended up telling him she couldn't stand him and their whole arrangement was caput. The poor guy professed his love and got dumped while she relieved herself of him and washed some dirt off her hands."

"Gross," replied Betsy.

"Insightful and helpful, Page. My respect for your gifts is growing. I see Lola seated over in the corner. Here comes Velma with our tray." Steve's hunger lit his face as she approached.

"Don't get fooled. Velma's a tease with her trays." Betsy's eyes caught a glimpse without turning her head.

"Here you go, honey. Fried fish basket with all the trimmings, well, except for me. I could be your dessert later if you say the word." Velma bent low and placed Steve's lunch on the table.

"Umm, Velma. He's with us, in case you haven't noticed. Curb the come on and give us our baskets," said Betsy already taking hers from the tray. "Don't forget my chocolate cake, or I might forget your tip."

Velma stepped back, sizing up her competition. "Sure, I get the message. Hands off this hunk. Know what, Miss Feisty? I've decided I like you."

Everyone burst into laughter, happy that Betsy's matching brashness had diffused an awkward situation.

"Hey, Velma? Thanks for the offer," hollered Steve, still smiling. "Let's eat, ladies."

"While we have time," finished Page cryptically.

CHAPTER 48

"Helloooo?" Betsy waved her arms like windshield wipers in front of her two distracted companions. Would you two please give the Lola lookin' a rest and feast your eyes on this scrumptious chocolate four-layer cake? Take your spoons and grab a taste. I'm generous that way."

"I can break surveillance for cake," said Page, filling her mouth with an impressive bite.

"I'll pass on the cake, but get a look at who just joined Lola," said Steve with a wink.

"Geez, it's Seedy. What's he doing with Lola?" asked a puzzled Betsy.

"And I wanna know why he's wearing a leather jacket in this temperature?" added Page.

"Are you kidding me? Now Ty's joining them." Betsy returned to her cake. "You two can work this one out while I eat."

Steve punched a button on his cell phone and positioned himself behind their booth's post to avoid being seen by the threesome. "Koch, the tip was good. Both men are here, along with our Lola. You've lived here since the dawn of man. What's her connection?"

Page and Betsy looked at each other, awaiting another puzzle piece.

"Ah, interesting. Thanks, but I can handle these guys. Back to you later." Steve tucked the cell phone in his pocket.

"Well? What's interesting?" cajoled Page.

Steve looked at each woman, pausing to build suspense. "Guess who Lola's ex is?"

"Not Seedy?" Betsy took another look, noting Seedy and Lola were cozy in the booth talking with Ty.

"Yep. Ole Seedy and Lola are recently separated, but by the looks of them, you'd never know it." Steve laid money down next to their ticket for a passing Velma.

"Are we leaving?" asked Betsy. She gobbled the rest of her cake.

"Soon. Sit tight, ladies, and chat or something," instructed Steve.

"Did you see that? Seedy passed a brown sack to Ty, and it ain't his lunch," said Page. "Ty is leaving."

"Stay here. I'll be back for you," Steve ordered.

Page grabbed her handbag, darting from the booth. "But… we can—"

"Stay put." Steve walked toward the door.

"We'll be here when you get back," replied Betsy to the air. "Wonder what he's going to do with Ty?"

"I guess it depends on what's in the bag. Lola's acting antsy, but Seedy won't let her out of the booth. That's funny. He just tried to kiss her, and she smacked him good." Page grinned.

Betsy stole a peep. "I bet you those two are up to something. They don't strike me as the types to do anything above board. You agree?"

"I do agree, and I'm hankering to know how Seedy fits in with Lola's little scheme with Garrett?" She had a good read on Evan, but the others still left her cloudy. She sensed time choking down on all involved. And Catherine's murderer? Unpredictable was the word that came to Page, which served to amp her worry.

"Excuse me for a sec, Page." Betsy headed for the cashier.

Page watched Seedy wave to a group of tough-looking dudes as he slipped out the Shak's screen rear door. She warred with her mind whether to go over to Lola and say hello. Steve returned, saving her the trouble. "Glad you're back and standing upright. So, what was in the sack?"

"Another gun. Seedy excels at selling unlicensed weapons it appears. Quite the versatile petty criminal." Steve patted the side pocket of his cargo pants. "Got me a little souvenir of our exchange. And I delivered Ty another invitation to visit Koch and explain what just transpired. It looks as if Ty's worried seeing Evan's business associates popping up all around town. He claimed he needed the gun for added protection but didn't want to waste time driving to Wilmington to get a gun the legit way."

"Let me try to guess. Ty's afraid that guilt by association will visit pain and suffering on himself. No doubt, being around Evan can be dangerous. Listen, we already know tomorrow night, Evan's supposed to hand over the missing Fabergé egg and gems. Time's running out, and he's stuck in jail, unable to..." Page's voice trailed off, seeing Betsy approach with a large white box tied with a bright red string.

"What'd I miss while I secured for our eating pleasure this delectable coconut pineapple cake with cream cheese frosting?" Betsy modeled the box.

"Oh, Steve's packing extra heat, thanks to Seedy's bad merchandising skills, and Ty is supposed to be heading to Detective Koch and explain why he needed that unlicensed revolver. Seedy's trouble radar clicked on, and he sneaked out the back door. And, Lola? Where's that hussy?" Page noted the empty booth and busboy clearing the table with about as much enthusiasm as being told he'd be clocking extra work hours.

"Lola's where you'd expect her, in the corner pool room with the bikers. I caught a glimpse of her a second ago, polishing some guy's cue. Betsy, don't say whatever you were about to let loose." Steve chuckled.

"I was only going to comment that Brakem must have given her the day off. I wasn't gonna say a word about all the other cues she polished." Betsy shrugged and pulled a face of innocence. She peeked in the cake box with her sampling index finger, ready to strike.

Page rolled her eyes and reached over and flicked her cousin's hand, closing the box lid. "No more cake. Reward later."

"As much as I enjoy the free entertainment, I need to drop you girls back at Hibiscus and get to the station. In the next few hours, I expect most of the reports back. We should have a pretty good picture of these suspects. Ladies, after you."

CHAPTER 49

Betsy waited for Page to close the front door. "Well, haven't we had a fascinating day? I mean getting invited to observe the interrogation, treated to lunch by the hunk next door, Velma deciding she likes me, and then the bonus of observing the three low-life diners at the Shak." Betsy transferred her cake to a plate and put Tilly's vintage milk glass dome over it.

Page watched, smiling at the care her cousin awarded the dessert. "Yes, today has propelled us toward knowing so much more. I'm anxious to hear what Ty's fingerprints reveal about his identity. That hint of accent piqued my interest."

Betsy poured them each a glass of lemonade and motioned Page to follow her and the drinks to the porch. "Why is Ty's accent significant?" asked Betsy, frowning and taking up residence in the hammock.

Page took a sip, thinking about how best to answer Betsy's question. "I'm not sure yet, but I believe we will know soon enough."

~*~

"I'm glad the Dowager Gertrude and I finally got to spend some time together this afternoon. She's making quite an impact on society in this second book. I felt guilty neglecting her and the Ton," said Betsy, placing the book on a nearby table.

"Yes, and while you attended some high society gala with her in Dorset, I worked on our suspect board," replied Page, pointing to the alterations she'd made. "I'm convinced that Evan and Brakem weren't involved in the burglary. Evan feared sharing the Member's names more than being arrested. And,

Brakem may have an addiction, but he's not desperate enough to break into a client and partner's home." Page gazed at the board.

"I'm with you. My money is on Garrett's involvement. Fine jewelry, inflated riders, an expensive girlfriend who's probably the brains…" Betsy paused, tapping her fingers on the armrest of the chair.

"Ex-girlfriend. Lola dumped him a few hours ago in the Shak's ladies' room and cozied up to Seedy minutes later," reminded Page.

"Yeah, her ex. Garrett's got his paws in this somewhere," said Betsy.

~*~

Their evening was almost enjoyable if Page's mind hadn't run scenarios incessantly on the suspects. No other inklings, nudges, or intuiting had come calling, and that disappointment amplified her frustration. She knew that lulls usually meant the one who'd committed a wrongful act hadn't made their next move. Page heard the doorbell and shoved the suspect board into the hall closet. She glanced in her mirror, seeing a face bare of makeup, and released a sigh. No time to primp now. "I've got it, Betsy."

"Okay, I'll be out in a minute. Just finishing answering some emails," hollered Betsy from the bedroom.

"How's it goin,' Tanner?" Page stepped aside, allowing him to pass. "Barnacle showed up for a visit earlier, which is why, I assume, you're standing at my door."

Hearing his name, Barnacle came charging toward Steve with a blue muzzle and a wagging tail.

"Page, I thought we'd agreed no more people food for him." Steve stooped to examine Barnacle while the blue tongue licked his face. "Page?"

"We didn't feed him. Rather, he fed himself a bowl of our blueberries meant to sit on top of vanilla ice cream," Page explained. "Yep, we ended up with plain, boring vanilla for dessert."

Betsy entered. "That's right, Tanner. Your dog's manners need some work. I'd placed the bowl of berries on the table and went to scoop the ice cream. When I returned, I was greeted with the face you see and my empty bowl."

Steve's face registered amusement. "I apologize. How about I make it up to you both and supply a case update from the last few hours? You, Barnacle, go to the porch and stay out of Betsy's hammock." Steve took a seat.

"Apology accepted. Tell us," replied Betsy, showing off her good mood.

Steve's cell phone interrupted. "Tanner. Finally, someone's nerves forcing them to act. I'm here and can tail him. Talk to you later, and thanks." Steve pocketed the cell phone and stood. "Koch had Ty under surveillance by an officer who just called in. It seems Ty has the urge to take a trip without our blessing. He's putting suitcases in his car at the Langes'. Sorry, ladies, I've got to run." Steve moved toward the front door.

Page felt the nudge. "Hold up. I need to go along, and I promise to do whatever you say." She grabbed her jacket and handbag, coming up beside Steve.

"You might as well let her go. She'll follow you if you don't," informed Betsy. "I'll stay here with Barn and have our second dessert of pineapple cake and coffee ready when you both get back."

Steve opened the door. "Let's go then. And, you'd better not do—"

"Whatever I'd better not do, I won't," said Page, jogging behind him towards the SUV.

CHAPTER 50

Page and Steve sat scrunched down in his vehicle's seats, watching Ty close the silver sedan's trunk lid. He glanced around the surroundings before climbing inside the car.

"Wow, that's cutting it close. Good that you were home for this surveilling. Look, Ty's leaving, and I especially admire how he's morphed into a heavy-metal rocker. Check out that blond wig he's sporting. Impressive disguise."

"He's quite the talent. Buckle up. Too bad he's about to make another big mistake. I didn't get a chance to tell you, but your guess about his real home was correct." Steve waited for a car to pass and then backed out to follow Ty.

"I'll bite." Page smiled.

"Curacao. And, get this other fact, the same island as Evan and his deceased father, who incidentally had been a founding Member. Quite the lineage the men share." Steve turned on his navigation.

"Seems to me every place has groups skirting the law and working nefarious agendas, even small island ones. Beautiful Curacao is no different. Still, these guys are connected. I bet Ty is leaving town because with Evan being in jail, there's no way the Fabergé Egg and stones will be found and delivered by tomorrow night. I'm thinking Ty is worried about that group coming after him." Page glanced over, noting Steve's concentration on driving. Page found her coral lip gloss in the bottom of her purse and did a fast application. Her faded jeans and top weren't a wow, but she'd had no time to change. And why did it matter? Because she liked Steve, and her mom always told her to look her best.

"Why don't you tell me more while I focus on being stealthy, as you call my moves?" Steve dropped behind two cars to blend in better.

"Did Brakem help Evan make bail and get released?"

"As a matter of fact, he did not. He stayed with the ponies all afternoon and then went home. As far as I know, he's not left his house. We're watching him."

"So, I think Brakem knows Evan is a dead man if he doesn't make the meeting with the goods. Maybe he thinks Evan is safer in jail than on the streets trying to track down the stolen valuables, or maybe Brakem plain doesn't care." Page looked out the window, trying on the theories.

Steve kept a reasonable distance from Ty's sedan and waited for the sleuth to share more insights.

Page continued, "Yeah, Brakem is an uncaring oaf. He's acting in his own best interest. Staying away from Evan is a healthy choice for him right now. Besides, he's got problems with the Members, like an impressive loan that needs paying and ongoing laundering to do for them. Nope. He'll not do anything for Evan unless directed by someone higher up. It's better for Evan to be sequestered with Brutus." Page acknowledged that inkling's correctness.

"Bruiser," corrected a smiling Steve. "Agreed. And, from what we can determine, Evan's at a dead end locating his stolen items. His sister doesn't seem motivated to help him get out of jail. The truth is, Gwen's probably reveling in having full control of the home. She's another uncaring one. All about herself. Hang on." Steve gave a voice command, "Call Koch."

"Koch here. What's up with Ty?"

"Be warned. You're on speaker with our local sleuth sitting next to me," said Steve, winking at Page.

"Why am I not surprised? That sleuth's wiles have you, Tanner." Koch laughed. "Page, be careful and give us some help if you can."

"My wiles and I are fully engaged, detective." Page reached into her handbag, feeling for her mini binoculars.

"Listen, Koch; I'm pretty confident that Ty is heading to Wilmington's airport. He's scared and on the run. He won't use his current alias, and we have no idea what other fake ID he's carrying, so there is no point checking passenger lists. Get some Wilmington detectives there and tell them Ty looks like he's just come off stage as a heavy metal band member. The wig of long blond hair is an especially nice touch." Steve laughed.

"I've got the picture. Will contact them now, and I'm not far behind you. Be careful. He's likely scored another gun from Larry. Out."

"Page, I need to find a secure place for you, so help me."

"We'll be shown our next steps when it's time. So, Larry is Seedy's name, huh?"

"Yes, and he's a talented guy. Your Seedy is known for petty theft and safecracking, his latest specialty. Fits perfect with his locksmith job. We're pretty sure now he's involved somehow with the most recent robberies around Shell and possibly the Lange safe. He and Lola may be separated, but they've forged some working relationship that included Garrett. What we don't know yet is if Garrett is on the periphery or in their inner circle? Any insights? Steve's face registered uncertainty.

"I sense Garrett's on the outside but still filling his pockets. He's too spineless for them to risk him knowing the extent of what they're doing. What's with the face?" Page looked ahead and had her answer.

CHAPTER 51

"Whose place is this? Not much to look at," offered Page, peering through the binoculars, watching Ty exit his car.

Steve pulled the SUV over and cut the lights. "I'm hoping you can provide that answer as soon as the front door opens. Am I glad you thought to bring your snoop glass."

"Funny. Hold on. It's Seedy, and he's dying laughing at, I assume, Ty's get-up. An envelope just passed from Ty...with cash. I see Seedy counting. Okay, let me zoom in more. Ty's looking at...I can't tell for sure." The inkling came. "He's gotten a fake ID from Seedy. Here comes Ty back to his car."

Steve snapped a few photos of the pair with his camera. "Well, guess Seedy has added even more to his resume. We're building quite the list of laws he's trampled. Here we go. The airport should be the next stop."

~*~

"Koch, listen up. Ty's at the airport parking garage unloading a tan suitcase and a plaid garment bag. Our rocker should be entering the terminal in less than five. I'm going to find Page a bench once inside, and I'll be right behind Ty. You and the others in place? Good." Steve clicked off and motioned for Page to follow him.

The airport terminal's architecture was an interesting blend of red brick construction with a green metal roof. Another insight interrupted Page's study. "I thought you'd appreciate knowing that Ty's going to do a bit of running, but he'll trip and become yours."

"Is that right?" Steve stopped and spun her around to face

him. He looked into her eyes and met with sincerity, staring back. "Well, okay then, guess I'm going to get another run in today. Nice to have you along, Wright."

"Just doing my part, but I'm still about solving this confounded case." Page released a sigh of frustration. "I regret this outing isn't getting me any closer to knowing who robbed the Lange safe and killed Catherine. The suspects are so intertwined." Page sent a fist skyward.

"We'll get a break soon enough." Steve put his arm around her as they approached the terminal sliding doors. Ty had gone through, and Steve recognized one of Wilmington's detectives following behind the rocker. "Here's your seat, and don't you dare budge. I'm going on."

"Sing out if you need me. I'll be right here," Page groaned, accepting her lot. She sat on the slatted oak bench, admiring Wilmington Airport's architecture with the atrium-like ceiling and tranquil color scheme. The gates fanned off the concourse like tentacles. Page noted the elevation renderings of the airport's latest expansion phase displayed on a nearby easel. The town's growing attraction to visitors was evident.

Founded around 1740, the city of Wilmington was located between the Atlantic Ocean and Cape Fear River. The town possessed a charming ambiance with its sea commerce and robust tourism. Page recalled the many restaurants and shops along River Walk, but the different town tours ranked high on her list for fun. Wilmington was awash in history and pirate doings that she'd like to explore more one day soon. She and Betsy could make a day of…Betsy. She'd better call before her cousin's every worry gene activated.

"Hey, Bets, I wanted to let you know we're at the Wilmington Airport. I'm parked on a bench inside for safety while Steve and the others follow Ty. Guess they're waiting for him to try and board before they arrest him. Oh no! Call you later." Page rang off before Betsy had a chance to utter a single word.

Page glanced toward the terminal doors in time to see Brakem hustle by with a satchel. *He must have dodged the officer watching him. What should she do? Steve told her to sit tight, but he needed to know the attorney was there, too.* Page grabbed her handbag, pulled out a ball cap to disguise herself, and took off after Brakem.

While she walked, her mind ran scenarios and best solutions. She looked for Steve and Koch, but they were nowhere around the ticket counters; however, Brakem was. Page remembered Steve had given her his card earlier. She rummaged in her purse, relying on touch to find it, while her eyes remained on Brakem, who was next up at the ticket counter. Page's fingers snagged the card and dialed the number.

"Tanner here."

"Umm, Steve, sorry to break protocol, but this is important. Brakem just arrived. I'm watching him.

"Brakem! Well, this is a surprise. Don't approach him. I'll send one of the officers. Page?" Steve's voice held concern.

"Yeah, I'm here. Brakem's purchased a ticket. You can't get someone to me in time; I'm going to follow him. Don't worry. I'll be discreet." Page took out her readers to hide her appearance better, but blast it, she needed to look over the glasses to walk.

"Do not tail this guy, Page. If we lose him, we lose him. I'm not going to have you risk..."

Page overheard Koch. "Steve, we've got a runner. Let's go."

"You guys go on. Remember, we've been told he's going to trip. You'll capture him easily. I've got to hustle and grab Brakem. Page just said the louse is trying to flee, too."

"Page? Where in the blazes are you?" Tanner's frantic voice shouted into the cell.

"We're walking toward the gates. Hurry, Steve."

"Stay on the phone with me. Page, are you listening?" Steve's legs were in a full run, dodging people like a basketball player dribbling his way to the basket.

"Yep, I'm here. We're at Gate Seven. He's in first-class boarding." Page dropped her glasses back in place. "Just great, he's almost to the front of the line. If you're not here in a minute, I need to delay him." Page moved closer to Brakem, her mind struggling with how to engage the attorney.

"Avoid Brakem. He's bad, not weak like Garrett. I'm almost there," Steve pleaded.

The attorney approached the airline employee, boarding pass in hand, along with a feigned affable smile.

Page put the phone in her pocket, knowing Steve could hear. "Mr. Brakem. What a coincidence." She yanked the cap off and put her hand out. "Page Wright."

Brakem turned and absently stepped aside, which allowed other passengers to move ahead of him. "Yes, yes. Ms. Wright. Please excuse me. I need to board."

Page grabbed his arm. "Oh, please give me a moment. They still need to board business class and the less fortunate. I have some news you might find interesting. Could you maybe step over to that corner with me?"

"Ms. Wright. I can't imagine anything you have to say that would be that important at this moment." Brakem turned to cut in the line.

"Hey, buddy, you stepped out. Get to the back," said a father holding a crying tot, exasperated with his charge.

Page scrambled to Brakem's side, waiting for her next guiding words. "Hey, did you know Ty's here too? At the airport with you. Isn't that a coincidence?"

"Ty's here? Where?" Brakem let his eyes dart around the gate's passengers. He locked on the face approaching him.

Brakem turned to bolt.

Page pulled her foot back and kicked the attorney with enough force to impress a goalie.

Brakem screamed out in pain and bent over to pull up his pants leg and rub his shin.

"Man, I bet that hurts like the blazes. Looks like a nasty bruise in the making." Steve took Brakem's satchel. "Let me help you with that. Why don't we take a seat over there and have a chat? You see, I'm curious why you were leaving town when we expressly told you to remain at Shell Isle." Steve looked up at the flight info. "And, you're going to Charlotte, I see, and then on to the Caymans. I hear the island is friendly to offshore accounts. Page, here's my credit card. Grab three sodas from the bar. Our friend here needs some reviving after you walloped him with those big buckle sandals." Steve smirked.

"I might bleed from that woman's kick. Maybe even need stitches," whined Brakem. He applied pressure to his shin with a handkerchief — the shock of having his leg harpooned by a buckle and his travel plans invaded by Page showing on his face. Steve's words hadn't registered as the pain trumped his waiting troubles.

"Treat yourself to a few deep breaths, Brakem." Steve spoke into his phone. "Koch, I've got Brakem with me, a little worse for wear. What's Ty's status? Great. We'll drive back to Shell Isle in a few minutes. Hang on." Steve tapped Brakem on the shoulder.

He rose from his ministrations. "What now, Tanner?"

"Do I need to handcuff you and have an officer escort you back to the station, or will you go cooperatively with me? Your choice, counselor." Steve pulled the handcuffs out to make his point.

"I'm an attorney. I know my rights. I'll go along without your needing to show off your perceived authority." Brakem returned to his leg, cussing Page.

"We're good here, Koch." Steve tucked his phone in his pocket. "Ahh, here are the sodas." Steve handed the drink to the attorney.

"Much obliged, Ms. Wright, for your assistance." Steve nodded.

"Sorry, Mr. Brakem, for causing you such pain," said Page, conjuring a pretend sympathetic smile. If she got a chance, she'd kick the other shin.

The attorney glared. "You've been a nuisance and a bother since the first day I laid eyes on you and that cousin of yours. Leave me alone."

Steve laughed. "If you only knew about her, you'd be sweating out of that designer shirt of yours. Let's go." Brakem limped, grumbling, toward the exit.

Once inside the SUV, Page texted Betsy she'd be going back to the police station to observe the two suspects' questioning. Her tired body relaxed as she settled into the seat, luxuriating in the cool leather. Her numbed senses offered no further insights, and for that reprieve, she felt grateful.

Brakem's presence brought only amusement to Page as he tried coaxing Steve to keep him separated from Evan and Ty. Fear surrounded him in the backseat as he explained to Tanner that returning him to the coop he was trying to fly away from didn't bode well for his well-being. Absent any response from Steve, the attorney retreated to fight his inner demons.

CHAPTER 52

"Hello again, Ms. Wright. You're going back to the observing room that you and Betsy visited earlier today. See if you pick up anything to steer us toward solving this case, assuming you're up to this? I'll gladly get a policewoman to drive you home." Koch's eyes reflected his regard and weariness.

"Thank you, but I'll stay. I'd appreciate a cup of strong coffee."

"Coffee. Can do. This day has been demanding for all of us. Tanner told me of your latest thoughts around our suspects, and, of course, I hear you can kick harder than my old granddaddy's mule." Koch enjoyed a chuckle as he escorted Page to the room. "We might need to register those feet of yours as lethal weapons." With his humorous side activated, he disappeared.

Page could hear the detective sharing his little joke with others as he went in search of her caffeine. She sat down, feeling the chair's hard plastic push against her tight back muscles, and wondered where Steve had gone. Looking through the glass window into the interrogation room, she noted the empty hot seat. Only the bright fluorescent lights and filled water pitcher testified to the suspect's imminent arrival.

Steve opened the door. "You okay? Here's your coffee. I brought sugar in case you needed extra pep." He placed the coffee cup and packets on the table and set a stern expression on his face. "I still can't believe you disobeyed my orders and went after Brakem. And, you gotta know I'm very unhappy with you."

Page grinned unabashedly. "No, you're not. You're just saying that. You know I was never in danger with Brakem unless you count his foul mouth. There were witnesses all around. Besides, when a nudge comes, I act. It's my way. It's how I help." Page blew into the cup. "This is hotter than lava."

Steve laughed and rubbed his jaw. "Page, I care about you, and that makes your safety primo." He saw movement out of the corner of his eye. "Showtime. See if you can read more body language — another specialty of yours. Ty's up first. See ya later, Miss Drew."

Page watched a cuffed Ty enter the room with Koch. The detective towered over a seated Ty as he Mirandized him. "Do you understand your rights?" asked Koch.

"Man, I understand, but you don't. I've told you over and over that I didn't kill Mrs. Lange, and I didn't rob them either. Yeah, I was leaving town, but if I don't, I'll be dead by the weekend. And I don't want to be dead. Would you?" Ty's voice pleaded for understanding.

Tanner appeared. "Well, Ty, I hate to see you back here with us, but truthfully, I'm not surprised after learning more about you, Lars Hoff, a citizen of the Dutch island of Curacao. I hear it's the most beautiful island in the Caribbean." Steve shoved the document over to him.

Ty glanced at the words. "So? I changed my name to be more employable." He pushed the paper back with an air of disdain.

The sleuth imagined the act would incite Steve's wrath. She sipped the coffee, willing it to keep her brain neurons firing — nothing to read yet.

"I understand your reasoning, Ty, but here's the thing, you've messed up big. Koch, you might as well start typing the list of laws this guy managed to violate."

"Good idea. Got my laptop right here and getting this first one down." Koch rewarded Ty with a sneer.

"You see, Ty, we in this country take exception to folks

buying guns illegally, using aliases and badly executed fake IDs, like your buddy, Larry, made for you tonight. There's a legal process for having your name changed, and you didn't follow that. And, your visa, Mr. Hoff? Well, that's expired. You're no longer a welcome guest of the United States. And, those disregarded laws are the tame ones compared to what else I suspect to uncover this night."

"Man, you don't understand my situation."

"Sure, I do. Tell you what. I'm going to give you one chance to make things easier. You've indicated you don't want legal representation and haven't done anything wrong other than the things we've just uncovered. I'm going to take you at your word for the moment and offer you help." Steve sat back in his chair, waiting.

"Okay. Sure, let's do it the easy way. I need to get out of town. Once I answer your questions, maybe you'll let me catch a flight? I'm no longer interested in citizenship, legally or illegally. I can disappear if you'll give me a chance. Save everyone a lot of trouble and paperwork. You guys hate paperwork."

"Well then, let's get about some answers. You've maintained you weren't at the Lange home around the time Catherine was killed."

"Nope. Not there."

"Let's jump ahead to your attempt to leave the country despite being told to remain here. I'm curious who you believe is going to kill you this weekend?"

"They're called the Members. Evan's screwed up big time and lost their rare collectibles needed for an upcoming business deal. Some Faberge Eggs and some rare gems I think. The trade of the pieces happens tomorrow night at nine o'clock, only it won't. It can't."

"Lost? No, I think it's because the pieces were stolen, and there's little hope of finding them," corrected Steve.

Ty registered surprise. "Okay, maybe you're right. Here's the thing. Evan's in jail and can't work his connections in the black market to determine who nabbed the valuables. It's bad, man. I'm cooked if you don't let me disappear."

"Forgive me, but why is this bad for you?" Koch jumped in, forcing Ty to try to appease both men.

"Because." Ty stared at the floor as if courage would flow up to him. "I'm one of the low-placed Members. Evan's dead father founded the organization along with three other men from nearby islands. Don't you get it? I'm in the States to ensure Evan lives up to his promises and delivers to the Members. Only this time, he can't, and that's on me. See, lately, Evan's been doing side deals, racking up some serious green. I had no choice but to inform on him. It's like this, man, Evan's dead, whether he finds the gems and eggs or not." The cuffs were chafing Ty's wrist. He glanced at the red marks.

Steve pressed on. "Evan told us some men are in town. Are these guys here to assist in tomorrow night's transaction, or perhaps if things go really badly, they'll mop up—"

"Right. Those goons will bop me, Evan, and that slime Brakem. That's what they'll do once they find out we've got nothing to hand off. I gotta scram tonight. Please. I'm begging you." Sweat trickled down Ty's forehead. "How about maybe loosening the bracelets?" He held up his hands.

"Maybe later. Where's Brakem fit in with this outfit?" Steve pulled another paper out.

"He's a lackey. They use him to launder money and set up offshore accounts. The Members loaned him big bucks to pay off his gambling debt to some wise guys threatening to remove appendages, but Brakem just transferred his problem to a group that he'll never be free of. I know."

Koch jumped in. "Why do you think Brakem wanted to get to the Cayman's tonight?"

"What? Brakem's gone? Man, he lucked out." Ty stared at his image in the double mirror. Traces of a fake tiger tattoo dressed his cheek as his eyes darkened with anger.

Ty's direct gaze caused Page to pull back, forgetting for the moment she couldn't be seen. So far, Ty was telling the truth. She almost pitied him for being caught up with the organization. He was indeed a caged tiger.

Steve laughed. "Oh, his luck didn't hold. We've got him in a cell around the corner. Why the Cayman Islands, Ty?"

Ty smirked. "That's a cell I'd not want to be inside. Probably because Evan and Brakem have stashed money in the Caymans. I heard they've bought homes and are set up to live well on the island. Not looking good for those dwazen."

"Excuse me?" questioned Koch, eyebrow raised.

"Sorry. It means fools in Dutch. About these cuffs? Come on, man. They're hurting me, and if you want more answers..."

Koch came over and released them. "Don't move from that chair, or I'll be calling you a dwazen."

"So, I've got Evan, Brakem, and you tied in with this group calling themselves the Members. And tomorrow night, you all have some big business deal involving moving these rare Fabergé Eggs and some pricey rocks, correct? Who's the buyer? Enlighten me," encouraged Steve.

"Look, I'm not in that circle, as you call it here. I'm the do-boy and spy on Evan and..."

"And who else?" that slip caught Steve by surprise.

"No one. Listen, the Members are always looking for cash. They put deals together to get US currency. Your dollars are valuable when you leave this country. Know what I mean? Wouldn't it make sense for the buyer to be some rich collector? That's what I think. I've been around those types. They have secret rooms for their collections."

Steve postponed the push to find out the name of the

person Ty held back. "It's my turn to confess, Ty. It might be helpful for you to hear that I'm part of a special unit with the FBI."

Ty's face turned ashen, but he said nothing.

"We've been watching Evan for a while, trying to connect him to money laundering and this group out of Curacao and the other islands. Right now, we've got enough to prosecute both Evan and Brakem. Evan told us earlier today that he'd prefer being behind bars than outside. Fact is, he begged Koch not to release him yet, as if we would. That goes along with what you've told us. Ty, you're earning points that may help your cause, but I'm going to need more." Steve went to pour some water.

"Do you have the names of the guys in town? Do you know where they're staying?" Steve placed the water in front of the suspect.

"No clue where they're staying or if there's more of them here, but they're watching us all the time. They know who you've got in jail. I hope my disguise worked. It's my only hope to escape this country with all my body parts. As for names, I know two of them. They've grabbed me a couple of times since they arrived to try and rattle me to find out more on Evan."

Koch stopped typing. "Names?"

"Yeah, Finn and Max. That's all I know about these two, other than they're good at inflicting pain. Ask my ribs."

"Koch, I need to step out and check in with someone."

"We'll be here." Koch nodded, knowing exactly where the investigator was headed.

CHAPTER 53

"You know why I came to you. I'm at a critical place with this guy." Steve shut the door and pulled up a chair.

Page nodded. "You're interested in what I picked up observing Ty. Everything he's said is factual. First, you can't think like an American when questioning him. If you want to understand what motivates Ty, you must place yourself in the world he's occupied probably his entire adult life or even earlier if his family, like Evan's, has been a part of this group. Find out the name he almost slipped and told you moments ago? He has protective feelings for that person." Page's sapphire eyes burned from weariness despite the coffee.

"Very insightful and helpful. You know, I'm developing my own special sense." Sleepy grey eyes matched hers.

"Hmm. Maybe I'm rubbing off, though I never had that effect on Betsy. What's your other sense telling you?" Page felt a tad intrigued.

"Ah, my sense tells me you've got a name to send me back into that room with."

"Well, aren't you something, mister?" Page paused. "Go force Ty to tell you who Catherine is to him."

Steve reached for Page's hand and bestowed a gratitude squeeze before disappearing.

~*~

"Okay, Ty, let's get this wrapped up. I've got Brakem waiting to sing louder than a canary." Koch chuckled and glanced at his watch. "Wife's held dinner. Won't be edible. And that gets me out of sorts if you get my meaning?"

"Come on, Ty. Why not explain your connection to Catherine Lange?" Steve leaned into Ty's face, fixing his best intimidating gaze on the man.

"Not much to tell. She was Evan's wife. He expected me to look after her when he was away."

"That's surface chatter. I don't pay attention to that. You kept her name inside of you minutes ago. I'm guessing because you have feelings for her." Steve pushed.

"Yeah, okay, I cared about her some." Ty fidgeted in his chair.

"Ty, don't make me drag this from you. I already know who Catherine is and what she was about with Evan. Did you hear me say FBI earlier?"

"Yeah, but first, I'd like to hear what you've got on that paper. Prove to me you're telling the truth." Ty swallowed. His eyes darted to the clock.

"Okay, I'm going to humor you, but in return, I expect some major information. Catherine is from Curacao, too. Her marriage was arranged to Evan to allow her to become an American citizen. And, we think she played some role for the Members as well. You know what her role was. You know why Catherine was trying to flee the country the night she got murdered. I bet you know who killed her. Was it you?" Steve's fist hit the table.

Page's face registered surprise with the pounding interrogation skills. Her intuiting of Catherine's name had proved accurate and supported Ty being involved somehow in her death. They were moments from learning his role and why. Anticipation followed her next inhale.

"Man, I've already told you I didn't kill Catherine. I... couldn't." Ty let out a loud sob and dropped his head. Seconds ticked by while he mustered control. "She was my...sister." Tears cascaded down Ty's cheeks. "She was my sister. And even though she always treated me like her slaaf...slave, I didn't wish her dead."

Koch tossed him the box of tissues. "Good performance there. What do you think, Tanner?"

"I don't know Koch. I think he did care some for his sister." Steve turned back to the man who still held more inside. "Ty, who wanted Catherine dead? I know you've got that information. Get it all out so we can bring that person or persons to justice for ending your sister's life. Help us."

"I guess there's no reason to keep quiet now. You've told me the FBI is into this mess. It's like this. Catherine overheard Evan and Brakem discussing their side work and cutting the Members out of some of the profits. They called it skimming. Catherine told me what she'd overheard and that she feared Brakem had seen her listening behind the corner. I told her she'd better let our contact know what she heard, which, of course, she did." Ty rubbed his face. "Can I get something other than water? Do you have bourbon?" Ty's voice sounded defeated.

"No booze here. It's a police station. I'll see about getting you something from the vending machine." Koch walked out whistling.

"Ty, I need you to wrap this. Your lot will improve once you've spilled everything. Here's what I'm wondering right now. Do you think Evan or Brakem killed her?"

"Man, I don't know. They're both capable if they thought the Cayman hideaway was in jeopardy." Ty grew thoughtful. "Guess I gotta tell you what rattled me a few nights ago. Proved the Members had escalated things. You see, Finn and Max gave me an ultimatum the night Catherine was murdered. They told me it came from Armand, who is high up in the organization." Ty paused to gather courage and pulled off his wig. He looked at Tanner straight on. "They told me if I didn't take my sister out, they would. And they'd make it plenty painful after they had their way with her. I had no doubt they meant every word. You see, Catherine made a huge mistake by telling our contact she was done spying on Evan and wanted to come home and resume her old life. My sister didn't understand there's no going home, at least not to the life she planned." Ty's eyes filled with tears. "She miscalculated her importance. She always did."

"So, that night, you went for a ride to decide what your next move would be and mentally prepare yourself to kill your sister?" Steve's experience told him one harder jab would get the whole story from Ty.

"Yeah, I went for a drive. Right then, I knew only two choices were out there. I take her life painless like or have those goons do it their way. I tried to find the guts to kill my sister. I had to keep those two monsters from touching her. They even demanded I bring proof of her death, like a body part. Animals." Ty spit in his glass.

Koch returned and plopped a root beer in front of Ty. "That's the closest I can get you to a real drink."

Ty released the tab. "Thanks, man."

Steve moved to unsettle Ty and get the last bits out of him. "I think I've got the picture of the pressure you felt. You were in a no-win. So, you drove around, I expect, with the bourbon bottle by your side. The booze gave you the courage to do the unthinkable. You went back to the Langes' and got Catherine to go out to the beach. The noise of the waves would drown out the bullet, assuming you didn't have a silencer on the weapon. You took care of her because if you didn't, they'd not only kill her but you too. Doing this proved your loyalty to the Members. Hard place to be, Ty. You had to shoot her." Steve sat back, waiting for the rest.

Ty jumped out of his chair and started pacing. "I told you I didn't kill my sister. I don't know who got to her first. Finn and Max, Evan, Brakem...it had to be them because you gotta believe it wasn't me."

Koch escorted Ty back to his chair. "Settle down, bud."

Steve's knuckles rapped on the table as he thought. "How about Garrett or Larry coming after Catherine?"

"Those two aren't the killing type. I know what it takes, and they don't have it."

"Gwen?" asked Steve.

"Nah, not her. She didn't like Catherine, but Gwen kept to herself. Took her meals alone. She stayed away from them and ended each night with some pill that put her in another orbit. If I had to guess, I'd say Evan's your man. He didn't care about Catherine and wasn't taking her to the Caymans. She was what you call a thorn in his ribs? Whatever. Evan doesn't care about anyone. He's all ice. Besides, Mr. Lange booked those two flights from New York, like you said when you brought us all in. Evan flew in early, using another name for a reason. A murdering reason. He killed my sister. Too bad for him that you figured out about the two flights. Go after that varkens...swine."

Steve studied Ty. "That's an interesting theory, but I find myself still leaning toward you murdering your sister, especially since you were tasked to perform the deed. Come on, Ty. Koch and I can sympathize with your plight. We can put in a good word with the prosecutor and tell him how you cooperated. That'll keep you from getting the chair," explained Steve, trying to find the key to ignite Ty's engine. He banked on Ty not knowing which states used the chair. North Carolina did not.

"The chair?" Ty screamed loud enough to wake the napping desk sergeant and send him knocking.

"Everything okay in here?" asked the bleary-eyed officer. The double shifts were evident on his face.

"We're good, thanks. Back to your desk and eyes open," instructed Koch.

Steve went over to Ty. "You've got more to tell me about Catherine's death. Prove to me you didn't kill her by telling me what you did do. I'm giving you one more minute before Koch books you for murder."

Ty returned to his seat and gulped the soda. "I gotta say this without any bourbon. That's inhumane. Okay, okay, I came back to the Langes that night, hoping I could convince Catherine to drive somewhere, anywhere in the States…just not leave on her flight. I knew the guys expected her to go to the airport if I didn't take care of the problem. I looked for my sister everywhere in the house and finally found her in Evan's study." Ty rubbed his eyes as if that would erase the memory.

Steve pushed. "And then what, Ty?"

"Man, she was already dead. Lying on the floor. I couldn't believe it. My sister was gone. I freaked out. I had to get her out of the house. I didn't want you guys coming around asking me questions. My life was still questionable." Ty finished the root beer. "So, I wrapped her in the rug where she'd bled out and carried her out into the ocean. I figured she'd wash ashore somewhere, and you'd think someone got her in a boat or pushed her off the pier. I don't know. I wasn't thinking clearly, and I didn't need trouble directed my way. I just knew I had to get the body out of the Lange home."

"But the plan failed. She washed back onto shore where you'd left her. And the medical examiner determined someone moved the body after death because her lungs were absent seawater. That conclusion proved unfortunate for your scheme." Koch held his poker face in check.

"Look, I screwed up. I get it, but it wasn't me that killed her. I couldn't do it. The only thing I did was cut a long hunk of her hair as Finn's proof. Just some hair. I swear."

Steve stood. "Ty, I believe your story. Sad as it is. One more question. Was the safe opened or closed when you found her?"

"I don't know, Tanner. All I could focus on was my sister

lying dead and what I needed to do to save myself. Sorry. I can't help you there."

"Okay, Ty. I appreciate your owning your role. We're going to give you some protection from the outside tonight. Finn and Max won't get near you, and we'll not make you bunk with Evan. Koch, he's all yours." Steve left the interrogation room, taking his exhaustion and appreciation into the room next door.

CHAPTER 54

Steve collapsed in the chair next to Page. "You delivered the goods again. Next is Brakem. And you're exhausted. Your face is showing me the drain of energy going on inside of you. Let me get you a ride home." Steve moved toward the door.

"Tanner, get yourself in this chair." Page smiled, patting his empty seat. "I've some insights saved for you. Ty delivered on everything he knew. And by the way, Ty gave you the name Armand as one of the top members. The same guy I'm betting Mickey told us about when we visited the Perk. Also, I may have forgotten to tell you that Armand happened to call Brakem's office the other day when Betsy and I were clue-gathering. That info should provide you with a strong connection to Brakem's involvement."

"That's solid info." Tanner rubbed his forehead. "Go home, Page. You've contributed enough."

"I'm here until Brakem is questioned, and barring any unforeseen mayhem, only then will I accept the ride."

"Stubborn, aren't we?" Steve winked.

"To the core. So, tell me, are you prepared for Brakem? No doubt he'll use his knowledge of the law to squirm out of talking. I bet we go home a lot sooner than you think." Page popped a peppermint into her mouth.

"You're right. Even if he killed Catherine and somehow got into the safe, he's not going to confess. Besides, that's the FBI's big case to prosecute against him and Evan. I'm going to focus on why he was leaving the country and connect it somehow to his killing Catherine. It's a dead end, but at least it keeps him in the country until I get an agent here tomorrow. Sure, you want to stay for this flop performance?" Steve grinned.

"I learn something every time I watch you, Tanner, even on a surfboard. Get about it." Page shoved him off the chair.

~*~

Brakem entered the interrogation room with his anger on full display. "You guys aren't getting squat out of me. And let it be known, I'm working in my head what I'm suing this department for, and the list is growing."

Koch rolled his eyes at Steve. "Sit down, you bag of hot wind. He's been read his rights. This lady's all yours." Koch stood by the door.

Steve studied the notes Koch had made for the arrest. "So, Mr. Brakem, you don't care to answer any questions for us tonight, huh? Not even why you were fleeing the country when told to remain here as you were under investigation? You didn't view that as a problem?"

Brakem glowered at Tanner, pretending to be bored.

"You sure offered zero help to your client Evan Lange. Evan's hoping to have you for a roommate tonight. I understand he's busting to tell you some things. Yes, he's been quite a talker once we offered a public defender to arrange bail. Of course, Koch went and blabbed about Max and Finn waiting outside. That got your friend Evan in a lather. I've never seen anyone beg to stay at our accommodations like Mr. Lange. Perhaps you know Finn and Max? Even Ty is acquainted and happy to remain with us tonight. Maybe you know Armand?" prompted Steve.

Brakem's head had developed a tremor. His eyes darted toward the door. "I refuse to share a cell with Evan or Ty. They're nothing but thugs. I'm an attorney in good standing. I deserve better treatment."

"You have to earn better treatment, Brakem. No one brought into this room deserves anything but mirandizing and a token phone call if charged. Want your own cell? Talk to us." Steve's impatience showed.

"All I'm saying, without an attorney present, is it wasn't me who killed Catherine Lange or stole Evan's precious whatevers. I had zip interest. Nada."

Koch came closer. "Does that mean you wouldn't mind if we escorted you to Finn and Max's black sedan outside? Maybe say howdy and ask them to buy you a cuppa? Maybe share your failed attempt at fleeing this evening? That little meet and greet is our next step. We like to get social, as my daughter says."

Brakem's tremor moved to a demonstrative shaking of his entire body. His lips parted, trying to speak, but words remained inside.

Page watched Brakem puddle. She respected how nimbly the two investigators had manipulated the lawyer into such a mental state of collapse.

"You're not looking well, Brakem. Are you still refusing to discuss the Lange case?" Steve joined Koch in front of the attorney, applying more intimidation.

Brakem managed a nod. His face matched the color of the red file resting on the table.

"Okay, Koch, we have a couple of options here. We can release Brakem and ask a favor of those men parked outside to see him home…safely. They seem overly concerned about the welfare of Ty, Evan, and Brakem. I bet they'd be willing to keep Brakem company. Or, perhaps we could invite Mr. Brakem to Ty and Evan's slumber party. The three of them have much to commiserate and discuss. What do you think, Koch?"

Koch chuckled. "Why not let Mr. Brakem choose."

Brakem coughed, finding his voice. "I'd…I'd like to stay over. Get my one phone call. And…and revisit this tomorrow with my attorney." He made fists to hide the shakes.

"Koch, he's all yours. I've got a couple of FBI agents

coming to Shell Isle tomorrow. They're anxious to meet our local attorney. Brakem, see how your popularity is growing? Enjoy the stay compliments of our generous taxpayers," said Tanner, making his way out.

CHAPTER 55

Steve turned off the ignition and faced Page. "Now that law enforcement has matters under control, are you ready to give up this sleuthing enterprise?" He motioned Page toward her front door.

"Nope, I still have a murder and theft to solve. Nor am I willing to give up having a piece of that Crab Shak's cake tonight if Betsy hasn't devoured the whole thing. Come on; you're invited." Page dragged Steve inside.

"Eleven o'clock, and judging by the looks of you two, all ain't swell." Betsy stood aside, letting them pass. "The coffee maker has trickled for the last two hours waiting, and the cake… well, there's enough left."

"Cake, coffee, and conversation. My favorite three C's," laughed Page, entering the kitchen. She moved to pour two cups of coffee while Betsy cut two slabs of layer cake. "Have a seat, Tanner."

Steve settled on the bar stool around the action. "You know, Wright, I've yet to figure out the mood you're in when you call me Tanner. I detect something in your voice, but…." He grinned at both women.

"I call you Tanner when you've pushed my buttons," interjected Betsy. "Does that help to know my Tanner rule of use?"

"Immensely, Ms. Ross. Happy to have your input on this subject," Steve volleyed back. "Page?"

"Betsy summed it up nicely. You should strive for more Steve's. That'll mean you've curried our favor. Here's your fork.

We owe Bets an update on our humdrum evening…Steve." Page winked.

~*~

Betsy entered her cousin's bedroom wearing a frown. "Page, your idea of humdrum has me ready to collapse in my bed, but first, can you tell me what next step you're considering? Has anything come to you?" Betsy parked in the swivel chair.

"Truthfully, I'm too exhausted to feel a nudge or anything else. My brain is mush, and not even that black syrup you served as coffee stirred me. The only suspect I've eliminated is Ty. He told the truth, at least the parts that mattered. The rest of them are back on the board. Go find your bed. Let the sun appear, and we'll see what direction beckons."

"Well, that's a plan of sorts. You've accomplished a major goal by proving valuable to Steve." Betsy walked her furry purple slippers to the door.

"Hey, don't discount your role, Mermaid. We're a team. Oh, remind me to call Larsen first thing in the morning." Page arranged her tropical printed duvet, still unable to ignore the giant coral squid smack in the center of her bed. Aunt Tilly's decorator gene was a mutation.

Betsy's head popped back inside the door frame. "Oops, I forgot to tell you Larsen called tonight." She decided it was better to stay out of Page's room delivering that news.

"Geez. This I didn't need. Well?"

"You know me—big blabbermouth. He got the case's condensed version out of me. Don't fuss. I know I royally messed up. Larsen excels at pulling things out of people." Betsy dropped her head in mock shame.

Page couldn't resist laughing. "Is he angry?"

"Nah, fortunately, I couldn't blab about tonight's hijinks because I didn't know any of it. But, I do know something you might find worthy of considering," offered a contrite Betsy.

"Prepare yourself. Larsen loves running the bookstore and wonders if you'd like to sell out and settle here at Shell? That's why he called."

"What? Sell my bookshop to Larsen?" exclaimed Page. She pulled the sheet over her head. "Leave me alone with Aunt Tilly's squid quilt."

"Let it marinate. I've found marinating improves almost everything except for your bed companion." Betsy's form evaporated with her laughter echoing down the hall.

CHAPTER 56

Friday morning's weather couldn't decide what to present out Page's kitchen window. She'd felt teased for the last two hours with grey clouds threatening a deluge, only to have the sun spread the clouds, displaying an azure sky. She'd risen early with her mind busy plotting steps to flush out Catherine's murderer, but none felt plausible. The case's complexities were wearing her down fast. Page knew her mind didn't have the answers. Frustration held her captive. She needed some reliable guidance. Her gifts never failed her. Were they now? That question only agitated her frustration. She turned her attention to a more pleasant subject... the one that had awakened her. Was it indeed time to make a huge lifestyle change?

Larsen's desire to buy the bookshop would provide Page with wings to become a seagull instead of a mountain bluebird. And since daybreak, she'd made a grand effort to unearth a sound and logical reason to keep her shop. None came calling that fused with her spirit's desire to set sail.

Distracting life-changing questions filled her head when she needed to be about solving a murder. Since she didn't seem capable of putting the idea aside, she'd just ring Larsen. Maybe he was only joshing Betsy.

The call went to voicemail. "Morning, Larsen. Knowing you, I'm envisioning you standing in a clear mountain stream, talking to the trout before you open the bookshop. So, here's the thing. Betsy told me you were interested in becoming its owner. Maybe sit down for this next sentence. Surprise, I find myself sort of smitten by your idea. Shell Isle has cast some spell on me during this visit. As cracked as this may sound, the beach feels like my next home. Let's explore your idea of owning the shop. Ring me, Larsen."

"Check that off. Ball to Larsen," mumbled Page. For now, she'd suspend pondering Hibiscus as home. She'd taken the first step and trusted the next one would be revealed. She grabbed the box of cereal, one of the two remaining bananas, and flicked the coffee maker switch. Page filled her bowl and moved to a stool where her glass of cranberry juice waited for company.

"Here I am, dressed in my comfortable beach ensemble, all ready for our day's adventure. What's up with the crazy weather?" Betsy created an encore of Page's breakfast bowl and joined her.

"The weather is mimicking my indecision with the Lange case. Today, I'm hopeful we'll soon know the who and why of it all. We must be on alert for signs. Betsy? You're not listening."

"Oh, I'm listening, but to that ridiculous sounding coffee machine. Do you see it's only dribbled out an ounce of almost clear liquid? I need my morning brew. What say we go to the Perk? I fancy their Raspberry White Chocolate Frappe. Mickey recommends it highly." Betsy tossed her half-eaten cereal and whisked Page's bowl away.

"I wasn't finished with my banana. And when exactly did Mickey share his frap rec?" asked Page, grabbing the keys from the hook. "And, I must say you've got quite a love affair going with chocolate. You're not planning a trip to Belgium again, are you? Because if you are, I'm placing my order for more of that dark hazelnut bark."

For once, Betsy walked faster than Page. "Start 'er up. I'm not going anywhere. I feel anchored to Shell Isle more and more. Feels homey. Makes me nesty. Is that a word?" Betsy pulled her cap down to block the sun's glare.

"Nesty isn't a word, but I like it...a lot. I'm feeling nesty as well. So, you know, I left Larsen a message testing his sincerity in buying the shop, and I'm still waiting on my answer about Mickey." Page pulled out, noting Steve's missing vehicle.

"It's nothing," Betsy groused. "I'll fill you in once we're at the Perk. Are you truly entertaining selling and moving full-time to the beach? Don't tease me." Betsy clasped her hands in excitement.

"I am. Yes, I most certainly am. You got me thinking. Shell does offer me an interesting life shift." Page came to a stop sign and turned to Betsy.

"It feels right somehow, Page, for me too. I could even buy my own cottage near Hibiscus. Doesn't that sound idyllic? I think so. I've been holding onto scads of fresh ideas of what we could do here." Betsy grabbed a deep breath.

"Goodness, you have been pondering things, Bets." Page waved back to some kids crossing in a golf cart.

"Yes, the initiative grabbed me straight away, and my enthusiasm hasn't diminished, which is unusual for me. You know I get bored at the speed of light." Betsy smiled.

"Do tell."

"Okay, so now I'm anxious to show you something when we get to town. Drive faster. Koch wouldn't dare stop you now. You're golden." Betsy remained suspiciously quiet until Page parked near the coffee shop.

"Before we go inside, walk with me one block," Betsy's face lit up and not by the sun.

"Sure, but I don't have a clue why you're so amped up." Page frowned and struggled to keep up with her cousin's excitement and pace.

"Stop." Betsy halted and pointed to her right. "Get a load. Feast your baby blues."

Page turned as directed. "I am staring at an empty store. Why are we here?"

"Because, you goose, this is the location for our next life adventure. Whilst you've been occupied chasing Catherine's murderer, I've been devoted to finding how we can become part of Shell Isle. Picture it." Betsy cast her arms upward, pointing to the place where a sign belonged.

"What am I picturing exactly?" Page stared above the double wooden doors.

"Honey Bees Shop." Betsy closed her eyes, imagining. "Yes, Honey Bees. That suits. Anyway, you were all aflutter reading that article about how bees are vital to our survival as a species. And I've studied them a tad. They're fascinating, and that queen…well, why don't we specialize in tasty honey treats, potions, creams, hair products, all things honey? I've been researching honey…the god's nectar. Let me tell you something. You have no idea of the many amazing benefits honey offers. Don't you see? We can do good right here at Shell Isle and still live our laid-back life."

"You are serious." Page peeked inside the building's display window, trying to absorb her cousin's pitch.

"Yes, I'm serious. I've been sitting on my big plan like a fat hen on a prized egg, waiting for the perfect time to present it. Listen, I even have a local beekeeper ready to supply us with different varieties of the golden nectar, and we can branch out globally to include other honey. I'm making my first honey cake after lunch with a special Old World recipe given to me that promises to have folks eating out of our hands, so to speak. I've so many exciting ideas and plans to share with you once we wrap up this case. Don't you see? Larsen wanting your bookstore is a sign the time is ideal for us to begin this new chapter. I feel it. Don't you? This is all too divine." Betsy flapped her arms and spun around like levitation would occur at any moment.

"She's fine. It's called a waking dream. Won't last long," Page explained to the puzzled couple walking their Lab. Page pulled her cousin's arm toward the Perk. "Come."

Betsy followed, bringing her enthusiasm. "You connected to my idea. I can tell. You're biting your lip. That's my proof," said Betsy, now in step with her cousin. "I hear Aunt Tilly singing. Maybe since Shell Isle is a small town, we'll have fewer mysteries to solve? Fewer expectations on you. Less of those inklings you must answer." Betsy's pitch was heartfelt.

Page put on a doubting face but retained her amusement.

"Okay, so mysteries to solve will still find us, but I know our life here will be simply fantabulous. Is that a word?"

"That's a word. I don't understand how you can declare something that doesn't exist as fantabulous." The logical Page had her say, but the spirited Page was catching her cousin's rogue wave to the land of honey cakes, orange blossom body butter, and an exciting new path. Having Betsy as a partner meant more free time and not being chained to a business as a sole proprietor. Catering might be a lark, too. Page put her arm around Betsy's shoulder. "You know, your sweet idea is growing on me. Fact is, it's a real honey."

"Please, none of your bad jokes. I'm bubbling with enthusiasm, never mind the shock. There's not even a man involved." Betsy opened the door to the aroma of coffee beans.

"Hiya, Mermaid. What brings those lovely size seven feet in the door today?" Mickey came over to greet Betsy. "Hi, Page. Remember me?"

Page directed her raised eyebrow the Mermaid's way. "I do. Hi, Mickey."

"I'll stop by your table in a few minutes. Try my lavender honey. The bottles are on the far tables. I think your taster will like it plenty. Got a delivery next door." Mickey held up the coffee carrier.

"Well, Mermaid, let's examine some of your statements. No man involved, but within seconds, I hear a guy talking about your lovely size seven feet, which you don't own; you're here because of a rec for a white chocolate something frappe, and last, I suspect he's your honey man. All very interesting from my perspective." Page's eyes sparkled.

"It's white chocolate raspberry, and I can explain. It's all quite innocent. Hardly worth the effort." Betsy placed her order. "I'll snag a table with the honey."

The barista looked at Page. "Guess you're buying again. What'll you have?"

"What's the most robust brew today? I want that over ice."

"Our Dark Night Espresso coming up. Be warned; you'll be buzzing like a bee the rest of today. Mickey will bring it over. Go join your friend." Angela woke up the hiss of the espresso machine.

Page tucked the surprise buzzing bee reference as another sign and found Betsy hiding behind a magazine. "Put it down. You forget that's my ploy. So, size seven, what ya got to say for yourself?"

Betsy dropped the magazine on the table and blew out a breath. "Mickey works part-time at the bowling alley. He was trying to charm me by giving me a smaller size shoe. All in fun. Trust me; he knew these tugs were a nine." Betsy lifted her foot for effect.

"More?" Page put on her smug face.

"He came and went at Ina's and my table when we stayed for the brews. That's when I learned about his passion for bees. Please recall the critically important info I gathered from Ina that evening before you bust me. As for the drink rec, that wasn't anything either. Mickey just thought my daytime drink might be this frap he's bringing over now. You behave." Betsy's smile broke out.

"Ladies, please enjoy. Umm, Betsy, are you bowling with the gals again next week?" Mickey tucked the tray under his arm.

"Well, I did promise Ina I'd fill in until the real Mermaid returns. No doubt I'll see you at the alley." Betsy made a big deal of peeling the paper from her straw.

"Then, I will be sure and have a nice pair of sanitized shoes just for you." Mickey nodded to Page.

"Well, isn't the bee man just the sweetest thang," drawled Page.

"Hush, you. I'm not getting involved with any men this summer. Mickey is just a friend who holds an opportunity for us that we can't ignore. Where are you going with your high octane?"

"I'm only funning you, cousin. We needed some levity. Enjoy your frozen concoction and Mickey's visit. Here he comes again. I'm going next door to the travel agency to make another attempt at buying Hannah's ticket for her July fourth visit. Be back in a jiffy."

CHAPTER 57

Page entered the travel agency, bringing her a nudge. A friendly college-age admin greeted her. The young lady's sparkling smile rivaled the promise of any whitening toothpaste commercial.

"Hello. If you take a seat, our agent on duty will be happy to assist when she finishes with the other customer." She motioned Page toward a grouping of chairs.

"Thank you." Page caught a familiar voice and nimbly tucked behind a decorative floral screen, pretending to look at the rack of travel brochures. She could see between the screen slats that Gwen was seated in front of the agent, but there was something much more mesmerizing to behold. Around her neck twinkled the canary diamond necklace that had once graced Catherine's neckline. The very one Gwen described and coveted belonging to her mother. The same diamonds her brother chose to give Catherine. Other expensive jewelry pieces dangled and bedazzled her wrists and fingers. Page finally understood the cliché *dripping* in jewels…and something else of far greater magnitude.

"I want you to check for a first-class seat to Budva, Montenegro. I understand that flying out of Wilmington requires plane changes; it's imperative I leave Shell Isle no later than six this evening. Tell me you have something," voiced a desperate Gwen.

"Oh, I see you booked a red-eye flight there last Friday. How nice that you're going back so soon?"

"I couldn't make that flight. Besides, my travel itineraries are none of your concern. Do your job. Get me on a flight." Gwen walked around to the agent's computer screen.

"I'm looking. Please give me a few moments, Ms. Lange." The agent's mouse flew around the pad as she clicked on screens. "Does it have to be Montenegro again? I can get you—"

"Yes, I've things arranged in that country. Dear girl, I've made myself clear. Budva is the destination. Not Paris. Not Milan. Budva." Gwen's usual condescending tone returned.

"Will this work? I can get you out of Wilmington at five this afternoon to New York and from there..."

Page heard what she needed and hurried back over to the admin. "I've got to leave. My cousin's waiting for me at the Perk. I'll try and swing by tomorrow."

"Sure, okay. Have a nice day," the young woman replied absently, engrossed with her cell phone.

Page flew into the coffee shop and pulled Betsy away from Mickey's explaining pollination. "Sorry, Mickey, I need Betsy. She'll see you again tomorrow. Hurry, Betsy," said Page, dragging her cousin out the door.

"I left half my drink. What's got you chasing windmills now?" Betsy closed the SUV door.

"We're heading to Hibiscus, and I need you to make one of those people-pleasing honey cakes and fast. Can you do it?" Page ignored the speedometer and all yellow traffic lights.

"Make a honey cake now? Gosh, I didn't expect you to be this eager about our new venture, but sure, I've got the recipe and ingredients at the ready. This is more than I could've hoped. I figured...oh, never mind what I figured. Get me home. I'm your baker." Betsy grabbed the armrest. "Honey cakes must have awakened your every sweet tooth judging by the way you're driving."

Page caught a red light and a breath. "Betsy, I know who stole the valuables from the Lange safe, and I suspect it's the same person who also killed Catherine." Page's eyes bore into her cousin's. "The case is solved."

"You know? How do you know? And why aren't we going to the police station now? Instead, you're insisting I make you a honey cake? Makes no sense."

"The honey cake isn't for me. It's a condolence gift for Gwen," explained Page.

"This isn't like you taking a cake to a stranger who happens to be on our suspect board, especially when you profess to know who did the deed. We always tell the authorities when we've solved a case. I'm all confused. Slow down. You went through that stop sign." Betsy took a road map from the door's side pocket and turned it into a fan.

"There was a stop sign? Sorry. We're almost at Hibiscus." Page turned on their street and made a decision.

~*~

"Betsy, come sit before I help with the dessert. Now that I'm not behind the wheel, I want to tell you what happened a few minutes ago. It will answer all of your questions." Page waited for her cousin to park next to her on the sofa.

"I'm listening. What did I miss this time?"

"I need your gifts. We're a team." Page grabbed a breath.

"Relax. I'm not budging." Betsy squeezed her cousin's arm.

"When I went into the travel agency, I saw Gwen purchasing a plane ticket to Montenegro. She's bolting later today." Page's cell phone dinged with a text. She glanced at Larsen's words and smiled.

"Is that text anything?" asked Betsy.

"It can wait."

"So, Gwen is taking off, despite being told as a suspect, she needs to stay at Shell? We are now up to three suspects trying to make off. Ty, Brakem, and now her. What a bunch of runners. Evan, no doubt, would be on the list if not for vertical steel decorating his room. Poor Garrett is either too dumb, too in love with Lola, or not involved with the murder to try to take flight," deduced Betsy. She grabbed a nearby notepad and pen.

"Betsy, what are you writing? I'm in the middle of sharing my theory."

"Oh, just an extra spice I thought might embellish the honey cake's flavor."

"Forget the spices and cake for a moment, will ya please? So, Gwen's escaping, but she's also fleeing, too. Listen to this. She was draped in her mother's jewels today. I do mean draped. I don't know how she could walk with all that gold weight hanging around her neck and arms. The earrings she had on were so weighty with gold and diamonds; her lobes could sweep the floor."

Betsy laughed. "That's a lot of moola on that dowager's body. I thought Gwen told you her mother left zip to her?" Betsy's expression exhibited her growing confusion.

"She did, but I have a strong suspicion of how the jewelry came into her possession."

"Yes, Evan gave the pieces to his sister to keep her quiet. He had them all along. Double dipping in insurance, claiming they were stolen." Betsy raised both palms for effect.

"Not quite, Bets. My theory goes like this. Gwen somehow found the combination to Evan's safe and emptied it. Gwen's path to freedom got interrupted that night by Catherine."

"Okay, I get Gwen stole the jewelry to start her new life, but who murdered Catherine? Evan?" Betsy scooted forward on the sofa.

"I believe Gwen shot her. I suspect Catherine found Gwen in the den with the valuables and confronted her. Probably threatened Gwen and eventually pulled the pistol she got from Seedy on her sister-in-law. Who knows? As awful as Gwen is, I don't think she's the type to premediate someone's death. The woman's self-absorbed and wants what she wants. She'd grown tired of being dependent on Evan for every crumb. Following me?"

Betsy bobbed her head. "Makes sense. So, Gwen and Catherine got into some major altercation, and Catherine lost. Gwen fled the den with the loot and pretended to be asleep in her room. Ty showed up to kill his sister but finds her already lying dead in the den. Not thinking clearly, he whisks her into the ocean and hopes her body gets taken away by the currents, but that doesn't happen. Nope. What happens is you and I get tapped into finding Catherine's lifeless body and get assigned another case. I've summed up that part right well?"

"Exactly, Betsy. But we're missing something crucial, and we have to obtain it in the next hour or two." Page touched her temple, willing the first twinge of migraine pain to recede.

"Ah, we are missing the proof. Do you have a plan that won't get us killed?" Betsy's expression shifted to worry.

Page's eyes crinkled. She leaned in and patted her cousin's hand. "I've conjured the perfect plan."

CHAPTER 58

"The doesn't-get-us-killed part of the plan, I noticed, wasn't confirmed. Lay it out, and then I'll decide whether to call Tanner on you." Betsy settled back into the sofa's cushions, arms crossed over her chest.

"I need your honey cake to have Gwen eating out of my hand." Page waited for the laugh that didn't come. "Fine. I'll skip the humor. We're going to make one of those magical cakes. I'm taking the sweet to Gwen and insist she and I share a slice and have a quick visit so that I can provide news of Catherine's investigation. She should bite on both of those morsels. Sorry. I couldn't resist."

"Very clever, and my special recipe will have a proper test, but I still don't like this plan. My danger bells are ringing."

"Hush. Then, I'm going to tell Gwen what I suspect happened using our trusted sympathy strategy to get a confession. Next, I'll hit her with the travel agency part to let her worry the escape is compromised. I may reverse the order of the setup. I won't know until I'm with Gwen and start feeding her." Page laughed at her double meaning.

"You can't distract me with clever humor. However, I understand your goals are to get Gwen to confess and test my honey cake's charms." Betsy grew thoughtful. "Now, I'm going to tweak your scheme. I will bake the cake. I will call Tanner and tell him what madness has taken you. I will demand he and Koch get to the Langes' and back you up. I will not allow you to go without support. Last, and most important, I will only accept yes to my terms."

"Since when did you become such a tough nut?" Page hugged her cousin.

"Your plan is the one we'll go with, but I want a bit of a head start, and just for our sleuthing record, it's what I was going to ask you to do. You can't call for backup until I'm at the Lange home, or Koch and Tanner will try to stop me. I spied Steve's SUV parked next door so that he can be inside their house within a couple of minutes. Don't fret. I'm getting my guidance on how to handle this confrontation. I will be fine. Gwen's an accidental killer."

"Okay, once I see you at their door, I'll jingle Tanner. He's going to go off like a stick of dynamite. Poor me. Just make sure you don't cause that vile woman to become an accidental killer again."

"Not in the cards. Time for our first charmed honey cake to go to work. Come on. Tell me how to help." Page hustled toward the kitchen, anticipating both their future baking roles.

~*~

The tempting honey cake rested on a vine-designed plate. Rich powdered cinnamon sugar dusted the top. Page grinned, seeing the second cake on a nearby white tray with Betsy's addition of lemon zest waiting for a later sampling and the first for the woman two doors down who was incapable of tasting the sweetness of cake or life. Bitterness had been Gwen's daily serving for decades and likely would see her to the last breath. Page trusted her plan, and now time beckoned her to implement it. She'd seen Gwen's black sedan return home and suspected the woman was readying to leave. Page breathed easier, knowing fate still had Tanner next door. The anticipated nudge came to act.

Betsy stood nearby, watching her cousin prepare herself for the performance. "Are you prepared? Guess I'd rather walk over to Steve's and attempt to explain what you've hatched. I hate male explosions. And I know you've set me up for a doozy; thank you very much." Betsy glanced out the sliding door and saw Steve tossing a red ball for Barnacle. "He's in such a good mood, too. All smiles. Wearing his favorite surfing shirt." Betsy offered a defeated shrug.

"You are a stitch, Betsy Ross. Don't worry. I'm going to be fine. Please tell Steve that I'll make sure the front door's unlocked so that he can slip in." Page lifted the cake plate. "Here's to your honey cake's magic." She hugged Betsy once more and walked outside.

With Steve in the backyard, he missed seeing Page stroll down the sidewalk. Smile in place, she rang the Langes' bell.

Gwen opened the door. Her attire was a total departure from the usual designer high-flair fashions. Instead, blue jeans hugged her long, slender legs, and a loose-knit shirt depicting the face of Monet on a muted color background covered the front. White leather flats asked for no admiration, and a well-worn beret sat atop Gwen's head. Large gold oval earrings finished the Avant Garde look. "Yes? What is it?" Gwen ignored the cake.

"Hello, Ms. Lange. Remember me? I'm Page Wright. We met the other evening aboard my neighbor's sloop?" Page put one foot on the threshold, forcing Gwen to step backward.

"So?" came the chilling reply.

"Well, I can only imagine how stressful your life must be with everything unfolding. I stopped by with a freshly baked honey cake. The recipe is quite delicious. My cousin tells me eating one slice promises answers and blessings. This recipe's gifts are a secret that few know about, making it more special. Old World stuff, I think she said." Page boldly stepped inside the foyer.

"I don't have time for eating cake. I'm busy. Just give me the dessert and be on your way." Gwen reached for the plate only to have Page rush past her.

"Please don't deny me five minutes to witness the lovely effect the cake's sure to have. I promise this honey cake will help you handle what the police recently learned about Catherine's killer and the theft." Page paused, watching worry wash over the woman.

"Of what new information are you speaking? I've heard nothing." Gwen came to Page's side with a changed demeanor. "Please, follow me to the kitchen. I find myself craving a slice of this…?"

"Honey cake," supplied Page with a friendly smile, relieved Gwen neglected to lock the front door. Page trailed her hostess into the expansive kitchen. "This room is incredible. I've never seen copper-toned appliances, and the cabinetry is exquisite. What kind of wood?" Page ran her fingers down a panel.

Gwen ignored the compliment and question, searching for the dinnerware and flatware. "Here's what you need." She laid a cake knife, forks, and Limoges plates on the apricot-swirled marble counter. Don't tarry, cut me a piece." Gwen perched on a metal stool and waited, arranging her facial features to look pleasant.

Page planned to serve Gwen an extra serving of shock soon. She peeked at her watch. Only a few moments left before Steve's arrival. "By all means, please enjoy the cake. Mind if I join you and share my news?" Page sat on the adjoining stool.

"Must you?" Gwen took a bite.

"Yes, and I'm sure you'll be thanking me soon for stopping by. You see, Gwen, I want to help you. I empathized with your story the other night. I know how difficult it is to be around a family that is incapable of caring about others…always focusing on themselves. You've suffered for so long and been deprived of things that you hold dear, like your mother's priceless jewelry collection that should belong to you. And the final insult, to see Catherine decked out in your mother's favorite canary diamond necklace and earrings…well, that was the end, right?"

Gwen kept eating, but Page knew she swallowed the cake and words.

The sleuth went to pour Gwen a glass of water. She counted on the length of the island to offer some protection for what words she delivered next.

Gwen paused, eating, and focused on her visitor. "Yes, that's all true, but what business is it of yours?" Gwen took a sip and returned to the cake with uncharacteristic zeal. "I must say this honey cake is quite good. I do feel rather…mellow."

"Yes, the recipe seems to know what the one eating the cake needs most. Pretty amazing, I know. Anyway, I saw you today at the travel agency booking a flight to Montenegro. I also happen to know that country doesn't extradite to the United States. And that got me to thinking. Why would my new friend Gwen be running off when the police are still investigating, and she's a prime suspect in that investigation?"

"I see. You're quite the little busybody. And, what did you deduce?" Undeterred, Gwen slid the second slice of cake toward herself.

"I deduced that you had done something pretty serious, and seeing that canary necklace and all the other jewelry hanging on you…well…I knew you'd been the one to empty the safe. Plus, I overheard Ty say he'd found Catherine's body in the den near the safe. And, I confess that I heard you and Evan talking on his yacht that night we rescued you. The police know all about that, too."

"Well, aren't you an unfortunate meddler? Those traits get people dead." Gwen's tone remained calm, but her eyes grew menacing.

Page made a quick adjustment to her plan. "Oh, but I'm the kind of meddler who wants to help you. But first, I need to make sure I'm clear on what happened to come up with a successful strategy. You see, I have an inside track of what the police have planned next, and you, Gwen, are that next. You need to trust me. Keep eating. Let me hurry things along so we can prepare your exit. Friends help each other. Okay?" Page wanted Gwen to enjoy the illusion of feeling in control.

Gwen studied the sleuth. The charmed honey cake called to Gwen louder than her worry about this woman's professed loyalty. "Keep talking. I'm most anxious to hear how you propose to help me, and I expect there's something in this for you."

Page heard the front door and went into a coughing spell to distract Gwen from hearing what she hoped was Steve arriving. "Sorry. I swallowed wrong. Here's what I think happened that fateful night. Please correct me if I've got anything wrong. You decided another day in the house with Catherine the Awful couldn't be endured. Somehow, you'd fortuitously found the combination to the safe, and its contents held your freedom ticket away from the intolerable Evan, who refused to give you rights to anything that should be yours. So, you had a plane ticket leaving Friday night for Montenegro, your suitcase packed, and all that remained was to obtain what belonged to you from that safe. You'd then disappear and live the life you richly deserved. And, to your credit, you even insured Evan had riders for a few of the pieces. I overheard you tell Garrett to do his job. I now know that job was issuing riders to lessen your brother's financial loss. See? That's another example of your kindness compared to Evan and Catherine. You knew they'd never give you a single item of your mother's. Right, Gwen?" Page needed to keep her engaged in the story and not thinking.

"Yes, though I don't know how you figured this all out," she hissed. "How I despise Evan and celebrate Catherine's being off this earth." Gwen's face hardened. "And, the bonus of finding the Fabergé Eggs and bag of gems is going to make my life in Montenegro even more pleasurable. You see, I've arranged a buyer of those rarities and other things from the safe that hold no interest for me." Gwen forked another bite of cake.

Page nodded, careful to maintain her distance. "Yes, it sounds like you've done an excellent job of securing your future. To get back to that evening, you have your treasures, and you're putting the pieces maybe into a satchel. Catherine comes in and sees what you're doing. Naturally, you both argue and finally, you tell her what's been pent up inside for so long. Unmoved, she pulls a gun and threatens to kill you if you take the jewelry and valuables. Of course, what choice do you have but to fight for your life and what belongs to you? You both get into some altercation, and the gun fires. It was an accident. You didn't mean to kill her, Gwen. You just wanted the safe's contents. Your mother's jewelry belonged adorning your beautiful self. So, you planned to disappear and never lay eyes on the two of them, but then Catherine ruined everything for you yet again. You did what you had to do to survive. You defended your life. More, Catherine's interference caused you to miss your flight that night, but at least Ty took care of Catherine's body." Page offered a sympathetic look. "Am I right about how this all unfolded? See, I told you that I understood your situation."

"Oh, you conveyed the story exactly how it happened, except that Catherine came into the study wearing the canary necklace. She flaunted the piece, telling me I'd never get what Evan had given her. I felt such rage." Gwen's smile turned dark. "I proved her wrong. I managed to get that necklace off her body before I slipped away to my rooms to make a new exit plan. Under no circumstances could I allow that loathsome creature to wear my necklace another second. Besides, the color of the stones was wrong for her skin tone." Gwen tugged the collar of her shirt.

The diamonds' sparkle winked at Page. "Ah, they do look perfect on you."

Gwen's expression shifted from confused to threatened. The

cake's effect had vanished. She turned on Page. "Unfortunately, I can't allow you to leave here knowing my story. Having you run to the police is something I cannot risk. You understand the situation." Gwen moved toward her handbag resting on the breakfast table.

Page lurched toward the handbag, failing to beat Gwen there. "I won't tell. I don't need to. It's your story, Gwen." Page recognized the pistol Seedy had passed to Catherine. She held the panic out of her voice. "That's Catherine's gun. Is that the one that killed her?"

Gwen pointed the weapon at Page and advanced. "Aren't you clever guessing about this gun? I regret that I must make use of it again before departing this country."

"Put the gun down, Ms. Lange. You're not going anywhere but jail." Tanner appeared, moving toward Gwen; his gun aimed her way.

Gwen raised the pistol, ready to fire. "I've watched enough police shows. I know we're equal here. I've nothing to lose by shooting this annoying snoop and then you."

Page stepped closer to Gwen. "You're wrong. You have so much more to lose. Listen to me. You didn't mean to kill Catherine. It was an accident. A jury may well rule kindly toward you. I bet you've got enough on Evan that he'd even say the jewels belonged to you. Please put the gun down and let Tanner make things easier for you. Right, Tanner?"

Steve moved within a few feet of Gwen. "Page is right. Catherine is the one who pulled the gun on you. There's self-defense involved here. Think, Gwen. Life in prison versus something so much less."

Page jumped in. "Gwen, you might even get off without any jail time. It was an accident. You told me it was an accident. I'm your witness. You didn't intend to kill Catherine. You were defending yourself. Let me live to help you."

Gwen studied Page. "You'd help me? Why? I've treated you terribly from the moment we met. You're lying."

Page's expression softened. "I don't lie. Listen. I will go with you to the station and give my statement. Come with me, Gwen. Tanner, you drive us." Page felt the nudge and moved to face Gwen. "We can take care of this matter as soon as you pass me the pistol." Page held out her hand. She saw Koch behind a wall a few feet from Gwen. His gun pointed at the older woman. "Please let me help you as I promised," whispered Page.

Gwen hesitated, considering Page's words. Agonizing moments passed before Gwen broke. Tears pooled in her eyes before she dropped the small pistol into Page's outstretched hand.

"Thank you, Gwen." Page stepped back and handed Steve the weapon.

Koch grabbed Gwen and put the handcuffs on her. "Sit down, Ms. Lange, while I read your rights to you."

Steve rushed to Page's side and wrapped his arms around her. "Ms. Drew, you and I are going to take Carpe out very soon and draft a new sleuthing playbook for you and Betsy."

"Here I am." Betsy shoved Steve aside and hugged Page. "Cousin, you were amazing and, as usual, perfecto on solving another case, but I'm with Steve." Betsy looked over her shoulder at the grinning investigator. "You write the playbook. I'll type it, and we'll sign it. I can't risk losing my new baking buddy."

Page kissed her cousin's cheek. "Hang on to that honey cake recipe. I don't know what ingredients you added, but it's enchanted." She released Betsy. "I'll see you in a bit. I've got to fulfill a promise."

Tanner and Koch were talking to a silent Gwen, her eyes vacant of emotion.

"If it's any consolation, Ms. Lange, we have a full house of your compatriots at the station. Let's see; there are Garrett and his two colluders, Brakem, your brother, and, of course, Ty. You'll feel right at home." Koch delivered a sneer.

Page approached the three and nodded toward Gwen. "Tanner, may I catch a ride to the station with you? I want to provide my statement.

Gwen looked at Page and said two words that seldom left her lips. "Thank you."

"You're welcome, Gwen." Page turned back to Steve. "Let's get this done. I've got a honey cake to experience and a new business venture to plan."

ABOUT THE AUTHOR

Multi-genre Author~Inner Explorer~Humor Chaser~Labyrinth Lover~Waterfall Wanderer

Author Tonya Penrose (pen name) is a storyteller who believes in the power of humor and narratives to touch her readers' hearts. She's always been moved by how a story can invite personal exploration and leave a lasting impression on those who read it. When Tonya sits in her favorite writing chair gazing at a lake, she's all about creating beguiling characters that leap from the page and capture a reader's fancy. Her characters aren't just words on a page. They become real people with their own challenges and quirks. She enjoys sprinkling her romps with moments that offer readers grins or even bursts of laughter.

But for Tonya, it's not only about the characters or the humor. The dialogue is where her stories shine. As a multi-genre author, she feels that engaging dialogue provides the heartbeat for any truly wonderful tale. It breathes life into the narrative and allows readers to feel they're with the characters along the way.

Whether you're seeking an entertaining escape or a thought-enlivening journey of inner discovery, Tonya's books are waiting to whisk you away. Embark on a path where humor meets introspection, and unforgettable characters await at every page turn.

Tonya invites readers to explore the familiar and enchanted settings with her. To uncover secreted truths, share inspiring moments, and awaken to her deeper message — that living in the *now is how*. Tonya's fiction and non-fiction stories are published in numerous anthologies, e-magazines, local press, and literary magazines.

Find Tonya Penrose listed in the Poets and Writers Directory. If you enjoyTonya's novels, please tell others.

VISIT:
Website: http://www.tonyawrites.com
X: @TonyaWrites
Instagram: @TonyaPenroseWrites
Threads.net @TonyaPenroseWrites
Bluesky @tonyapenrose.bsky.social
Substack @TonyaPenrose

BOOKS BY TONYA PENROSE
Old Mountain Cassie: The Three Lessons
A Secret Gift
Welcome to Charm
Venetian Rhapsody
More coming…

RECIPES

Betsy's Red Chili Pepper French Toast with Goat Cheese (Served on page 24)

5 organic eggs from nice hens
1 cup organic coconut milk for sweetness
1 T spicy mustard for zing
2 tsp. dry mustard
2 tsp. herbs Provence (*I mix my own concoction*)
2 garlic cloves smashed to smithereens
1 tsp. Celtic salt
1-2 T chili pepper (*I've been known to use a smidge more.*)
1 3-day old French baguette sliced 1 inch thick
1 stick of organic butter chunked

In a lovely ceramic bowl, whisk eggs until frothy. Add the milk to marry the eggs. Next, fold in the dry ingredients into the liquid. Bathe the slices of bread in the mixture. In a medium-hot iron skillet, melt a few chunks of butter. Add the bread slices. When golden brown, flip. *HINT: If one side gets too brown, simply serve it on the bottom.* Remove to a warm plate. Top with goat cheese and a really generous drizzle of the bee's nectar. Beverage recommendation: A Very Virgin Mary with extra hot sauce.

Savory French Toast*
5 extra-large eggs
1 cup milk
2 tsp. fresh thyme chopped
3 tsp. fresh chives chopped
1 tsp. dry mustard
1 T grained mustard

1 tsp. sea salt
¼ tsp. white pepper
¾ stick of butter
8 thick slices of day-old French bread

Whisk eggs in a medium bowl until frothy. Add milk, herbs, and spices and stir until well blended. Bathe the bread slices in the mixture. In a non-stick skillet, melt the butter. Add slices of bread and cook until done and golden. Transfer to a warm plate. Sprinkle with more chives and serve with a dollop of sour cream or Brie cheese. Beverage suggestion: A Mimosa

Betsy's Sardine Sandwich Delight (page 86)

2 cans of whole sardines packed in olive oil
½ English cucumber
1 carton of fresh organic raspberries
2 multi-grain organic bagels (*We all need extra fiber*)
Betsy's homemade mustard sauce (*recipe follows*)

Coarse chop the sardines in a bowl. Add the diced cucumbers and toss ever so gently. Fold in the mustard sauce to liven up the mixture. Spread onto one side of a lightly toasted bagel. Mash the raspberries a touch and spread them in a lovely and colorful circle around the bagel. Leave the top off to garner compliments. Serves 2 happy ladies.

Betsy's World Famous Mustard Sauce

1 T horseradish
1 T grainy mustard
A few splashes of hot sauce

1 small jalapeño pepper finely minced.

Sunday Sardine Surprise Sandwich*

2 cans of sardines in mustard
1 T white wine vinegar
1 tsp. lemon zest
1 tsp. fresh dill chopped
10-15 capers
Dash of black pepper
1 ripe avocado mashed
Extra virgin olive oil
4 multi-grain bakery bagels

Combine lemon zest, dill, capers, vinegar, pepper, and salt. Toss in sardines. Let marinate for 10-15 minutes. Drizzle olive oil over both sides of the cut bagels and broil until golden. Remove from the oven and spread the mashed avocado generously over the bagels. Top with sardine mixture. Place a lemon wedge on each plate. Serve with a side of orange sections and fresh mint.

May substitute smoked salmon for sardines and eliminate the vinegar.

Betsy's Sunny Surprise Sipper

1 cup cold triple espresso
½-1 cup heavy strawberry syrup with a dash of cayenne (*maybe 3 dashes*)
1 cup organic sweetened cashew milk whipped to a frothy cream
1 cup canned pineapple juice

In a tall, frosted glass, layer espresso, syrup, milk, and pineapple juice. Be careful not to jiggle or stir the layers. Well, you can if you so choose. Serve with a long colorful straw. Compliments will be forthcoming from sipping this sunny beverage—lots of them.

Refreshing Pineapple Espresso*

2 ½ cups of fresh pineapple juice
¾ cup cold-brew concentrate
4 T Kalua or a flavored syrup

Mix liquid in a shaker and pour into two tall, chilled glasses. Garnish with a skewer of fresh pineapple chunks and cherries.

Betsy's Happy Happy Hash Browns (page 166)

5 cups frozen diced potatoes
6 T olive oil
½-1 tsp. Celtic salt
1 tsp. crushed pepper medley seasoning
½ tsp. sweet paprika
1 chopped white onion
1 chopped yellow pepper
1 chopped red pepper
1 chopped green pepper
1 carton of organic grape tomatoes halved
1 smashed clove of garlic
1 cup shredded aged gouda cheese
Fresh parsley

Prepare the potatoes according to directions. When done, add the salt, pepper, and paprika and toss. In a large skillet, sauté the seasoned vegetables in olive oil until soft. Add the still-warm potatoes to the vegetables and stir gently. Do not mush those spuds. Pour into a ceramic casserole dish and top with shredded gouda. Broil a couple of minutes until cheese melts. Sprinkle with parsley. Serves 4 big eaters. Well, maybe 3 big eaters. *NOTE: This recipe of Betsy's was a hit with Page. The author cannot improve on it without risking Betsy's wrath.*

Betsy's Enchanted Honey Cake

Betsy agreed to share the basic honey cake recipe but confessed what makes her cake enchanted is the kind of honey she uses. That's her secret ingredient, and she won't divulge the source of this amazing nectar. It seems our Betsy can keep her yap shut when it comes to creating magic for garnering a confession and closing a murder case.

3¾ cups all-purpose flour (sometimes I use a tad less flour.)
1 tsp. baking soda
½ tsp. Celtic salt
1 T baking powder
1 cup quality vegetable oil
1 cup of the honey bee's magical nectar
1½ cup organic sugar
½ cup dark brown sugar
3 large organic eggs from those happy hens
½ cup orange juice
2-3 T Kentucky Bourbon (optional)
¾ tsp. vanilla extract (*Don't dare use imitation extract.*)
1 cup coffee freshly brewed (*I use a nice dark French roast.*)

Set the oven at 345 degrees. I find most ovens run hot. Spray a 9 x 13 pan liberally with butter-flavored baking spray (*Page likes a Bundt pan, but I don't. Too finicky to remove my cake.*). In a rainbow-colored ceramic bowl, (No eyebrow-raising. You are making magic here.) mix the flour, salt, soda, and powder. In a separate bowl, combine the oil, ¾ cup of the honey nectar, sugars, eggs, coffee, vanilla, and juice. Mix. Add the wet mixture to the dry until everyone looks nicely married. Pour the magic into the pan. Drizzle in a lovely pattern the remaining nectar atop the batter. Bake until done. I start testing with a toothpick after 30 minutes. Let the honey cake cool before removing it from the pan. *I drizzle more nectar on top, but that's just me helping Page solve our latest caper.*

*These are the original recipes that inspired Betsy's culinary debacles.

www.ingramcontent.com/pod-product-compliance
Lightning Source LLC
Chambersburg PA
CBHW021503240626
47154CB00002B/485